SHROUDS OF DARKNESS

BROOKLYN SHADOWS BOOK 1

BY BROCK E. DESKINS

I let out an exasperated sigh. "Cut through the bullshit, Vincent, and tell me what you want."

"There has been a rash of killings, mostly in your district."

"So? It's Brooklyn, and not the nice part either. People are always getting themselves killed."

"These killings are not caused by humans. You should know me well enough to know I would not inflict your presence upon myself for anything so trivial."

"I still don't see why you're asking for me. Send your dogs out. It's their damn job."

I can see Vincent struggling to maintain his composure as he responds. "They have more pressing business, which is why I am telling you to do it."

"Yeah, I'd like to help but you fired me, remember? It's a Sheriff problem, so kindly go fornicate yourself. Fornicate is today's word from my Word of the Day calendar," I explain.

I see Quinn twitch almost spasmodically as Wyatt restrains him with a glare. Vincent saves me complete disappointment as his calm façade slips.

"You are still a warder of your district, you little shit, and you will deal with it as is required! I strongly suggest you find out what is happening rather quickly, because right now you are my prime suspect!"

Damn, he has me on both counts. A warder is like a land¬lord or baron. Any vamp who wants to hunt in your district is supposed to get your permission. On the flip side, you are responsible if people in your district are fucking up. And if your car gets stolen, people generally look at the neighbor who has a history of stealing cars. Metaphorically speaking, I have stolen a lot of cars.

CHAPTER ONE

Martin Goldstein, accountant to several of New York's less savory inhabitants, exits his Brooklyn office. Marty hesitates in the shadowy doorway of the old brick building before shrugging his narrow shoulders and stepping out into the darkness of the city street.

A light spring rain is falling, wetting his beige trench coat and misting his round, wire-framed glasses. The mousey, fortyish-looking accountant looks left and right, hoping to spy a cab, but he is not surprised when none enters his view.

This is not a neighborhood where cabs run at night unless you call ahead. It is late, well past normal business hours, but tax time is nearing and he has several important and dangerous clients who will not look kindly upon a late filing or any errors which might gain the attention of the IRS.

His wife is waiting at home, keeping dinner warm for his eventual return. It is not a far walk, and it will be much quicker than waiting for a cab. Even if he called for one, drivers often find any excuse to delay picking up the fare. There are many other fares in the city in far better locations than this.

The unassuming man wipes his spectacles on a clean handkerchief and peers into the darkness through squinted eyes. He scans the area around the few working lamp posts and sees nothing more than an occasional vagrant.

Marty has lived here all his life, and most people willing to cause another harm know Marty is a protected man. Dropping the name of one of his clients is a powerful deterrent for all but the most ignorant or desperate of criminals. Marty is a nervous man, however, and even this knowledge does little to take the edge off his anxiety.

With a final sigh of resignation, Marty steps off the curb and takes brisk strides into the night-shrouded canyon of multistoried buildings.

He knows it is foolish for anyone but the most apathetic homeless with nothing to steal or the most hardened of gutter scum to traverse the dark streets of this neighborhood. Nevertheless, he takes a measure of confidence in his position as accountant to the Mob and his own knowledge of the streets to see him home safe where his wife waits for his return with eagerness.

His mind drifts to his wife, Beverley. Tall and fair-haired, he thinks of how she is far too smart and beautiful for him. Women of her quality do not often see the kind and gentle man lying beneath the pathetic, scrawny, intellectual exterior. However, she does, and has given him two wonderful children, who are grown now, along with twenty-nine years of absolutely blissful marriage.

Marty's street sense snaps him out of his reverie. A furtive glance over his shoulder reveals two men shadowing his movements. They are walking straight toward him, closing the distance separating them. The accountant's heart rate doubles in an instant.

Marty knows this bodes ill for him. The thugs have marked him and his wallet. If these miscreants are very stupid or uninformed, his life may be in peril. He breaks into a run, skirting the debris littering the sidewalks with a grace that belies his apparent lack of physical prowess.

All he needs to do is make it another block and a half without getting caught, and he will exit the concealing confines of the concrete chasms and emerge onto the busier streets of the city. Marty redoubles his efforts as he spies what he prays will offer a measure of sanctuary in the glow of the streetlight just a few dozen strides ahead.

His Oxford shoes slide on the rain-slicked asphalt as another figure steps out of the shadows and into the light ahead of him. Marty whips his head about, searching for another path of egress. His pursuers are almost upon him, and the new figure is now advancing with malicious intent.

Marty's voice cracks as he shouts in desperation, "I am a protected man! Very dangerous and powerful men will come after you if you hurt me!"

The man advancing from the end of the street begins to laugh. "Oh, we know who you are, Marty."

Oh God! This isn't a mugging, it's a hit! Martin realizes as a fresh wave of terror courses through his body.

His options for escape are limited, and he darts down the only path available. His flight takes him down an even narrower and darker alley. Having lived in this very neighborhood for the better part of fifty years, Marty knows the layout of the streets and alleys as well as anyone. This alley empties out onto a wider avenue, which he can then take to the busier street his newest assailant denied him.

Marty's luck is off tonight and he is unaware of the construction on one of the towering buildings near the end of the alley. A ten-foot chain-link fence blocks his retreat. Martin spins around as pounding footsteps close in on him.

The footsteps slow as they near, and the men begin to laugh as they stalk toward the feeble accountant now hunched in a squat with his face buried in his hands, whimpering for divine intervention.

"Oh God, no! Please, God, no, don't let this happen," Martin chants in a desperate mantra.

His assassins are amused by his pleading. They take great pleasure in his stark terror, laughing as if they share the greatest of jokes while they leisurely advance on the cowering man.

Had the petty thugs-turned-killers known the true reason for Marty's desperate pleas, they would have found absolute terror instead of malicious joy. Marty is not praying for his own salvation. He is praying for theirs.

A loud popping, like someone wringing bubble-wrap in their hands, sounds out over the chorus of laughter as the frail-looking accountant's body begins to twist and contort. His pleas for salvation change to pain-induced grunts before becoming an ominous, deep rumble of uncontrolled fury and power.

The transformation is so rapid the lead thug has little time to recognize the change in what is supposed to be their helpless prey. The gang-banger's death is so swift the source of his demise never has time to register in his brain.

A lunge and single swipe of the powerful, fur-covered paw, which just a moment ago had been the dexterous digits of an innocuous accountant, takes the head from the attempted murderer's shoulders. The power of the blow hits with so much force, the decapitated cranium strikes the brick wall of the building hard enough to shatter most of the bones encasing the pathetically weak brain.

The second man has just enough time to register the four-legged monster standing before him and recognize the death promised in the creature's eyes before the lethal, extending jaws of the werewolf tear out his throat. The wet gurgling of blood-inundated air leaving his lungs for the final time is the only sound the doomed man is able to make.

The third assailant isa man fleet of foot and actions. Seldom caught by surprise, he turns and runs back down the alley in the direction from which he came the instant he sees the inhuman creature pounce on the leader of what had been their small gang. He does not even see his other friend die as he races toward what he prays will be the safety of the populated streets, waiting just a few hundred feet away.

Although the alley is less than a hundred feet long, he fails to reach even the midway point before something swift and heavy strikes him in the back with the force of a speeding automobile and bears him to the ground.

The long canines sprouting from the inhumanly powerful jaws of the werewolf sink into the flesh of his neck and crush the bones of the thug as though they are made of papier-mâché. The werewolf is furious with the men who forced it to kill and takes out its rage upon their corpses. The monster, who had once been Martin the accountant, raises its muzzle to the dreary, drizzling sky and releases a howl of rage, sorrow, and uncontrolled primal instincts.

CHAPTER TWO

Like a fierce but patient jaguar, I crouch on my chosen ambush point, scanning the city around and below me with eyes able to pierce even the deepest shadows. I wait for my prey to present itself. My perch is no tree limb or towering rock, but the ledge of a building so narrow even the pigeons choose better spots to roost. Considering this narrow outcrop, the constant, drizzling rain, and the twelve-story drop to the unyielding concrete below, one might think I was suicidal.

I'm not. A fall from here might not even kill me. It would hurt like hell for sure. I chose this spot with deliberate intent and without fear. Along with my keen eyesight comes unparalleled balance and reflexes. The longish nails growing from my fingers are almost as strong as steel and assist me in maintaining my grip on the concrete and mortar.

I used to curse the kind of chilly, soggy weather I have chosen to put myself in tonight, but that was a lifetime ago—a couple of lifetimes for some. I ceased caring about the cold and damp long ago.

I was turned, or cursed depending on your point of view, on December fifth, 1933. I remember the date so clearly because a lot of things happened to me that day. The first event of any significance was the repeal of prohibition. The streets of New York were alive with all manner of people drinking and toasting strangers. The fact there could be so much booze in the hands of so many so soon gave testament to the uselessness of outlawing alcohol.

That was how I met her. She was the most beautiful thing I had ever seen in my life, with alabaster skin and long, black tresses hanging past her slim waist. Long hair was out of fashion back then, but it made her look more exotic to my nineteen-year-old eyes. It was the height of the Great Depression, but that night I was anything but depressed.

Even her name made me quiver with excitement—Lesile. Her voice was soft, yet it held a strange power. The slight French accent was even more intoxicating than the champagne we shared. Little did I know champagne was not her drink of choice.

She was intent on taking control of our liaison, and I had no problem giving her the reins. I was no altar boy. Times were tough, and I had taken to running the streets when I was thirteen. She was an older woman and had things she could teach me, and I was more than willing to learn. She looked to be in her mid-thirties, or possibly even one of those women in her early forties who somehow maintained an incredible body and a timeless complexion. Not a line marred her perfect skin, and every other part of her body was a work of perfection, as if sculpted by the hand of God.

She led me to where she said she lived. The fact she lived in an abandoned theater never occurred to me as being the least bit odd. Her domicile was the last thing on my mind. I thought it was the booze jumbling my mind, but later I was certain she had somehow bewitched me.

Lesile took me deep into throes of passion such as I never thought possible. The encounter was so raw I may as well have been a virgin. I winced when she sank her teeth into the nape of my neck, but I was so far gone the pain was lost in the ecstasy. When she told me to return the bite, I didn't think twice. She kept telling me to bite her harder and harder. Her skin felt as if I was trying to chew through the soft hide of a leather sofa, but I soon tasted the copper tang of blood as it seeped into my mouth.

I don't remember how I got home, but I awoke in my shabby little apartment feeling as if my blood was on fire. Agony as I had never thought possible flared through every cell in my body. At first, I was afraid I was going to die. As the pain intensified, I was terrified I wouldn't.

It was a good thing I lived alone and in the worst part of New York. The only attempts at intervention were my neighbors pounding on the walls, floor, and ceiling, shouting at me to shut the fuck up or have enough consideration to die. Losing consciousness was a blessing after what seemed an eternity of hellish agony.

When I awoke once more, I felt cold so I donned every piece of clothing I owned and wrapped myself up in blankets, but nothing raised my body temperature. I had no heat in my apartment and ice covered the outside and inside of my small window, but I soon discovered I got no colder either.

I shed my blankets and extra clothing before stomping out into the snow and biting cold. As I grew accustomed to my own frigid body temperature, the freezing air outside did not bother me. I saw everyone blowing out thick puffs of fog as they breathed. Everyone, that is, except me; I wasn't breathing at all.

I rubbed the base of my neck, expecting to feel the remnant of the bite my beautiful, dark seductress had given me, but my skin was unblemished.

I was a big fan of the moving pictures back then, and I loved to be scared. I had seen Vignola's *The Vampire* and F.W. Murnau's *Nosferatu* a dozen times, and I began to put things together. At first, I thought these crazy ideas were a result of whatever illness had struck me, but then I recalled Kipling's The Vampire. His poem had gotten me interested in the undead when I was a kid, and Bram Stoker's Dracula had clenched it.

I almost convinced myself the entire idea was an insane delusion brought on by this mysterious ailment. Realizing I had started to believe in vampires pissed me off, and I vented my frustration on a large trash bin in the alley.

My kick sent the quarter-ton steel bin sliding more than ten feet. As I stood staring in shock at what I had done, the hunger hit me. My stomach was gnawing at me with a voraciousness I had never felt before, and I was no stranger to missing a meal or five.

The smell hit me a moment later, the scent of blood pumping through the veins of another human, and it was nearby. I walked further into the alley, and I could sense I was getting nearer.

I saw him picking through rubbish bins for anything of value. The bum was looking to scrape up enough for a bottle of the relegalized booze. He flashed me a grin, thinking I was not so far from him in society's social standing. He turned back to his barrel to resume pawing through its contents.

He pulled his head back out and looked at me warily as I stalked closer. It could have been the look of intent in my eyes, or the fact I was literally salivating, but he went on his guard and backed away. He cast his eyes about for a weapon or a way to escape, but neither was within view.

"Look, buddy, I ain't got nothin', OK?" he told me in a nervous voice.

He was wrong. He had precisely what I wanted, what I needed. I covered the fifteen or twenty feet separating us in a second. I broke his neck with a quick twist at the same time as my teeth tore into his throat. I never knew a body could hold so much blood, but somehow I seemed to consume most of it.

As my stomach settled, my brain began to issue disturbing rumblings of its own. I dropped the transient down into the shallow carpeting of snow. I looked down in horror at the dead, accusing eyes staring up at me from the scarlet backdrop contrasting so starkly with the layer of white all around.

I wiped my face with my sleeve and scrubbed away the blood on my face, neck, and hands with handfuls of clean snow. Images of a beautiful woman and an old theater flashed through my mind. Disjointed memories began to align themselves into a coherent pattern. I knew what had happened, and I knew who had done this to me.

I sprinted out of the alley and down the sidewalk, forcing myself not to run faster than the black cars speeding down the street beside me. Block after block I ran until I stood facing the once majestic hall where actors once performed the works of Shakespeare and Molière.

I walked through the formerly grand lobby and up the stairs still covered in a red but moth-eaten carpet. A swift kick shattered the door to Lesile's boudoir, and I stormed in with rage and fury etched all over my face.

If I thought to put fear into this woman, this creature who

had done this to me, I was disappointed. She pursed her ruby-red lips into an amused look of disapproval at her ruined door.

"Leonard, look at what you have done to my beautiful door. That door was an antique. I do so love antiques, being one myself," she crooned, lost in momentary recollections.

I shouted at her, "Don't fucking call me Leonard! My name is Leo!" Although I lowered my voice, I still trembled with rage. "What have you done to me?"

Her laughter made my anger spike once again. "Oh, Leonar—Leo, you poor boy. I have made you better. I have made you eternal."

I shook my head back and forth. "No, no, you turn me back. You fix this right now, or I swear I'll kill you!"

This amused Lesile even more and her laughter was like a hammer driving nails through my flesh. "You are perfect now. Perfect for me, and we can be together forever—or until I tire of you."

Tire of me, and then what, toss me out like a piece of trash? Like I was nothing? Her lilting laughter, something I would have found melodious in other circumstances, was like a thousand paper cuts to my soul. I was a man of my time, and nothing was worse than being laughed at by a woman, or so I thought. Lesile showed me the error in my thinking as I lunged across the room, my hands outstretched and reaching for her delicate alabaster neck.

There is one thing more damaging to a man's ego than a woman laughing at him, and that is getting his ass kicked while she's doing it. She moved with a speed and struck with a strength that would be formidable to me even now. Her blows shattered the bones in my legs, crippling me in seconds. A blow to my spine ended my struggles and the agony of my ruined femurs.

There was still plenty of pain to go around from the numerous other broken bones and ruptured organs in my body as she strapped me down to a heavy oak table. Why she had a device with its thick, leather straps was beyond me until I realized this was not the first time she had done this.

She looked down on me as I lay pinned to the table, her

infuriating smile never leaving her perfect mouth. "The problem with making new vampires is a lot like bringing home a
new puppy," she sighed. "You have to train them."

"Let me go, you bitch!" I raved at her with all the scorn I
could put in voice.

Renewed pain radiated from my broken jaw and shattered
ribs, and I winced. I felt no need to be polite or placating. I
would never leave this room alive. Even if I did, I was crippled.
My spine had snapped and I felt my legs go numb when she
kicked me. Or was I?

Already I felt the tingling sensation of feeling returning to
my legs. I tried to wriggle my toes and succeeded. If not for the
fact I was strapped down on a table by a psychotic vampiress, I
would have whooped with joy.

She spoke, as if reading my mind. "You see the power of our
kind now? How fast you can recover from even the most severe
of injuries? Our rapid healing takes a great deal of energy, however, and you will need to feed again soon. I will leave you for
now, and when I return with your meal we shall begin our
lessons."

I had no idea what kind of lessons she was talking about,
but I had a good idea of what kind of meal she would be bringing back and the thought horrified me. Well, until the hunger
began to return as my body repaired itself.

Lesile returned in less than an hour with a middle-aged
woman in tow. I figured the woman was a prostitute on the
downhill slope of her career. The vampiress sent the woman
sailing into the room with a casual flick of her wrist, as if tossing a bag of groceries onto the counter.

The woman crawled to the far wall where she hugged her
knees and wept. Lesile glided across the room to where I lay
strapped down and smiled at me.

"Feeling better?" she asked in a sweet voice.

I was, but I still hurt and told her to fuck off.

"Such language to a lady," she responded with disapproval.
"I think our first lesson must be on manners."

I didn't like the sound of that at all. I cried out as she
snapped the bones in my lower left leg and then my right arm.

Fire erupted in my chest as she once again destroyed the bones that had been well on the way to healing.

Still smiling, she said, "Now, how much and for how long you are in pain is up to you. You have the ability to block the pain from most wounds you suffer and force them to heal at phenomenal rates as well. You see how fast you heal naturally. You can increase this severalfold by sheer effort of will. Do you have that? Do you have the will, Leonard?"

"Don't call me Leonard, you crazy broad!"

She slapped me hard like a regular, angry woman. "You belong to me, you little shit, and I will call you whatever I damn well please."

With her soft French accent, her profanity-laced rebuke was almost cute, but I hated this creature with every fiber of my being. I was also terrified of her almost beyond reason, so I kept my mouth shut and let her call me whatever she wanted.

Lesile continued. "A new vampire often takes months, even years, to learn such control of mind and body. I will teach you in far less time. I hope I can do it before I get bored with you..."

I didn't like the way she trailed off and got a hundred-yard stare in her eyes, so I swore to myself to be a quick study. And I was a quick study, if you consider two weeks of having your bones broken and your organs skewered quick. The worst was when she gouged out my eyes with an ice pick. I think it was then I began to learn how to direct my healing and block pain. I was so terrified of the darkness I put everything I had into seeing again.

At the end of two weeks, Lesile was satisfied with my progress, and after breaking most of my bones one last time, she disappeared. I have never seen her again. Rumors about her reached me from time to time throughout the decades, particularly after I became a Sheriff. She was often the topic of conversation within our little circle; she was a legendary criminal everyone was afraid to go after.

She was insane, everyone agreed. But even though she lived her life toeing the line of acceptable behavior, she seldom crossed it to the extent the council and the Sheriffs had to act. The laws regarding the conduct of vampires are few; you can do much of what you want, as long as your activities do not bring about the attention of the mortal populace. The rules are simple enough, but stupidity knows no boundaries, and violations happen often enough to make the Sheriffs necessary.

The movement of a shadow cast by the backlit body of a man through the window of the next building over and three floors down snaps me out of my mental time travel. It's what I have been waiting for. The voice of a young girl drifts up to my ears, my hearing being as acute as my vision.

"Daddy, no please, don't," the tiny, frightened voice begs.

But her words fall on ears deaf with drunkenness just as they have so many times in the past. Tonight will be different though. Tonight, her pleas have been heard. Like I said, I picked this spot with a purpose. Tonight, the girl would experience fear once again, but a different sort of fear than the one she has experienced for much of her young life.

This was no chance encounter. Despite my surly disposition, I do have a few friends in certain well-placed positions who occasionally inform me of people this world is better off without and who won't be missed. A concerned teacher had brought this man to the attention of Social Services, but there was insufficient evidence to arrest the father or even perform more than a cursory investigation. I'm not the type who takes joy in the necessity of killing to maintain my existence, but at times like this I'm happy to make an exception.

I don my black neoprene mask so my face is covered from the nose down. There will be a witness to my actions tonight. The half-mask will help me maintain my anonymity, and it makes me look scary as hell with the hood of my black trench coat pulled over my head. With a quick flex of my powerful muscles, I launch myself from the wall toward the fire escape, landing fifty feet away and thirty feet down from my perch. The span is an easy leap for one like me.

I make the barest whisper of a sound as my feet strike the wet metal grating of the platform. My boots make contact with the slick surface for a fraction of a second before another thrust of my legs propels me through the open window of the little girl's room with such velocity only my trench coat brushes the sill.

Directly ahead of my headlong flight into the room, a man stands in the open doorway wearing a stained, formerly white wife beater and nothing else but a lecherous grin and the overpowering reek of cheap whiskey.

I am behind him with my hand and its scalpel-like nails around his throat before his lust-filled sneer has time to turn into a look of fear. His first instinct probably makes him think the cops have come to arrest him for abusing his daughter. He might pray to be so lucky, but those prayers will never be answered.

The girl, ten or eleven years old, is sitting up in her bed with her back pressed against the wall, the blankets held in a tight wad under her chin. She looks from my eyes to those of her drunken, lecherous father, unsure of who is the most terrifying. I return her stare, using my gaze to penetrate deep into the region of her consciousness that understands the balance of power between predator and prey.

"Go to sleep," I command in a firm but low, grumbling voice. "In the morning, you will call the police, and they will take you somewhere safe where no one will hurt you again."

OK, that was probably a lie. In this world, people get hurt. Pain is unavoidable, but it is a pretty sure bet she will be safer and put up with far less shit than her father has forced her to endure.

"Do not go in your father's room for any reason. Do you understand me?"

The girl gives me an imperceptible nod before sliding down into the bed and pulling the covers over her head. Despite the sudden shock of tonight's turn of events, she will most likely go to sleep just as I ordered. This is where the old wives' tale of vampires hypnotizing their victims comes from.

Hypnosis has nothing to do with it, at least not in the classical sense of the term. No, it is the powerful influence a top-tiered predator like myself can have on a creature who knows it is prey. It's like a deer freezing in the headlights of an oncoming car, or a rabbit going stiff and immobile when it realizes a predator has it locked in its sights, and there is not a damn thing it can do to change whatever fate has in store.

I drag the filthy, disgusting man from the room with almost contemptuous ease. He doesn't struggle much, but resisting wouldn't have mattered anyway. Like the rabbit, he knows there is nothing he can do. He is the deer, I am the car, and the power of mypresence paralyzes him.

I don't do this often, preying on humans, especially to the point where they die. Don't get me wrong, I'm no saint. I am not doing this out of any sense of good or saintly quality I wish to personify. I have a job tonight, and I need the lifeblood of a human to make sure I am at the top of my game. Vampires can exist on bagged blood or drink just enough from a human so their prey survives the incident, but only for a limited amount of time. I seldom take the life of humans more than three or four times a year unless it's business. When I do have to feed, I choose those so-called victims who are not going to be missed by anyone who matters.

The girl will tell so many horror stories about her father, the cops will not be terribly inclined to find the man who ended his tyranny. I suppose I take a bit of satisfaction in ending this man's abuse. Perhaps a tiny spark of compassion is still glowing beneath the cold, passionless ashes of what was once my humanity. Maybe I'm just fooling myself. Maybe Ionly pretend I give even the tiniest shit about the vermin called humanity so I don't turn rogue again.

The council takes a dim view on vampires who go rogue: feeding without discretion and drawing enough attention to us that people start seeing a bit of truth in what we all try hard to ensure stays wrapped in myth and folklore.

We all have to feed, and we all need to take lifeblood. The frequency with which we do is based upon our personal tolerance and age. The older a vampire gets, the more they have to feed. I don't know what is in the last little bit of blood we suck out as the human dies. Some sort of life energy or the soul if you believe in that kind of crap. Whatever it is, it is a necessity for our survival.

I had a friend once, a doctor, who tried to deny this

requirement. He spent years trying to develop a way to over-come the necessity of killing even infrequently. He still had to kill, even though he struggled to keep it down to once a year. God, how he looked like shit in the months before his nature forced him to take a life.

You could never get me to care enough about humans to put myself through so much torture. I guess he was just better than I am. When he did take a life, it was from a terminally ill patient, but even this was more than he could bear. He gave up his search for a non-lethal solution after several fruitless years, and with the last bit of sanity left to his blood-starved mind and body, he dowsed himself with gasoline in the middle of his living room and torched himself.

Burning is one sure way of killing a vampire. Let me tell you about vampires. Ninety percent of what you have read or seen in the movies is complete bullshit. A stake through the heart? Please. When we are turned, significant changes occur throughout our bodies down to the genetic level. This massive change to our DNA is why we do not consider ourselves human any longer.

The first noticeable thing is we no longer need air to survive, and our hearts stop beating. We have become an anaerobic creature. However, we are not dead, and most of our other organs must remain viable; most importantly, our brains along with skin, muscle, and nerves. Keeping our important bits alive is why we must consume the blood of humans.

We are able to consume vast amounts of blood, and through a process similar to osmosis, the blood is shunted throughout our system. Our bodies also create or take in vast amounts of stem cells and supercharge them. These cells are why we are able to heal at a phenomenal rate. These turbo-powered stem cells rush to the site of any wound we receive and attempt to repair it, and they do so with a great deal of success.

We are not invulnerable and, if you cause enough damage, we can die, but death does not come easily. As a vampire ages, he or she learns how to control a great deal of their body, even their blood. We can move our own cells almost as easily as you move your hand. It's difficult at first, but one learns.

Our senses become super acute. We can detect the tiniest of sounds, see in near total darkness, and have a sense of smell far greater than even the best of humans. We are also able, with practice, to control our nerve endings. We can block out pain that would leave a normal man wailing in agony before he passed out from shock.

Our bones become stronger and more flexible; our muscles become dense and many times stronger than even the burliest of men.

Fire is a great fear, because just like humans, burns are hard for us to heal. Sunlight? Not so much. Our skin loses pigment and leaves us vulnerable to the effects of the sun, but proper clothing and a good pair of sunglasses allow us to move about in daylight even if most of us prefer the dark.

We do not have huge, conspicuous fangs, and we do not bite the throats of our victims—usually. Biting is far too messy. Some use a small, sharp knife to open a vein or artery, while most of us just use a sharpened thumbnail.

I leave the drained corpse on his bed without much of a mess. I am a rather fastidious eater. I hope the girl will heed my warning about not coming into her father's room. If she doesn't then that's her problem. She can talk about it with whatever state-paid shrink she will be seeing for years to come.

I use the window in the trash and booze bottle littered living room to make my exit. After a quick climb up the fire escape and a leap up onto the roof as I near the top, I vanish once more into the night. I have a job tonight, and I need to get myself over to the Perestroika club on time. My employer despises tardiness.

I use the rooftops as my own personal expressway, leaping the wide gaps between buildings with a graceful ease. I am jumping to the roof of the fourth building when a scream cuts through the darkness. I pause, more out of curiosity than any sort of concern for whatever trouble a woman who was not smart enough to avoid has found.

I don't hear anything more and back up a few steps for my running jump to the next building. The woman screams again, followed by the voice of a man warning her to be silent.

My first instinct is to leave her to her fate. Whatever trouble she has found herself in is hers, not mine. Probably just a whore getting slapped around by her pimp.The soft thump of a fist hitting flesh is followed by the pathetic mewling of pain and the loss of hope that comes when prey knows a predator has them.

Damn my chivalrous nature. I blame my intervention on being pumped up on fresh lifeblood. I take a hard left and leap to the next building, run across the roof, then drop to the ground fifty feet below.

Amidst the trash-strewn alley, I see a woman cringing against the wall as a young black man holding a knife in his left hand cocks his fist back for another blow to ensure she stops struggling and crying out. At first, I think it is just as I had suspected, some pimp smacking his prostitute around. The girl is young however, sixteen or so. It's not unusual. Many runaways are forced into prostitution to survive.

Then the air currents shift and I pick up their scent. This girl doesn't smell like a whore. Ten to one odds she had met a boyfriend somewhere and was now sneaking back home. Like a stupid little twit, she thought it a good idea to take a shortcut so she could get back before curfew or Mommy and Daddy found out she was even gone. That is the more likely scenario. You would be surprised how much information you can get from a smell and a few decades of experience.

I shout at the kid holding the knife, about to bust the cowering girl in the chops again. "All right, dickhead. Let the girl go and get the fuck outta here."

I'm both impressed and annoyed when the kid turns and looks at me with a sneer. Granted, I'm not what most would consider an imposing man, but I have a presence that usually makes people think twice before screwing with me. It could be because it's so dark. It could be the knife gives the kid a big set of stones, I don't know.

"Fuck off, white boy," the kid says contemptuously. "Get'cho ass outta here before I gut you too."

I blame my smile on the buzz fresh lifeblood gives me as I advance on the youth and the crying, cowering girl.

"Don't move, bitch," the kid orders the girl like he would a dog. "I'll be back for you in a second."

Yeah, the kid has balls all right. He would have fared a hell of a lot better with less balls and more brains. It is apparent neither one of us is intimidated by the other. That will change in a moment as the two night-time predators assert their dominance for their territory.

When we are within six or seven feet of each other the kid lunges forward, knife leading and aimed straight at my heart with a darn good bit of skill and speed. It is obvious this is not his first knife fight, but it is definitely going to be his last.

My left hand darts out faster than the eye can track, and I grab his wrist in a vice-like grip, stopping him dead in his tracks. A slight flick of my own wrist snaps both the bones in his arm as if they were dry spaghetti noodles.

"Mother fucker, you broke my fucking arm!" the kid cries out more in anger than pain.

Luckily for him, depending on how you look at it, he will be dead before the shock wears off and he feels every bit of pain such an injury produces.

He takes a swing at me with his free hand, but I slap it down with the ease of fending off the wild flailing of a tantrum-throwing toddler. I release my grip on his ruined arm and open-palm slam him in his chest. I feel the ribcage compress and hear the bones crack as I send him flying backward, knocking him senseless on the unyielding brick wall.

I look over at the girl just now getting up. She is unsure if her nightmare is over or just beginning. She holds the torn ends of her blouse together in fear and modesty. Judging by what I can smell, she was not so modest before she left her lover's house.

"Go on, go home, kid," I tell her in a half growl.

She walks shakily toward me and the end of the alley. With a nervous glance at her assailant, she rushes at me, weeping.

"Oh God, thank you," she cries as she tries to wrap her arms around me.

I grab her by the front of her ruined blouse and send her windmilling toward the street. "I said get out of here, you stupid little bitch! Go home and think about this the next time you want to make a booty call in the middle of the night in the shittiest part of the city!"

She squeaks in terror, sprints down the alley, and flees out onto the street. Yeah, I know, I'm an asshole. I've gotten used to it. I look at the kid crumpled against the wall and wonder what I should do with him. Be a shame to let a perfectly good meal go to waste.

I am just finishing my second meal of the night when my phone rings. I wipe off my chin with my hands then clean my hands on the kid's jacket before I answer it. I already know who it is. I'm late and I am being reminded of it.

"Mr. Malone. I assume you are waiting for me at the club?" the heavily Russian-accented voice asks through my Motorola.

"I will be, Yuri, don't worry," I reply more calmly than I feel.

I am really buzzed and edgy right now. I haven't had two full meals back to back since I was in Vietnam. Nobody missed people back then in such a hellhole. It was a shitty war, but there was some damn good eating.

Yuri is not pleased with this answer and he tells me so. "Mr. Malone, you have one purpose this evening, and you cannot fulfill it if you are not where you are supposed to be when you are supposed to be there. Do not make me wait."

Yuri hangs up on me before I can answer, which is a good thing. I had nothing to say, and it avoids what could have been an awkward silence. Yuri pays me well because he knows I am worth it, and the meeting he has arranged is serious enough for him to contract me instead of simply relying on his usual body-guards and mobster compatriots.

Yuri Poplonovich, also known as Molotov for his tendency to burn up those who piss him off or get in his way, is a Russian—or is it Ukrainian?…whatever—mobster. Yuri is a ruthless man, but he also conducts himself with a certain standard you do not often find in your typical criminal types these days.

I guess you could say he is your old-school type of mafia. He grew up reading about America's old mobsters from the days of prohibition and watching movies like *The Godfather*. He charges various businesses in his territory for protection like any good mobster does, but unlike other crime organizations, he actually protects them. He does not terrorize or threaten those he calls his clients. He simply lets it be known throughout the criminal underworld who is under his protection and who is not. It's an effective way to keep a good customer base.

Yuri deals in cocaine, ecstasy, and stolen goods, but he is adamant about keeping crap like meth and crack off his streets. I don't know if I would go so far as to say I like Yuri, but we have a mutual sort of respect for each other. I'm not real quick to judge the lifestyles of others.

I hang up then select the first of the few presets programmed on my phone.

"Yeah," the disinterested voice speaks through the phone.

"I need a cleanup, fast."

"Screw you, Leo. Clean up your own mess."

Damn, I hate caller ID. "I'm sorry to interrupt your jerk-fest, but I can't. I'm on a job, and there was a witness, so I need you here now."

"Fine, what's the address?"

I give him the exact location of the corpse. The cleanup crew will be here in minutes and remove all traces of the kill. I don't know why they always give me a hard time. Since I was fired as a Sheriff, I have to pay out the ass for this, which really puts me in a bad mood. It's not like I can add it to my client's bill as an expense.

I snap my phone shut and take the nearest set of stairs leading to the rooftops. I am really buzzing now, and I'm more full of energy and life than I have been in a long time. It was a serious danger and the warning signs set off alarms in my brain. It is too easy to become addicted to the feeling gorging oneself gives our kind. The feeling of having so much power makes me feel invincible even beyond my normal scary-strong and fast self.

The buildings and lights are a blur as I sprint across the roofs and leap across the yawning chasms between buildings. I drop four stories onto the roof of the Perestroika club before scaring the shit out of a valet by dropping down right behind him just as Yuri's up-armored 1955 Bentley pulls up to the front of the club.

The front passenger-side door swings open almost before the car comes to a complete halt. The valets are smart enough not to make the slightest attempt at opening the door or, even more foolishly, try to park the big, black car. A tall, blond Slav pivots on his right heel the moment he steps out of the car and, with a quick look around, holds open the door for his boss.

Yuri steps out in a well-made but non-ostentatious Italian suit and gives me a nod of recognition before slipping the valet a twenty simply for formality's sake.

"Mr. Malone, I trust everything is proper?" he asks without making it a question.

I give him a curt nod. "All looks secure. It does not appear Mr. Hanako has arrived yet."

"Bah, of course not," Yuri replies with a disgusted snort. "Would not be seemly for little peacock to be on time, much less waiting on someone."

Tommy Hanako is the leader of an influential and rapidly growing Asian gang bordering Yuri's territory. Hanako wants to fill what he sees as a void, namely the vast assortment of drugs that Yuri doesn't allow.

"Come, Mr. Malone. We will wait inside as is proper. I will need a drink or five to deal with this little prick, I think."

Another twenty is exchanged with the doorman as I lead my employer into the club. The big Slav does not follow us in, but rather stays with the driver to guard the car. It is a testament to Yuri's well-deserved faith in me.

I drape my black trench coat over my arm and pass it off to the coat check girl. I slip the ticket stub she gives me into the front pocket of my black slacks. A black sports coat and black shirt finish off my rather drab ensemble. I know what you're thinking—typical cliché vampire getup. It was no statement of style, however. Bloodstains aren't so readily apparent against the black material. I like to stay practical, and it's easy to accessorize.

My casual suit is acceptable, but I won't win any fashion contests. No tie, you see. I fucking hate ties. Stupidest damn thing ever invented by man. Come to think about it, a woman probably invented it. No self-respecting man would put a noose of silk around his neck to dangle in front of him as if he were just waiting for the scaffold to be built to finish his hanging.

My steel-toed combat boots aren't exactly a great leap toward being fashionably elite either. I'm a practical man, as I said, and my ability to out-kick a mule makes them eminently suitable to my work conditions. At least they're polished brilliantly enough a man can use them as a shaving mirror.

I hate clubs. The noise and press of people is almost stifling, and the smell makes me want to vomit. Too much sweat mingling with cologne and the disturbingly frequent smell of sex turns my stomach. Whether it's due to my presence or Yuri's, people get out of our way as I carve a path toward the stairs leading to the exclusive seating area reserved for VIPs. Two heavy-set bouncers follow behind at a discreet distance to ensure no one disturbs Mr. Poplonovich as he finds his table.

The two shadows peel off as smoothly as they attached themselves the moment we reach the stairs. Precisely one minute after Yuri takes his seat, an attractive young woman comes and takes his order. He does not bother to ask me if I want anything. He knows I will take nothing.

I choose to remain standing and will do so for the rest of the night. I can literally stand for days without twitching so much as a muscle. As a sniper in Vietnam, I often did precisely that. I was assigned to an elite Special Forces unit where I acted pretty much on my own initiative. I refused a spotter as I preferred—demanded—to work alone. I doubt I could have found one accepting of my peculiar culinary requirements.

Those were the best and the worst days of my existence. I had so much fun I damn near destroyed myself. While everyone else was getting high on weed, hash, heroin, and the medic's ample supply of morphine, I was glazed to the gills on the essence of human life. I had developed such a fearsome reputation amongst the Chinese and Vietcong I had to move my sniper position often, not because of fear of discovery, but because I had scared off the enemy. I was the ghost in the jungle, leaving nothing but blood-drained bodies to be found when the sun came up.

Every night those poor squints found another one of their buddies dead on his sleeping mat, in his watchtower, or even leaning against the tree he had propped himself against to take a piss. I was everywhere, and I was living high. So great became my lust, I nearly turned rogue. Hell, there's no nearly about it. I was a rogue, and a bad one. In Vietnam at the height of the war, no one really noticed; or if they did, they didn't give a shit. What was one—or a few hundred or thousand—dead squints when there were over a million more pouring over the border from China?

Yeah I said squint, so what of it? I'm from a different time, and I've fought three major wars against the shifty little bastards. Don't get me wrong. I'm not a racist. I don't hate them any more than I hate everyone else in this world. I would have to give a shit about them to hate them, and I sure as hell don't; not them, not these screaming, gyrating monkeys in this club, and not those walking dead outside.

I've seen too much and done too much to care. So why did I save the little girl and the stupid bimbo tonight? Saving the girl was just a side effect of my need to feed. It's what I tell myself anyway. The little slut? I don't know. Maybe I like to pretend I still have a tiny shred of a conscience left to help me maintain the slight bit of humanity I possess.

It's possible, and this is a stretch, the pretense is me not giving a shit. Maybe I am pretending to be a heartless bastard so I can go on doing what I do without becoming a complete basket case. How would you feel, with your so-called humanity, knowing that in order for you to exist others must die? A lot of others, and the body count just climbs higher and higher, faster and faster, the older you get. My shrink hasn't been able to give me a definitive answer in nearly twenty years of on and off therapy, so I doubt anyone else out there will be stepping forward with an answer not reeking of bullshit.

It's been twenty minutes, and Yuri is on his third vodka tonic. He's drinking slowly. He must be taking this meeting seriously. My flashback is broken when I spy an immaculately dressed Asian man flanked by two of the biggest bodyguards I have ever seen ascending the stairs.

Tommy Hanako. The man is nearly enshrouded in a kind of mystical aura from the club lights reflecting off the suit a million silkworms gave their lives to make. My blood is running hot, and it takes more than a bit of my resolve to keep from hopping the table and slapping the ever-present superior smirk right off his face.

I'm sure he feels immune to any sort of overt confrontation next to his two hulking escorts. The one on his right is huge. He is six foot eight, three hundred fifty pounds of sheer muscle and bad attitude. The bulge in his too tight-fitting suit jacket is mostly there as added insurance to discourage anyone so incredibly stupid as to still try to make a move. I think I'll call him Tiny.

The man on the left is a whole other magnitude of freak. He easily tops seven feet and has the face of a man who got in a head-on collision with a freight truck, only he wasn't in a car at the time. I put odds on the truck coming out on the losing end.

He too wears a suit big enough to have been made from five other suits stitched together by a skilled artisan, and still they could not get the front to button. His jacket hangs open to reveal his own piece. It is a .50 caliber Desert Eagle in a quick-draw shoulder holster. I hope like hell he is smart enough to put the weapon safety on because I can see the trigger guard has been removed to accommodate his sausage-sized finger. In lieu of a hacksaw, I bet he just chewed the thing off.

Oh man, I want a piece of him bad. Normally I wouldn't care, but tonight I am pumped, and one of the few pleasures I can still claim is putting huge, vicious men like these two in their place. Guys like Tiny and Freak go through life with a skewed sense of reality. They think they can do anything they want to anyone they want because they are big, scary men. They don't know the meaning of scary, but I'll educate them. Just let the bell ring. Class is in session.

All three men look at me like I'm a kid at the table reserved for grown-ups at Thanksgiving. Tommy's mouth twists into a derisive sneer so great I think he will tie his lips into a knot. Freak actually snorts at me. I'm almost certain he is about to sniff my ass then piss on the table leg in a show of dominance.

I keep my cool and smile politely as if I am the only one in on a private joke. Yuri knows the punch line too. Yuri likes a good joke—especially the ones where someone he doesn't like gets hurt. And I know Yuri doesn't like Tommy any more than I do. Less even. He actually still cares enough to hate.

"Please forgive me for being late, Yuri," Tommy says as he takes his seat. "I hope you have not had to wait on me for long."

Tommy Hanako is original Yakusa, but rumor has it he fled Japan to save his finger when he pissed off the wrong squint. He is something like fifth or sixth generation Yakusa, and his wanton cowardice did not sit well with the rest of his gang. So he packed up and came to New York to start his own little ninja clan. Lucky New York, lucky me.

If you look at Tommy and expect to hear the broken English of Jackie Chan, you are going to be disappointed. Tommy speaks with the clear basso of George Takei without any of the charm. The man is both snake and weasel. I don't know what part of the Chinese calendar that falls on.

I don't know if it's a vampire thing or just my own special physiology, but my tongue is host to a small but quick brain, and it often takes over at the most inopportune times. Like right now.

"Did you get stuck behind one of those slow Chinese drivers or did you have to stop off for more film for your camera?" I ask.

I know Hanako is Japanese, but Chinese stereotypes are easier and it only adds to the insult. Tiny and Freak's hands twitch toward their guns, and Tommy narrows his eyes at me. It makes him look like he just had a narcoleptic episode, and I'm not sure if he can still see me or not.

"You would do well to teach your servant manners, Yuri," the Mob boss warns through his false smile. "It would be a shame if I had to set my dogs on him."

Yuri nods, but he doesn't return the smile he knows to be as fake as the silk flowers adorning the table. "Yes, a shame indeed. Then you would have to go back to the pound for new dogs. Of course, you would save a fortune not having to feed those two."

Tommy looks at me, then studies Yuri's face for a tell that would reveal the joke he must have intended. He doesn't find one but laughs as if he gets it anyway. Freak grins at the top of my head as if I am a dessert he desperately wants to break his diet for. I pucker my lips and make a kissy face at him.

I'm sure he is going to pull his piece. I smile, a real smile, as his massive hand shoots inside his jacket and the handle of the .50 cal. disappears under its ridiculous amount of flesh.

It's starting to look like I am going to have a good time after all. I was so afraid I would be bored to tears. Tommy wrecks my fun with a quick twitch of his head. Nobody lets me have any fun. Oh well, time to be a professional again. I blame my bad manners on the blood. Too much blood in one night. Have to work harder on my manners.

Yuri is talking to Tommy again. Men like Tommy never waste so much as a single word for a hired gun like me. A bullet perhaps, but not something as important as showing I am worth even the slightest moment of his attention.

"Mr. Malone is a professional and I am sure he will act as one from here on out," Yuri assures his guest.

He says it to Tommy, but I know a reprimand when I hear one. My bad. My mind starts to drift, again, as the two gang leaders begin talking business. I have little interest in their discussion beyond wanting to see the look on Tommy's face when Yuri politely tells him to eat shit. I know Yuri well enough to know he has no interest in doing any sort of business with the likes of Tommy Hanako. Only professional courtesy got Tommy this meeting.

It's not easy for me to ignore the pervasive scent of the two goons flanking me and our bosses' table. I really struck a nerve tonight with my charming personality. Both of them wear the aroma of barely suppressed violence; I smell it oozing from their pores. I can tell how much they want to hurt me and how confident they are they can do it.

I receive a sharp look from both Tommy and Yuri as a small giggle escapes my lips at the thought. I am as chagrined by the visual rebuke as I am by the fact I actually giggled. I don't giggle. Not ever. I silently sigh as once more I come to the realization I drank too much tonight. I wish I could hold my blood as well as Yuri holds his vodka. I try to forgive myself as it's the first real mistake I've made in a long time. Surely, I can allow myself this small error in judgment.

I distract myself once more with fantasies of going toe-to-toe with Tiny and Freak. Barehanded and two on one, it could provide a good twenty or thirty seconds of entertainment. Vampires are strong and really fast, but we are not unbeatable, and those two goons bring a lot to the table for normal humans. Well, normal when compared to present company.

I let myself get distracted, which is my second mistake of the night. The mistake gets elevated to full-blown fuckup when I fail to take note of the two men climbing the stairs and approaching our party. By the time I am aware of the intrusion, guns are already drawing a bead on the two distinguished occupants at the table.

It takes me a fraction of a second to take it all in. There are two men. One is a large, hairy man with a thick, brown beard covering a powerful jaw. He is a heavily built man with a stern, focused look upon his face. He seems surprisingly calm, given the chaos he is about to cause, as he raises a mean-looking .44 revolver. I track his eyes to Tommy Hanako.

The second man is a squirrely little shit and almost certainly tweaking on something. His movements are fast but spastic. I would have dismissed him as the lesser threat if it weren't for the Mac-10 he is pointing in Yuri's direction. Not that it matters where it's pointing. With the weapon's fire rate and a clip nearly long enough to use as tripod, he could take down Yuri, Tommy, Freak, and Tiny along with half the people occupying the upper floor of the club in seconds.

I peg him as the bigger threat right now. This is my third mistake and second major fuckup of the night. Before Tweaker's half-glazed eyes can even focus on his target, my .40 cal. appears in my hand as if I'm Criss Angel or some other street magician. I don't even see my front sight post; instinct tells me I have him dead to rights.

I feather the trigger and put a bullet right between Tweaker's barely focused eyes. A neat little hole sprouts in his forehead and makes him look like a man who just discovered Hinduism. The back of his head erupts in a spray of blood, bone, and brain matter. I am sure the people on the dance floor below do not appreciate this in the slightest.

I catch Furball's movement out of the corner of my eye. I figure with my reflexes I can even save Tommy's useless hide before the hairy man pops him. I'm wrong. For a big man, he moves with incredible swiftness. He instantly recognizes my speed and the destruction of his partner's head and realizes if he is going to finish the job and come out of this alive, I need to go. His barrel traverses away from Tommy as he swings the hand cannon my way.

There is a sudden shift in the air currents, and I realize why the guy can move so fast. He's a gods-be-damned half-were-wolf. A freaking mongrel. This just keeps getting better and better. Half-weres, or mongrels as most call them, are not nearly as strong as their full-blood kin, but it's a big mistake to take them lightly. This guy would give Freak a beating in a three-round cage match. They're quick too, which is the biggest problem at the moment.

Had the guy been human, I could have easily beaten him to the punch and dropped him before he could discharge a single round. But he isn't, and this is going to be problem. For whom is still up in the air.

I don't have time to line up a perfect shot, so I stroke the trigger as soon as my gun is pointed at flesh. My hollow point strikes him high in the chest, just where the left arm attaches to the torso. He looks more pissed than hurt. His eyes widen as he realizes I am more than human myself. We both know he is not going to walk away from this table alive.

As realization dawns, he stops the traversing of his gun and points it directly at Yuri. A swift sidestep puts me between my employer and 240 grains of flesh-rending, bone-shattering copper and lead. The cacophonic boom of the big hog's leg puts the sharp crack of my .40 cal. to shame. I grunt as the slug punches me low in the ribs.

I can feel the round strike an iron-like rib in my back and stop dead. I'm hurt bad, but I can take it. With a mental urging as easy as breathing, I send stolen blood platelets to staunch the bleeding. Without a heart beating to put my bloodstream under pressure, my dark clothing absorbs what little blood does escape from the wound. The pain is intense, but I extinguish the flame by cutting off the nerve endings around the site. Half my chest goes numb as if I just received one hell of an epidural.

I manage all this without losing focus on the assassin. I continue to shift my aim and caress the trigger one more time. My bullet carves a nice trough about two inches deep along the left side of his shaggy head. To my surprise, he actually manages to give me a shit-eating grin before his eyes cross and he loses touch with his own existence. I put two more rounds in his heart just for good measure. If I am really good, it will look like a single entrance wound. I like to take pride in my work.

The entire chaotic event unfolds and meets its conclusion in less than three seconds. I take a quick look around for any more signs of trouble. All I see is Freak and Tiny, standing there with their mouths hanging open and their guns gripped in their trembling, meaty fists. Neither of them had time to so much as squeeze off a shot. They may as well have been standing there shaking their cocks at the assassins for all the good their hardware had done them.

I'll give Hanako credit; he composes himself quickly. He stands up, straightens the lapels of his ten thousand dollar suit, and gives Yuri a short bow before turning to me.

"Mr. Malone. It appears I owe you my life. I would reward a man like you greatly if you would come and work for me."

I manage not to spit in his eye. I'm so proud of myself. "As I have told Yuri many times, I am strictly freelance and amazingly choosey about whom I work for."

Tommy does not take rejection well. I see each of the muscles in his face twitch like a swarm of little subdermal worms fighting for dominance of his facial expression. Apparently, the humble ones win the battle.

"Then perhaps I can reward you by having you for dinner some time at my restaurant?"

I give a smile most people confuse with polite friendliness. "Or perhaps I'll have you?"

It sucks being the only one who gets a really good joke.

Tommy gives me one last fake smile before glaring at his two goons. "You two! What the fuck am I paying you for? You are fucking worthless! A fucking rented gun saves my life and

I pay you for what, to stand around and look stupid? Take me to my car, you fucking retards. Can you manage that? Can you walk to my fucking car? Can you even fucking spell car? Grunt once if you understand!"

Freak and Tiny are pulled along in the wake of their irate and still cursing boss as they make a beeline for the parking lot before the cops arrive. The crowded dance floor below is in chaos, but Tommy and his entourage are not slowed in the slightest as his bodyguards do what they do best and hurl anyone aside who foolishly gets in their way.

Yuri has been quiet the entire time, but with Tommy out of earshot, he can properly vent. "What de fock was all that? Who de fock are dees fockers?" Yuri demands in his accented English.

Yuri's accent gets worse when he is upset.

"Not friends of yours, I take it?" I ask with only a bit of sarcasm in my voice.

Yuri does his best to ignore my remark. "You took a bullet. I saw it. How are you?"

I put my hand over the new hole in my body.

"It hurts like hell," I lie. "Thank God for vests, huh?"

Yuri looks at me skeptically. I don't know what he's thinking, but he lets it go. "You moved fast—real fast. Those two giants, they were useless. I owe you—again."

I shake my head. "You got what you paid for."

Yuri gives me a noncommittal grunt. "We should get de fock out of here before cops show up."

I shake my head again. "We need to stay put. A couple hundred witnesses can put us all at the scene. We leave and the cops just follow and arrest us later. We haven't done anything wrong. We were the victims. It's best if we stay right here."

Yuri hates the idea, but he knows I'm right.

"I focking hate cops," he mutters, but he sits back down and gulps his unfinished vodka.

I pull out my cell phone. I know I'm in the right, but sometimes it's hard to convince the police. It's why we have lawyers, and I have a really good one—a really good and expensive one. This call is about to cost me most of what I make tonight.

"Will," I say into my phone as soon as I hear the other end pick up, "it's Leo."

"Oh shit, who'd you kill now?" he groans through the receiver.

Will knows me too well. "I don't know. A couple guys tried to kill Yuri and Tommy Hanako a few minutes ago. I did my job."

I hear my lawyer breathe out a sigh of relief. "So you were on duty; good, that's good. Are the cops there yet?"

"Not yet, but I can hear the sirens."

"OK, don't say more than you have to. Try not to say anything until I get there!" Will says anxiously.

I growl back into my phone. "I know what to do."

"I know you know what to do! The trick is getting you not to do whatever the hell you want anyway! Just try not to fuck yourself so bad I can't pull the dick back out of your ass. OK?"

Oh, ye of little faith. "Yeah, I got it. I'll behave."

Will scoffs, "Yeah right, and my next fart will smell of lilacs."

Will clicks the phone off as I assume he hurries out of his luxury apartment to pull my ass out of the fire. It isn't the first time, and it won't be the last.

I hear cops outside shouting commands to each other and at the crowd to restore some kind of control. Most of the mob is gathering in the street and the parking lot by now, but there are still plenty milling about inside to make a wreck of any crime scene.

I scan the ground floor from my elevated position as uniformed cops burst into the club and begin trying to separate and group up witnesses. I mark the Hispanic man mounting the stairs as a plain-clothes homicide detective. The cheap suit amongst the uniformed officers indicates he is a detective. The dead bodies lying near my table put the odds on him working homicide. See, that's what makes me a good private investigator. I have an eye for details.

I also know him as Angel Lopez, whom I almost consider a friend on the force. Several years ago, Angel had to testify against a major Mob syndicate operating in the area under the direction of a man named Falcone. Word got out this gang put a hit on Angel and his entire family all the way down to first cousins. Of course they were all put in protective custody, but PC is about as safe as a fishnet condom, so Angel hired me as a private bodyguard for his family.

Late one night, the two police officers tasked with protecting Angel's family both went outside to "check on a suspicious noise." It was no coincidence it was the exact moment Falcone's men struck. The official body count that night was seven dead Italian mobsters. Unofficially, you can add the owners of the thirteen trigger fingers I personally dropped on Falcone's desk, two of which belonged to two police officers who decided to retire early—and permanently.

Falcone never made it to court either. He decided to take a dive off the balcony of his penthouse suite with a little assistance from yours truly. I then convinced his replacement to pack up his operation and move it elsewhere.

Normally, a man on a cop's salary would never have been able to afford to hire me for that kind of work. But a double mortgage and a steep discount for police favors procured my services. I know; I'm a regular saint.

"How did I know you would be in the middle of this?" Angel pants as he crests the top of the stairs.

Angel has really let himself go lately.

I shrug my shoulders. "Just lucky, I guess."

"Not for them," the detective replies with a snort and a nudge of Tweaker's corpse with the toe of his shoe. "What happened?"

I shrug again. "Not much. Yuri's dinner was interrupted when these two came at the table with guns drawn, so I put them down."

Angel is scribbling notes on a small pad as I talk. "So Mr. Poplonovich was dining alone?"

I purse my lips as I think on how to answer the question. "My job is ensuring the safety of my employer. Any other details are not my business."

I should become a lawyer, or a politician. I have a knack for evasive answers.

Angel is a pro and lets my bullshit answer go. "So Mr.

Poplonovich was entertaining a guest, but I doubt either of you are going to share any information with me, are you?"

Yuri glares at the detective over his glass. "I don't focking talk to focking cops. You fockers put a boot on my Bentley last week!"

"Well, Yuri, you can't go parking in a loading zone, or those kinds of things happen," Angel calmly explains with a wry smile.

"It is my focking building, I park where I want!"

Personally, I think the entire Q and A is going great until a Latina-laced accent pierces the still chaotic din down below.

"You uniforms get control of this crowd, now!"

I knew it was inevitable, but I still blow out an invective-tainted sigh as Detective Sergeant Anna Castillo tromps up the stairs. Her dour expression turns into a maliciously gleeful smile as her eyes meet mine a few steps before she crests the top of the stairs.

Anna Castillo is a hard-nosed, honest-to-a-fault cop. She has more guts and determination than almost anyone I know. I could respect that, even like her, if only she weren't such a god-damn bitch. With her tan complexion and dark, bobbed hair she could be attractive, I suppose, but her constant sneer and pissed-off expression kind of ruins it. It's possible she looks better when she's not around me. I have that effect on most people.

"Well, well, well. What a surprise to find Leonard Malone standing amongst yet more dead bodies," she chortles without an ounce of friendliness.

Her evil smile drops as she spies my holstered piece inside my unbuttoned jacket. With commendable reflexes, she jerks her own automatic free from its sheath at her hip and points it directly at my useless heart.

"Why hasn't this suspect been searched and disarmed, Angel?" she shouts at her partner.

Angel looks abashed and his face reddens. "He's a body-guard, Sergeant. These two tried to kill his employer, and he did his job. It's Leo."

"Oh you have the case all wrapped up, do you, Detective?" Castillo snarls. "I know exactly who Leonard is and how many murders he's gotten away with."

She knows I hate the name Leonard and is trying to provoke me into doing something stupid. She has arrested me no less than twelve times over the years, and each time my lawyer is able to get me off, or there just isn't enough evidence for a conviction, and it pisses her off beyond reason.

"Put your hands on the table, Leonard. Angel, do your damn job and search him properly."

Angel shoots me an apologetic look as he steps behind me and begins patting me down. He pulls the .40 cal. from my shoulder holster and sets it on the table behind him. He works with the efficiency of a veteran, starting at my jacket collar, working down my right side to my ankle, and repeating the process once more on my left.

By the time he finishes, he has an impressive assortment of weapons placed on the table behind him. Along with my trusty .40, he has collected a 9mm auto I keep in the small of my back, a .38 revolver from my ankle, two flash grenades from the inside left pocket of my jacket, and my blade.

I love my blade, as it is one of the more effective weapons I carry to deal with my own kind. All Sheriffs are required to carry some kind of sword and be highly proficient in its use. Severing the spinal cord, or even better, the entire head, is the best way to put down a vampire other than incineration.

Most carry a semi-traditional sword. Mine is a simple length of highly tempered, razor-sharp steel. It is crafted along the lines of a katana, except it is a little over two feet long and half again as wide. The handle is simply the flat steel stamped into a diamond pattern for grip and slightly rounded. The tip ends not in a point as a normal blade would, but flat like a chisel and every bit as sharp as the blade. With my strength, there is no need for a pointed end to pierce flesh and organs and it is not a part of its design. It is a vampire-killing weapon, and the chisel end is designed to slip between the vertebrae and cripple my opponent so I may then take his head almost at my leisure.

Anna's gleeful smirk returns as she looks from me to my assorted weapons. "Quite an arsenal you have there, Leonard. I see at least twenty years laid out on the table."

I shake my head. "You know damn well I have a permit for those."

"Explosives, Leonard? Your licenses allow you to carry explosives into a nightclub?" she asks, looking at my flash grenades.

Technically, they are not explosives. I left those at home. I thought a light load would be sufficient tonight. And yes, I do have a permit and not only for the grenades. I am also a certified demolitionist and have permits to obtain and use all manner of construction-grade explosives I then turn into non-construction related devices.

"I sure hope you have those permits on you," Castillo continues. "Our computers have been real slow lately, and it could take a couple days to retrieve them from our database."

She was really enjoying this. She knows she can never get me for the two corpses bleeding all over the floor, but she can still put me through hell. It wouldn't be the first time she's done it to me. Castillo takes personal delight in stepping behind me and snapping on cuffs far tighter than I deem appropriate.

I am saved from further abuse, both verbal and physical, when Will practically leaps the last few stairs and slams his Gucci briefcase down on Yuri's table, nearly toppling the mobster's glass. No big deal, it had long been drained dry.

William Stepanek, my lawyer. As crafty and utterly immune to a nagging conscience as any man I have ever met. It's what makes him such a good defense lawyer, which in turn makes securing his services so damned expensive. But I despise inconvenience more than I like money, so I am willing to trade the latter for the former.

I don't know if it is intended or not, but Will seems to purposely look precisely like the sleazy rich guy he is. From his patent leather shoes to the silk shirt unbuttoned far enough to show several gold chains and a patchwork of graying chest hair, his ensemble makes him look part lawyer, part seventies porn star.

Will seems immune to the glare Yuri gives him for his abruptness, and releases the gold clasps on his leather attaché case and begins laying out several documents.

"Here is my client's permit for the handguns, one for the knife, and here is the one for the non-lethal suppression devices."

Detective Castillo's face contorts in anger and frustration. She hates Will almost as much as she hates me, which is an accomplishment worthy of a trophy.

"Now, if you will kindly remove the handcuffs from my unlawfully detained client."

Castillo has had enough and snaps at the small man. "He is a suspect in two murders, and you expect me to let him go because he has a permit to carry the murder weapon? Are you out of your rotten little mind?"

If she hopes to intimidate my lawyer, she is bound for disappointment. Will hands his cell phone over to Castillo. I can see the line is open as he passes the expensive device across the table.

"I have taken the liberty of calling your captain and explaining to him the circumstances of my client's involvement. This was verified to him by a statement from one of the uniforms downstairs, after said uniform talked to several witnesses."

After a few 'yes sirs,' the angry detective drops the phone onto the table. "How the hell do you sleep at night defending scum like this?"

"On two thousand thread count Egyptian cotton sheets and firmly wedged between two gorgeous bimbos," Will replies without missing a beat or a hint of shame. "Granted, two is just an average."

My lawyer grabs my hands and inspects my wrists. "This looks a lot like bodily injury resulting from police brutality," Will exclaims as he snaps several photos of my bruised and creased wrists with the camera on his phone.

Castillo steps within a few inches of my face, and the smell of smoker's breath is almost overwhelming to my sensitive olfactory receptors. "One of these days, your slimy little lawyer is not going to be there to save your ass. You will slip up, and neither he nor any of his powerful friends will be able to keep me from strapping you into the chair where I will personally throw the switch and fry your ass."

"Aw, does this mean I'm not invited to your *Cinco de Mayo*

party?" I ask with my most infuriating smile.

It is all I can do not to laugh as the detective's face contorts in barely suppressed fury. "I'm Puerto Rican, you stupid son of a bitch, not a damn Mexican!"

"Oh, now this is awkward," I reply innocently, then face Angel. "Aren't you Mexican, Angel? It sounds to me like she is really offended someone would think she is Mexican, like they are inferior or something."

I take delight in watching Castillo's anger at me deflate like a ruptured tire in humiliation. "Angel, you know I didn't mean it like that." She turns back toward me. "You fucking prick!" She gives Angel a nod as she storms away. "Bag the murder weapon as evidence. At least we can get it out of his hands for a few months!"

"Self-defense weapon, thank you," Will sings out at her retreating back as he places my various licenses back into his briefcase.

I can hear her downstairs screaming at the uniformed officers, venting her frustrations at every tiny imperfection, real or perceived. Angel lets out a long breath he has probably been holding for several minutes.

"Why do you provoke her? She already hates you enough without you throwing gas on the fire. I have to ride with her, you know."

"That fire is so out of control by now it doesn't matter what I do," I reply with a soft shake of my head. "Besides, it's so easy and so much fun. Is it just me, or is she an even bigger bitch than usual?"

"Come on, Leo. She's my partner and a good cop. Cut her some slack." Angel sighs once again as he too shakes his head. "We were at another scene near Classon and Willoughby when we got the call to come here. Fucking bodies—parts of bodies— everywhere in an alley on the other side of the borough. Most disgusting thing I ever saw."

"Mafia?" I ask, thinking that normal street violence is usually swift and reasonably clean.

"It looked more like animals got them. Could be a pack of wild dogs. Pit bulls would be my guess, but whether they were

torn up before or after they were killed will be up to the forensics team to figure out."

Will snaps his case shut and shakes my hand. "I thank you
for your services, Leo. My Manhattan penthouse thanks you,
and my new boat thanks you. I should make you a punch card.
For every nine times I keep you out of prison the tenth one is
free. I better print a few of them."

"Are you going to prorate that?" I ask as I carefully squeeze
his outstretched hand so as not to crush the delicate human
bones.

Will looks horrified at this suggestion. "Are you kidding? I'd
be working for you for free until I retire! Besides, I have my eye
on this sweet little Beechcraft Super King turboprop."

Crisis averted, Will descends the stairs and exits the club,
completely unimpeded now that a semblance of order has been
established. Angel asks Yuri and me a few more questions
before letting us go just as the forensics team and a pair of coro-
ners show up.

I retrieve my trench coat as I walk Yuri out of the club and
to his car, where a uniform is just finishing up asking his driver
some routine questions. Thor, as I refer to the big Slav, snaps to
attention and opens the rear door of the classic Bentley. Yuri set-
tles heavily into the soft leather seat and looks up at me through
the open window.

"That man with the beard. He moved fast, but you were
faster. You stepped in front of that bullet. Never have I seen
anyone move that fast. Many things I see tonight I do not like."

Again, Yuri gives me that suspicious look I saw earlier, and
I try to deflect it as best I can. "Adrenaline can give a man pretty
good reflexes. Like I said, thank God for vests."

Yuri looks at the spot where I took the bullet, but I have
already donned my trench coat and there is nothing there to
see. Even if I hadn't, there would no visible clues other than
another ruined shirt I'll have to burn. With a noncommittal
grunt and a flick of his finger, the sleek car pulls away from the
club and into the slow-moving traffic.

CHAPTER THREE

I'm too tired to go hopping rooftops back to my home, and it's not as though there are so many buildings close enough together I can go where I want like Spiderman. I descend the steps of the nearest subway entrance with more than a little trepidation. I find the flickering of the fluorescent lights and the stench of human existence almost nauseating.

Despite the late hour, an active nightlife is going on below the streets of New York as well as above. I keep away from the zombies milling around which the darkness has drawn out of whatever hole they hide in during the day, pressing my back against the far wall as I wait for the next train to show up.

In a recessed alcove, a couple of thugs are shaking down a guy foolish enough to get himself picked off from the herd. I know I'm not the only one who sees the crime in progress, but the other late-night riders care about as much as I do and feign ignorance. If ignorance is bliss, Disneyland is the second happiest place on earth. I'm sure the people's avoidance islargely based on the fear of becoming victims themselves, but it goes deeper than that. Humanity has become inured to violence, noticing and caring only when it happens to them or someone they love. Or whenever the television tells them they should care, like when a pretty little white girl goes missing.

I have no fear of these pathetic parasites, but I still do not intercede. I may be superhuman, but I am no superhero. I don't think I can pull off the whole wearing tights look. One of the muggers notices my attention to their activities and thinks for a brief second I may provide another means of quick cash. A forceful glare makes him think again, and he wisely turns back to his cohorts and their current victim. I'm glad this one is smart enough to realize I am not to be trifled with. I am not in the mood to walk to the next station after flinging his body onto the tracks. Killing someone, even garbage like him, in the middle of a busy subway station is sure to get me another visit from Castillo, and I'm really not in the mood for that.

I find to my relief the train is sparsely populated, and I won't be forced to sit next to a stinking bum, or worse, an old sow determined to share her life story with me. My sour demeanor is usually enough to keep most people at a distance, but there is always a special person so twisted up in their own head nothing short of tearing their arms off will bring them out of their fantasy world.

It's not a long ride and I am still replaying tonight's events in my head as I climb out of the dank subterranean passage and walk the remaining ten blocks to my dwelling. Tommy was trying to convince Yuri to allow him to expand his drug trade into Yuri's territory, promising to sell the crap his competitor did not and give him a thirty percent cut of the profits. Yuri was doing his best to politely tell the little squint to fuck off when Tweaker and Furball arrived on the scene.

I have an excellent memory for detail and I freeze-frame each of the faces of my attackers in my mind, studying them for the tiniest clue. My first instinct is to pin it on a setup by Hanako. A subtle cue, perhaps a wire, to let them know to come in and kill Yuri if negotiations are not going his way.

I discard this notion as I flip between the faces of my three suspects. The assassins caught Tommy unaware, and his surprise and fear were genuine. Tweaker and Furball were set on killing both mobsters at the table with no regard for bystanders. It was a major hit by someone with enough resources to hire a mongrel. The most probable scenario is a rival family, perhaps someone new, trying to carve out an empire of their own after removing the competition. A new player taking on two established crime bosses at the same time? The odds are against it, but I stopped underestimating human stupidity long ago.

I've been around a long time, and I am familiar with most of the other players with territory butting up against Yuri's. Some are larger and stronger, but they let Yuri run his business since he is not an expansionist and is fairly benign as far as Mafioso go. They know him as an honest dealer, and they are content with having him as a neighbor.

This leads me back to a new entity, picking a smaller operation as its target to take over. But it was two targets, and although few would miss Hanako's ninja clan, some would take offense to new competition. My conjecture is getting me nowhere, so I shelve my thoughts until my mind is clearer and return to my lair.

I live in a large, brick building in a mostly abandoned part of the borough. It was once a factory for turning out wrought iron for things like fences, gates, and decorations. I make my home on the main floor while I keep my office upstairs. A sign pointing to the external steel stairway directs people to it and warns them not to try my front door.

Heavy bars cover the few high windows, and the door itself is half-inch steel. If the mission at the Alamo had been similarly built, Davy Crockett and his crew could have stood off the entire Mexican army.

The sturdy door squeals on its hinges. It's a feature, not a sign of my neglect, and makes a heavy clanging as I pull it shut and set the hundred-pound bar in its cradle, securing it from the inside. Nothing short of explosives will gain anyone entrance, and the door leading to my office is of similar quality.

I strip off my ruined jacket and shirt and toss them into the forge that once smelted iron. Now its only purpose is to dispose of things I do not want found, like evidence or the occasional body. A quick look at my wound shows little more than a puckered red weal, which will be gone by morning.

I cross the dark, cavernous interior of my home to the corner serving as my kitchen—a kitchen consisting of nothing more than a refrigerator of bagged blood, a sink, and a gas stove. I forego heating the pan of water I would normally use to warm my meal and sip it right out of the bag like some kind of macabre Capri Sun.

I sit down in my recliner, one of the few items of furniture I own, and once again replay my evening's escapade. I chase the

possible reasons of the attempted hit around in my head like a
dog after a squirrel until I surrender and let it remain a mystery
to me. With any luck, someone will make another attempt and
perhaps then I will have enough pieces of the puzzle to begin
putting together a clear picture. I don't know why I bother
myself with something I'm not even being paid for. I guess I like
to figure out puzzles, especially ones in which people shoot me.

I decide I have spent enough time in useless conjecture and
give the wooden arm on the side of my chair a pull, laying the
back down and kicking my feet up. Vampires have no physical
need for sleep, but after suffering serious injury, we often relax
and enter a sort of meditative trance so the body can focus most
of its energy on healing. I do just this and sink into a relaxed
state.

I enjoyed sleeping when I was alive, and I still cling to the
habit like a wino to his bottle of Ripple. Somehow, it makes me
feel more human, almost like I am alive again. Why I want to
feel like something I have convinced myself I despise is beyond
me. I refuse to contemplate the meaning or significance of such
a mindset.

I find myself inside the dark confines of a grass hut in the sultry
nighttime air. Beyond the flimsy walls of the single-room dwelling lies a dense jungle gone preternaturally quiet. It is the type
of silence only the greatest of predators can create by the power
of its presence.

In stark contrast, the scene inside the hut is utter chaos. A
woman of Asian heritage is screaming and chattering away
in an incoherent babble. I assume she is begging for her life.
I speak passable Vietnamese as well as Chinese, but my lack
of humanity cannot process the words. She and I are the only
ones inside. Correction, the only ones alive. Another correction,
she is alive. I died nearly fifty years ago, yet I still go on. I am a
walking nightmare.

I see her huddling against the far wall amidst the bodies of
what I assume are her family and a mass of wailing children. I
don't know where the kids came from. Maybe my animal mind
completely ignored their presence, or maybe they are a figment

of my twisted imagination. I take another step toward her and she screams with renewed effort. Perhaps she is crying for help. No one is coming. Even if there is another soul left alive in the tiny village, which I made sure there isn't, there is nothing they can do.

I smile with evil glee as I approach, wearing nothing but a suit of blood like a second skin, my clothing surrendered to the decay-inducing climate of Vietnam long ago. Besides, I am an animal, and animals have no need of human trappings. I do not need food, nor sustenance from this wretched creature. I have already gorged to overflowing a dozen kills ago. This isn't about the need to feed, not a belly hunger anyway. The carnage is to feed the animal I have become, a longing for power and control, to quell a thirst I can never slake, but oh how I try.

As my clawed hand reaches out for her slender throat, I bolt upright from my recliner with a ragged gasp. The strangled cry from my nightmare echoes through my home as if the dream scream had followed me into wakefulness.

I stagger to my kitchen and splash cold water on my face. I scrub hard enough to leave my skin raw, but some blood can never be washed away no matter how much I scour. This blood has seeped through my pores and into my very soul.

As I search for my phone, I curse myself for slipping into a deep sleep. I knew the dreams would come, especially after a double feeding, but I did it anyway. I think I do it to punish myself. That's what my shrink says, but they're all quacks, so what do they know?

I fumble with my phone and manage to press the buttons in the correct order despite my palsied hands. Looking at my shaking digits serves to make me angry at my apparent weakness.

"Dr. Morison," I say into the phone before the person on the other end can even mutter "who the hell is this?"

Dr. Stanley Morison is my shrink and one of the few living people who are aware of the existence of vampires. I was referred to him after becoming a Sheriff for the council. He is trusted but carefully watched in case he has a sudden change of heart and feels the need to warn the rest of the world of the danger walking amongst them.

"Leo?" comes the answer from the other end. "Jesus, do you know what time it is? You're lucky. I'd tell most of my clients to call my office in the morning and hang up on them."

"Most of your clients won't eat you in a moment of pique," I reply.

Stanley disregards my threat. "We both know you are not going to eat me. Bad dreams again?"

"Yeah."

"Tell me what happened tonight."

I tell Dr. Morison about my midnight meal, my seconds, and the attempted assassination with my usual aplomb. This is far from the first time I have related similar stories, and he stopped being shocked years ago.

"It sounds like quite a stressful evening."

I give a shrug he cannot see, but he knows me well enough to interpret my silence.

"Deny it all you like, but inside you dwells a conscience that is only going to continue to haunt you until you face it and accept its existence."

"Not possible," I growl into the receiver. "A conscience would be extremely inconvenient given my condition and occupational requirements."

I hear him sigh into the phone. "Nevertheless, it exists, and it will not be ignored. Because it is part of you, it is as stubborn as you are. We haven't sat down and talked in a good while. Why don't you schedule an appointment with my secretary? I'll tell her to make room for you at your convenience."

My first inclination is to reject his offer. "Are you an aspiring pilot too?"

Stanley doesn't get the reference, but he's a smart guy and knows it's a shot at his hourly rate.

"All right, I'll call Jeanine tomorrow even though it's a waste of time. You've had twenty years to fix me, you old fraud."

I hang up the phone, cutting him off in mid-laugh. There is no way I am going to rest again now, so I decide to put my idle hands to work. I pull out a loose brick and press the button hidden behind it. With a hiss of hydraulics, a section of floor raises up a few inches and rolls back enough for me to navigate the short flight of stairs beneath the cement slab.

Fluorescent lights flicker to life at my approach, revealing racks of weapons of all makes and models. Several water pipes, gas lines, and electrical conduits run behind the various handguns, rifles, submachine guns, smoke and flash grenades, and a host of other lethal devices.

I converted the old maintenance passage into my armory and hid the entrance when I bought the building, over twenty years ago. Along with my host of lethal weaponry, a couple of workbenches take up much of the remaining available space. One side is dedicated to machining, with a grinder, a drill press, a small metal lathe, and a few other things necessary to fabricate those tools I cannot buy on the open market. Across from my gun bench lies a host of electrical components from which I make my transmitters, detonators, and other nifty little James Bond toys.

I select a weapon at random, break it down to its smallest parts, clean them, examine the pieces for wear, and put it all back together again. I have become highly proficient over the years, and even this level of scrutiny and care takes only a few minutes before I move on to another one and repeat the process.

Some people would call me anally retentive; my shrink calls it obsessive compulsive. I call it taking pride in my work and respecting the materials of my trade. Few things are more annoying than pressing the button on a transmitter connected to several pounds of plastic explosives, only to have it fail to detonate because you allowed the moist air to corrode the contacts.

I am adrift in my ritual and have lost track of time when I hear a chime indicating someone has walked into my office upstairs. I have company. The fact they followed the sign instructing them to climb the stairs to my office indicatesit is likely a client. Despite feeling a bit taxed from my gunshot wound, I am glad I might have a paying customer so soon after having spent a good portion of last night's paycheck on my lawyer and dessert cleanup.

I reassemble the Brugger & Thomet TP9 I am performing my maintenance on and stalk back up the steps into my converted home. The place always looks cavernous after spending a few hours below ground in my little armory. I grab a fresh shirt and slip on my trench coat from the closet containing no less than a dozen identical replacements.

Slipping my blade and an M1911 .45 into my pocket, I ascend the inner stairs to my office. I use as many of my senses as I can to ascertain the situation upstairs. Halfway up, I can hear two voices, one male and one female. The male's voice sounds a bit hostile. As I near the top of the stairs, I get the faint whiff of perfume. The scent is pleasant and lightly applied. The voices become distinct to my well-attuned ears even through the thick, steel door.

Despite its weight, the door opens effortlessly and without appreciable sound, as only I know how, and I step into my inner office. The pair waiting on me is beyond the closed wooden door leading to my outer office where a sign tells people to either wait or call for an appointment. Apparently, they have decided to wait.

The man appears displeased with the decision to come and see me. I listen to him as he says several unkind things about me, most notably the fact I am a vampire. If this weren't enough to give me pause, I receive an olfactory slap in the face that rocks me on my heels and causes my mostly healed wound to throb in sympathy. Beneath the pleasant scent of perfume lies the distinct fragrance of half-weres.

Now this is really getting interesting. I can go months without getting a whiff of a mongrel or full werewolf; suddenly I cross paths with three in the matter of a few hours. I'm not the type to believe in coincidence and go on alert.

The voices cease as the mongrels' own keen senses detect my presence as I near the room. I open the door with my left hand while maintaining a firm grip on the .45 in my jacket pocket with my right. I examine every detail of the room in a second. Nothing seems out of the ordinary, with the exception of the two supernatural creatures within.

A young man stands with an aggressive posture next to the cheap, vinyl couch that is the only piece of furniture in the room. He is tall, handsome, and well-built. With his muscular body, blue eyes, and blond hair, he looks like he was pulled right out of an underwear commercial. It must be Fruit of the Loom because he gives me a look as if he just bit into a lemon. I can feel the tension in the air like static electricity.

Sitting on the ugly orange sofa is a young woman of extraordinary beauty. Her long golden hair cascades over her shoulders better than halfway to her narrow waist and seems to glow with a light all of its own. She has the same blue eyes as the younger man standing defensively over her, but the physical similarity is where any comparison ends.

She is poised, even amused, and flashes me a broad smile as I stand in the doorway. With feline grace, she rises to her feet and steps toward me. Her brother, I am beyond certain that is what he is, attempts to grab her arm to stop her, but she slaps his hand away and approaches me, leaving her sibling red-faced behind her.

I turn and stalk back into my office, snubbing her attempted handshake and cutting off her greeting in mid-sentence. I flop into the chair behind my heavy desk and watch them enter the office in my wake.

"Have a seat or curl up on the floor, whatever you prefer," I say in a snarky tone.

She sits in one of the two empty chairs in front of my desk, while the young man looms over and behind her right side. The kid looks about to reply with a rude comment of his own or possibly jump across my desk in hopes of throttling me for my less than gracious demeanor. His sister stops both of these with a raised hand and smiles at me once more.

"Mr. Malone, I can see you know what we are, and you probably know we are aware of what you are," the young woman says.

With my usual charm I reply, "Yeah, hard to miss the wet dog odor in my lobby. You must hate this kind of weather."

I think she knows I'm intentionally being an ass and refuses to yield to my attempt to provoke her, but I won't give up easily. I want my clients to get angry so they let something slip they don't want to talk about. Her brother, on the other hand, takes the bait with eagerness but once again is interrupted before he can verbalize a response.

"Mr. Malone, I have been told you are very good at finding people. We need you to find someone; the situation requires discretion and may not be suitable for involving the police."

I have a real good idea where this is going, but I want to see how much information she is willing to give me without having to wring it out of her later, so I remain quiet and let her continue on her own.

Seeing I am not going to ask, she continues. "My name is Katherine Goldstein, and this is my brother, Roger. Three nights ago, my father, Martin Goldstein, did not come home, and we have not heard from him since."

Despite her outward calm, I detect a quavering of true concern in her voice.

"Maybe he got a whiff of a nice poodle in heat and got distracted," I say.

I finally struck the nerve I've been tweaking since I first saw them. I find people are more honest when they are angry and unable to think up lies or hold things back. My methods don't exactly endear me to my clients, but it makes my job a great deal easier.

"You son of a bitch!" the high-strung kid shouts as he lunges forward, arms outstretched and hands reaching for my throat.

His mongrel blood is apparent now. The kid is fast, but his sister is faster. Katherine practically leaps from her chair and plants herself between her enraged brother and my charming self. She stiff-arms him hard in the chest and stops him cold. Granted, it has as much to do with him not being willing to bowl over the young woman as it does her own formidable strength.

"Roger, don't," she orders, staring straight into his hate-filled eyes.

"Yeah, Roger, don't," I parrot with a wry smile.

Katherine spares a moment to shoot me an exasperated look before facing her brother again. "We need him to find Dad. Please, he's trying to make us angry, and you're falling for it. Just be still."

"Yeah, Roger," I pipe in once more, "why don't you go curl up in the corner over there and lick your balls while the grown-ups talk?"

To his credit, Roger is able to compose himself. "Jealous?"

"I'd have to like you a whole lot more to be jealous."

The kid doesn't lie down like a good dog, but he does pace to the corner of the room a few steps away, where he stands with crossed arms and a look of barely suppressed violence on his face.

Satisfied her brother is in control of himself, Katherine turns back to me, plants her palms against the top of my desk, and gives me a hard look similar to the one she used to halt her perturbed sibling. Uh-oh; I think I may be in trouble now.

"Mr. Malone, if you are through playing your little game, may we please get to the business of finding my father? I am perfectly willing to tell you anything you wish to know if it will help you find him."

I lean forward and return her gaze, my own hands planted firmly on the desktop. "The problem, Ms. Goldstein, is the client often thinks it is for them to decide what information is necessary for me to get my job done instead of me. You seem like a woman accustomed to being in control. Can you let go of that control and let me decide what I need to know?"

That beautiful smile creeps back on to her near perfect face. "And are you ever not in control, Mr. Malone?" It is obviously a rhetorical question and she continues before I can answer. "I will answer any question you have, honestly and fully, to the best of my ability, if you feel it is important."

I am surprised to find I actually believe she means what she says. I gesture back to the chair she recently vacated. She straightens her skirt before resuming her seat, folds her hands delicately in her lap, and attentively awaits my questions.

"Very well, Ms. Goldstein, tell me about your father."

"Please, call me Katherine. May I call you Leo?"

"No."

I hoped to put her off with my simple rejection but discover only disappointment. My contrariness only seems to amuse her. I find that infuriating yet strangely becoming. This woman is trouble in high heels.

"My father is an accountant. He is a kind and gentle man who dotes on his family. He is deeply in love with my mother, so your presumption that he ran off with some bitch, human or otherwise, is beyond reasonable assumption."

"Did your father have any enemies? Did he owe anyone money?"

"No and no. My father is very responsible and rather innocuous. He is also extremely honest and would never do anything to cause a problem with any of his clients."

The way she phrases her response tweaks my interest. "You think that some of his clients have the capacity to do something to someone who displeases them?"

I get an 'aha!' moment as I see conflicting emotions cross that lovely face of hers. This is where my clients start to lie to me and hold things back. I've seen it too many times to be fooled. She disappoints me again by being honest.

"My father's responsibilities include accounting and book-keeping for some dangerous people, people who are capable of making someone disappear, but my father would never cross them. He is a businessman and a very good one."

This complicates things. In a situation like this, it can be safely assumed Martin somehow ran afoul of one of his Mob clients and got himself whacked and disposed of. However, my guess is that these people are unaware of their accountant's ability to shift into a flesh-rending killing machine and would have found themselves on the losing end of a couple of hundred pounds of angry, nigh unstoppable death machine.

Like a flash of lightning, a thought strikes me swift and hard. "Where did you say your father disappeared?"

"He called my mother from his office Friday night at around 10:00 p.m. and said he was on his way home."

"And where is your father's office located?"

I pull up a mental map as she tells me the address. It is a couple of blocks from where Angel said they found the torn-up remains of three corpses. Maybe a client had tried to rub him out and found out the hard way it was going to be no easy task.

"Please, Mr. Malone, help us," Katharine urges.

I nod my head thoughtfully. "Very well, Ms. Goldstein. However, you should be aware that my rates increase substantially any time I have to deal with werewolves or vampires."

The sour look upon Roger's face turns even more bitter, but without even a backward glance, a raised hand from his sister cuts short his argument.

"That is certainly understandable, Leo, given the inherent risks involved in dealing with our kind," she says with a smile as she stands and extends a delicate hand toward me.

I ignore the polite gesture again, but I am surprised to find I have to resist the urge to do so. I have no problem admitting to myself she is an attractive woman, but her true charm is the strength of personality emanating from her like the heat of a bonfire. Fortunately, decades of being a surly, cold-hearted prick makes it little more than a minor nuisance.

As she retracts her hand, she smiles at me as if her gaze pierces my invisible shield and sees my little emotional battle. She turns with military precision and makes for the door with Roger close behind her. He turns to me just before crossing the threshold of the doorway.

"You had better be worth this expense," he warns me with a parting glare.

Upon the advice of my shrink, I got myself a dog several years ago. Stanley seemed to think that since I was unwilling to tolerate human company, a pet would help me maintain a sort of social dependency or some crap. It was right after I started seeing him, and Dr. Morison was not accustomed to tailoring his advice to best suit his few undead clients. First of all, dogs do not care for the presence of vampires or werewolves. It took me two years to build enough trust just so the little shit wouldn't bite me every time I walked into the room. When he died, it served to remind me I would continue to watch those around me die off as I continued my unnatural existence, forcing me to change my identity every few decades.

"Roger," I call out as I reach into the wide, center drawer of my desk, "you were a very good boy," I tell him, then toss a dog biscuit at him that is years past its freshness date.

Given his obvious temper and lack of humor, I expect him to hurl it back at me with a sharp invective, but once again, I am surprised as he catches the treat in one hand and takes a large bite from it. With a self-satisfied grin of triumph, he tips the biscuit toward his brow in a mock salute and saunters out the door.

Damn. Now why did he have to go and do that? If he keeps that up, I may start to like the angry little mutt.

I lean back in my chair with my hands behind my head and mull over what Angel told me last night. Tracking down a werewolf means I will have to go and talk to other weres. Not an appealing prospect. It's a good thing I'm such a likeable sort, or getting information out of them could be difficult. I am still formulating my plan of attack when the phone rings.

"Malone," I say into the receiver.

"Leo, it's Raj, from the coroner's office."

"Thanks for the clarification. I thought maybe it was Raj from my Hindu prayer group."

"It's always a pleasure talking to you, Leo. Anyway, I have some…things down here I need you to take a look at."

Raj is this borough's chief medical examiner and the only other human who knows what I am. We crossed paths years back while I was a Sheriff hunting down a rogue who was leaving the bodies of his victims around for the normals to find.

Ordinarily this isn't too big of a problem, but Raj was far too smart and curious for his own good. He began investigating and asking questions that were going to get him killed real fast. I thought it was better to have someone in his position in on our little secret society than to quiet him—permanently. So I told him everything.

He impressed me with the calm with which he took this disclosure. Most people would be in a panic at finding out their species is not at the top of the food chain. They are especially put off when informed having that simple knowledge marked them for immediate extermination.

Raj, on the other hand, found the entire thing fascinating. And he assured me he understood that if he so much as breathed a word of our existence to another living being, including vampires, *especially* vampires, it meant instantaneous death.

He is an unofficial informant, and if the council ever finds out he knows, and I am the one who told him, we will both be in a lot of trouble. Now I have someone who contacts me anytime he gets a body with the telltale signs of a supernatural cause of death.

Raj continues the explanation for his call. "I have three bodies down here in various stages of disassembly I think you should take a look at."

"Let me guess. Three toughs made extra tender around 123rd?"

"How did you know that?"

"Angel mentioned it last night after Castillo grilled me and took some of my office supplies."

"Ah, yes. I got your latest handiwork in a couple of hours ago. I haven't had a chance to give them a full examination. They seem fairly routine as far as gunshots go."

"The big furry one is a mongrel," I inform him.

Raj's voice lowers in concern. "Is this going to create problems for you, or worse, for me?"

I shrug my shoulders unconcerned. "It shouldn't, but you can never tell with weres. I doubt it. Purebreds aren't too concerned with mongrels, and he brought it upon himself, but you can never really be sure with their kind."

"Well, I'm pretty confident of what I have here, but I thought you may want to see for yourself. It might interest you and your guys," Raj said.

"Yeah. In fact I was just thinking I might stop by and take a look at them," I tell him.

I don't see any need to let him know it is a case urging me to pay him a visit. Let him assume I am interested because I care about the goings-on of werewolves and vampires. I tell Raj I will come by later in the day and have to cut him off as my cell begins to chirp with another call.

I look at the caller ID and think to myself well, aren't I just the pretty princess at the ball, when I see Yuri's number.

I hit the answer button. "Malone."

"Mr. Malone, I hope you are well. I know taking a bullet, even wearing a vest, takes its toll on a man, but I have urgent need of you once more."

"What's the job?" I ask with obvious trepidation.

"I need you to find a man for me. It is very important."

I can't help but smirk as I reply, "Yuri, I'm not really the matchmaking type. Have you tried eHarmony?"

Yuri seems to ignore my little joke. "I need you to find my accountant. He is missing, and he is only one who knows how to do my taxes...properly."

Now he has my attention. "What's his name?"

"Martin Goldstein."

Now I am very interested. "I'm really sorry, Yuri, but I just took on a big case that's going to take all my time."

"I pay you double, triple, your usual fee. Mr. Malone. I need this man found, and you are only one I trust to do it."

I try to make the inflection of my voice sound as though I am reluctantly doing him a favor. It's not easy when you want to start dancing like an old prospector who just struck gold.

"Alright, Yuri, but only because you're a friend." I cock an ear toward the door. "I hear someone coming up the stairs. I'll call you back for more info later."

"Good. Mr. Malone, I consider you many things. Funny is not one of them," Yuri growls in reply to my earlier attempt at humor, then hangs up.

I flip my phone shut, toss it on my desk, and lean back in my chair. Now things are looking up. Do I feel guilty getting paid twice for the same job? Not at all. I figure this will be a simple case, and the double-dipping just makes it sweeter. Yep, this should provide me with quick, easy cash.

Half a dozen darkly dressed figures stride into my small office and suck every bit of feel good right out of me. Sheriffs never bring good news, and I'm not enough of a fool to think this is a social call.

Wyatt, captain of the Sheriffs for this region, steps in front of my desk, hand gripping the handle of a weapon beneath his duster. "Leo, we need you to come with us."

Yeah, this is definitely not a social call. My good fortune never does seem to last long. Story of my life.

CHAPTER FOUR

Wyatt stands with his hand gripping the hilt of his undrawn blade waiting to see if I am going to accept his invitation. Behind him, mimicking his posture and preparing to jump at the slightest hint of a threat, is his posse.

I strum my fingers on my desk as I consider my options. I drag out my response in part because I want to see what these clowns are made of, but mostly I just like to screw with them. I have a rather dark reputation, and I've earned every bit of it. It makes a lot of people nervous.

Besides, the fifteen pounds of plastic explosives and fifty pounds of ball bearings backed by a half-inch steel plate making up the entire front of my desk ensure any attempt at force will end up much worse for them than for me. Yeah, I'd have a killer headache and my ears would ring for a week, but I am coming out on top—on top of a bunch of dead vamps.

Wyatt's face is easy to read, as usual. He does not like being here any more than I do. His guilt is in a three-way battle with duty and fear.

The other clowns are also readable to varying degrees. There are five in all. I pick out the second in command. He is tall, athletic, and has a smug, self-assured look on his face. I dislike him immediately. I find there are a finite number of arrogant pricks I can tolerate in one enclosed space and I like to call dibs.

Next, I search for the weak link. There's one in every group and it isn't hard to find him. Lean and twitchy, he stands nearest the door with an appropriate amount of fear on his face. I assume he has heard of me. I like it when young vamps are afraid of me. It shows they are both capable of respect and smart enough to be afraid.

The other three are also young and their respect to fear ratio varies. They try their best to keep up the poker faces, but I've been reading expressions a long time. When you have been where I have been and done what I have done, reading faces can mean the difference between a good evening and a bullet in the head. I prefer it to be my bullet and someone else's head, so I became a quick learner.

"To what do I owe this unexpected visit, Wyatt?" I ask as nonchalantly as a guy can with six highly-trained killers ready to cut him down if he so much as twitches.

Wyatt's response is interrupted by the smug little shit obviously aching for a fight. "Shut your mouth and do what you're told. We'll ask the questions."

Wyatt knows me well enough to know the smile spreading across my face is not a sign of amusement, but the prelude to a level of violence not seen outside of the Old Testament.

The Sheriff captain spins around with a speed I haven't seen from him in a long time. The weary sag of his shoulders vanishes as his hand flies away from the hilt of the sword hidden under his black duster.

He points a quavering finger at his upstart lieutenant and barks, "Shut the fuck up, Quinn! He used to be one of us, and you'll treat him with respect!"

Quinn glares past his leader and our eyes shoot lasers of pure hatred at each other. We both know in that instant, someday we will cross blades and no quarter will be given. I don't know what reason I seem to have given him that's made him want to fight me. I certainly don't need one. I'm almost disappointed as I pull my finger away from the button of my giant, makeshift claymore. I've never had an opportunity to use my desk bomb, and I was kind of looking forward to seeing how well it worked.

My smile does not slip a bit as I reply, "Yeah, kid, play nice or you'll get a time-out."

The hostile young vampire lunges forward, blade half drawn before Wyatt intercepts him.

"Quinn, enough! Are you so stupid you can't see you're dancing to his strings?"

Quinn glares at his leader as if trying hard to keep from turning his blade on him instead of me. The kid is so full of rage he is trembling.

Where did Wyatt find this guy? I ask myself.

When I was a Sheriff, this kid's attitude and lack of control would have kept him from even passing the initial interview. I realize I do not recognize any of the faces in the room other than Wyatt's. All are new, and I don't mean just unfamiliar. None have been vampires for more than a few years if my intuition is correct.

The kid is still venting. "We outnumber him six to one! We don't have to pander to his ego!"

"And if I thought I was going to have to use force, I would have brought another six if I had them!" Wyatt argues back.

Through an amazing effort of will, or divine intervention, the kid clamps his mouth shut. Taking advantage of Quinn's momentary control, the Sheriff captain turns back toward me.

"Leo, will you come with us—peacefully?"

I give him a small shake of my head. "Sorry, Wyatt, but I can't do that."

My former friend lets out a sigh of exasperation and trepidation. "Why not, Leo?"

"Because you didn't say please," I reply with a smirk.

"Goddamn it! I'll give you a please and thank you as I ram my sword up your ass!" Quinn screams, practically frothing at the mouth as he once more tries to pull his blade from the scabbard hidden beneath his trench coat.

It takes Wyatt and two of the other young Sheriffs to pin the upstart's arms to his side and force a sense of control back into him. Wyatt leaves his protégé in the grip of two other members of his posse.

He rubs his temples as if trying to massage out a migraine—or a stroke. The fact I can still aggravate him to such levels of frustration amuses the hell out of me.

"Leo, would you please come with us?"

"I want him to ask me—nicely," I say, indicating the hothead with a point of my chin.

"Goddamn it, Leo!"

It's not often you can make a vampire flush. And I thought this wasn't going to be any fun.

"Oh fine," I say with a casual flick of my wrist.

"Leave your weapons here," Quinn orders.

I give Wyatt a look.

"Please, Leo. It will make it more comfortable for everyone."

I shrug my shoulders as if the request does not bother me in the least. I stand and drop my gun and blade on the desktop then give everyone an intent look.

"If I need a weapon, I'll just take one of yours," I promise them all.

Quinn's smirk says he'd like to see me try. At this point, I do my best to ignore him. He's a puppy just aching to try out his new big-dog teeth. Ihave better things to do with my time, so the more I cooperate, the faster I can get this over with and be on my way.

I'm flanked on all sides, but my escorts are wise enough to stay beyond arm's reach. Despite every one of us wearing heavy boots, our combined footsteps hardly make a sound on the steel steps. Waiting on the curb at the foot of the stairs is one more vamp, standing next to a black panel van with the sliding door open. I'm almost relieved to see a face I recognize.

"Greg," I greet with a nod of my head.

"Leo," Greg replies, trying but failing to keep an amused grin from his face.

Greg was a Sheriff before I joined. He is a big man, and the only vampire I know who keeps a full beard. We get along mostly because we share similar ideologies. We both despise politics and the bullshit that always accompanies it. He's just better at accepting things beyond his control, which is one reason he's still a Sheriff and I'm not.

I am allowed to enter first and take a seat on the bench running along the inside of the van. Wyatt and his entourage pile in after me. I am wedged between an Asian girl and a lean black woman with a shaved head. Wyatt and Quinn sit in jump seats that fold down from the sliding panel door. Greg flashes me a look of regret and possibly an apology as he climbs into the driver's seat. That concerns me more than just a little.

I'm not too worried. Despite there being numerous people who want me dead, if someone ordered me killed, the attempt would have been made already. I do not need to see out of the windshield, the only viewable port in the van, to know we are heading for the Brooklyn Battery Tunnel. Nor do I need the salty smell of the air to alert me to the fact we are now crossing under the bay. I've dumped so many bodies here that if you fished them all out, the water level would drop three inches.

The benefit of taking the toll road is it takes us just half an hour to make the fifteen-mile trip. Quinn slides the door open and rudely shoves me out almost before we come to a full stop.

I pause for my escort, looking up at the tall, black building stretching up to the sky with its hundreds of silvery reflective windows. Bloodsucker headquarters, also referred to as the Tower. It is where many vampire-owned companies and corporations keep their corporate offices. It is solely occupied by our kind. Having an enormous tower in the heart of Manhattan is a testament to our ability to keep a secret.

Quinn shoves me again. "Move it, asshole. What are you, a fucking tourist?"

I just smile at him as I rehearse in my mind several gruesome ways in which I will kill him. A growled warning from Wyatt makes him back off, and we march in unison through the huge glass doors and into the lobby.

The interior is as decadent as one would expect from a den of evil. The walls are black marble and granite. Near the center of the five-story atrium, in a mocking contrast to the masters of this warren of iniquity, is a thirty-foot-tall alabaster angel standing upon a ten-foot dais, holding an infant. The woman has her wings outstretched as if welcoming everyone who enters the building, and is smiling down serenely at the babe in her arms. Few visitors understand it is the smile of a vampire just before it sucks the lifeblood out of a human.

The two guards sitting behind the large security desk nod to Wyatt and let us pass without a word of challenge. The security in this building is run by one of the few other vampires I consider something of a friend. The doors of the elevator open as we approach, as if it has been waiting just for Wyatt and his crew. Wyatt uses a key to gain access to the top floor.

Despite the towering height of the building, our ascent is swift and the doors to our elevator open to deposit us into another foyer, though less grand than the one on the first floor. We march past a second security station, turn down the first hallway on our left, and step into a large open room occupying a significant amount of real estate in one of the building's corners.

Other than a few concrete pillars, the room is rather spartan in appearance. The only exceptions are a couple of couches, a large television, and a foosball table in the corner of the room. I have more than a passing familiarity with this room. It is the dayroom and training room for the Sheriffs. When not hunting down troublemakers, the Sheriffs gather here to relax and beat the hell out of each other.

No one is offering me any information, and I'll be damned if I'm going to ask. I wonder how hard it will be to make Quinn go for me. Probably not very, and I'm minutes away from finding out just to break the boredom with something more entertaining than challenging someone to a game of foosball. Fortunately, the sound of familiar voices entering the far end of the room breaks the tedium before I start breaking heads.

"I don't understand why you're blocking this, Vincent. My people are stationed at the monitors at all times. It will help us keep track of not just our own people, but we can spot potential prey, clean up the gutter trash, and most importantly, make me some damn money."

The speaker is Percy LaRoche. He is one of the few people here I can tolerate. Percy is an old southern gent who seems to hold few grudges for being on the losing side of the civil war. He is a big fellow, a bit on the heavy side, and his greying hair makes him appear vested in his early fifties.

The other half of the polite argument is Vincent, which is an apt name since he looks a great deal like Vincent Price when he was in his sixties. Vincent is the head of the enclave, an elected position. Being nominally in charge does not make him an uncontested power, however. The position is mostly that of a figurehead, though he does guide the politics and workings of the local vampire community and wields a veto power for anything brought before the council.

Vincent is an old vamp too. I don't know how old, but I am pretty sure he was around for the signing of the Declaration of Independence. I would bet my left testicle he supported the losing side too, and is still bitter about it.

He is *not* my friend, and is the primary factor in my self-employed status. Several years ago, a German diplomat friend of his came for a visit and began abusing our hospitality. Vincent and I had a disagreement about the limits of diplomatic immunity. I was also tired of cleaning up his messes.

Vincent politely asked his friend to leave. My solution was less subtle but far more permanent. Baron Von Wurst-in-Ass was not only a vampire but also a "former" Nazi so sadistic his antics would make Himmler puke. While he was in his luxurious hotel suite packing for his return flight, I packed the floorboards and inside roof of his town car with C4.

I used shaped charges so the explosion made a glorious Nazi sandwich. Other than blowing a crater in the street and shattering every nearby window, there was almost zero collateral damage. I wasquite proud of myself. Vincent was not.

He told me I had overstepped my authority and risked exposing the enclave due to the overwhelming attention from the feds my solution attracted. I argued my oath of upholding the laws of the enclave and expeditiously destroying rogue vamps overruled his political convenience. The result was my being fired and earning the enmity of the most influential vampire in the western hemisphere.

"Mr. Malone, how nice of you to stop by," Vincent calls out with veiled hostility as he breaks away from Percy and stalks toward our little group. "I seem to recall saying if I ever found you anywhere near this building I would have you killed, you miserable little prick."

I glance at my escort. "I don't recall being given a choice."

"I don't recall having made a distinction."

I roll my eyes at his attempted wit. "What's the matter, Vincent, you miss me?"

Vincent steps close to me, totally violating my personal space. It takes all my self-control not to move away. "The only thing I miss is functional kidneys so I may piss on your grave when someone puts you down like the rabid dog you are."

"I'm so sorry my continued existence brings you so much disappointment."

"Don't be too sad, I have already commissioned a latrine for the homeless to be constructed atop your gravesite. I shall take my pleasure in the end."

"I always thought you did. Good of you to finally push your coffin out of the closet. Now I know why you hired Quinn."

I know it is not the prudent thing to do, provoking the leader in a room full of already hostile vampires, but my mouth has long overruled my brain. As I suspect, Quinn is eager to jump at me. High-strung kids like him, convinced of the near immortality and the feeling of invincibility their recent vampirism gives them, are quick to test themselves.

It's a lot like the Old West. A gunslinger gets renowned for being the meanest and fastest gunman around. Most people are smart and leave him the hell alone. But there are always a few hotshots who just have to test him and beat him so they can immortalize themselves. My reputation for being particularly lethal is well-deserved, and all Quinn needs to do is kill me to claim top dog.

I know he is going to jump even before he does, and I am ready for it. I already have my target picked out: the nervous kid with the shifty eyes. I lunge while Quinn is in mid-flight, yanking the sword free from the scabbard he keeps beneath his long jacket before he can even register the fact I moved.

I spin toward Quinn and catch his blade with the one I borrowed inches from my face. The young tough would surely have pressed his attack, but Wyatt punches him in the side of his head and sends him sprawling to the floor.

"Why the fuck did you do that?" Quinn shouts at Wyatt as he springs to his feet and glares daggers at his superior.

"Two reasons," Wyatt explains. "First, no one ordered you to kill him. You need to learn to act on orders and not your own personal desires!"

I can't help but feel the rebuke is partially directed at me. I mentally shrug my shoulders.

"Secondly, I don't want to have to assign someone to clean you up off the floor."

"He's not so tough. I almost had him," Quinn replies, sulking.

Quinn thinks he has my measure now and finds it lacking, or at least not living up to the hype. I do not intend to dissuade him of this notion. The fact is, he still knows nothing of what I am capable of, but now I know exactly what he is made of, and I am not impressed.

Everyone relaxes when I give Shifty his sword back. "I told you I would take one of yours if I needed a weapon."

Shifty grabs the proffered blade as if I am handing him a live snake and backs away.

"You may want to take care of that nasty nick," I tell him, indicating the notch made by the colliding blades.

"If you are through playing, perhaps we can discuss the business at hand," Vincent says with as much snobbery as he can muster—which is a considerable amount.

I let out an exasperated sigh. "Cut through the bullshit, Vincent, and tell me what you want."

"There has been a rash of killings, mostly in your district."

"So? It's Brooklyn, and not the nice part either. People are always getting themselves killed."

"These killings are not caused by humans. You should know me well enough to know I would not inflict your presence upon myself for anything so trivial."

"I still don't see why you're asking for me. Send your dogs out. It's their damn job."

I can see Vincent struggling to maintain his composure as he responds. "They have more pressing business, which is why I am telling you to do it."

"Yeah, I'd like to help but you fired me, remember? It's a Sheriff problem, so kindly go fornicate yourself. Fornicate is today's word from my Word of the Day calendar," I explain.

I see Quinn twitch almost spasmodically as Wyatt restrains him with a glare. Vincent saves me complete disappointment as his calm façade slips.

"You are still a warder of your district, you little shit, and you will deal with it as is required! I strongly suggest you find out what is happening rather quickly, because right now you are my prime suspect!"

Damn, he has me on both counts. A warder is like a land-lord or baron. Any vamp who wants to hunt in your district is supposed to get your permission. On the flip side, you are responsible if people in your district are fucking up. And if your car gets stolen, people generally look at the neighbor who has a history of stealing cars. Metaphorically speaking, I have stolen a lot of cars.

Vincent continues a bit more calmly. "We have cleaned up several messes over the past two weeks, but several mutilated bodies were found by the police before we could get to them. This last killing points toward a rogue werewolf, but I do not want to rule anything out, as the previous deaths appeared vampire made."

On the bright side, I am already dealing with what he is ordering me to investigate. The problem is since the council is involved it makes it an official issue between the vamps and the weres, and that is not pleasant to deal with at the best of times.

"All right, I'll look into it," I reply in surrender.

"Excellent. Now get the hell out of my building before I decide it would be far easier and preferable simply to hang it on you and have you summarily executed."

Quinn darts forward as if to grab me by the arm and force-fully march me out of the building, but Percy's intervention saves him from drawing back a bloody stump before he can latch on to me.

"It's all right, Quinn, I will escort him out," the elder vam-pire informs the little punk as he strides across the large room toward us.

As we walk toward the elevators, I ask him, "So what were you and Vincent arguing about?"

"What do you know about London?"

I shrug my shoulders. "They talk funny, drive on the wrong side of the road, and eat the vilest food known to western civilization."

Percy rewards me with a grin. "Certainly all true, but they also have over ten thousand security cameras watching the streets, and I want to replicate that here."

"In New York?"

Percy nods. "As a start, but I hope its success will provide my company with contracts in all the major cities across the country. It would create thousands of jobs desperately needed in this economy."

"It would also create millions of dollars for you," I point out, quirking a knowing eyebrow at him. "Besides, as loath as I am to agree with Vincent, having cameras record our particular activities seems like a pretty bad idea."

"That's just the thing. We would know where the cameras are, and my people would be the ones watching. There is a lower risk of discovery because we could direct hunters to prey with no witnesses around. And it's billions, Leo, Vincent is cockblocking me out of billions of dollars in contracts."

"You and Vincent not getting along these days?"

It's Percy's turn to give me a noncommittal shrug. "No more or less than usual. It's all politics, and there has been a shift in political tides these last few years. More people are thinking it is time to elect a more progressive member to lead the council. Even we are not immune to this decaying economy."

"It always seems to be about money," I reply, my lack of understanding of what I see as greed obvious in my reply. I wonder if it is because I am always broke.

"It's more than just the money. People need a leader who will take them higher, put them up where they belong. We are at the top of the food chain, but we hide inside our giant prison, afraid of the humans outside."

"Well, there are a lot more of them than us."

Percy dismisses my comment with a wave of his hand. "I'm not talking about taking over. Vampires who think like that do not often enjoy a long life. But there are key political and corporate positions we should be involved in that will grant us a great deal more influence, freedom, and power."

"And money, we mustn't forget the almighty dollar."

Percy stops, shakes his head, and grins at me. "Why are you

so resistant to showing a profit?"

"We hate that which eludes us," I reply philosophically.

Percy enjoys a good laugh as we exit the elevator and cross the enormous lobby. He holds the door open for me and I step out of the building.

"Leo," Percy says in a warning tone, "watch yourself. There's something off about this whole business."

"Rogue vampire, rampaging werewolf, what's off about that? It seems pretty normal to me."

Percy grunts a short laugh and disappears back into the building. I see no one is waiting to give me a ride home. Oh well, I'll just put the cab fare on Katherine's bill. And Yuri's of course, and if I can find a way to swing it, I'll even bill Vincent.

CHAPTER FIVE

I take a cab back to Brooklyn since I am about as fond of subways as I am of nightclubs, and for the same reasons. Thanks to the creative route my driver uses, it takes twice as long to get back.

The taxi deposits me in front of the medical examiner's office on Winthrop Street. I don't know why all government buildings look like county jails. I guess they use the same uninspired architect.

Raj has a visitor's badge waiting for me at the front desk, and I grab it before heading toward the examination room, something I am more familiar with than can possibly be healthy.

I push through the doors of the exam room without registering the sudden drop in temperature. I recognize Raj right away despite his paper gown and blood-spattered face shield. He is hunched over a corpse, not one of mine since it is intact, and using an electric oscillating saw to remove the top of the skull.

Despite the noise of the blade, he is aware of my presence and gives me a nod of recognition while he finishes his gruesome task. Steady hands and exceptional skill make short work of the procedure. He sets the top of the skull down like a macabre bowl on a steel tray.

"Leo, I'm glad you stopped by. Your guys are over here," he tells me, then motions to the lockers as he tosses the contaminated disposable gown in a waste bin.

Raj slides the drawer out and unzips the thick, black body bag, exposing its contents. What I see inside would turn the stomach of the most hard-core veteran. The bag is nothing more than a container to keep the various pieces of anatomy together. It looks like the parts bin at a Barbie factory, except bigger and a lot grosser.

"Jesus Christ, is that one guy?"

"No, I put off identifying and separating them until you took a look."

"Thanks, you always get me the nicest things. So what makes you think this is for me?" I ask him.

Raj pulls a metal rod out of a pocket of his lab coat and starts picking through the pieces, pointing out anomalies.

"The puncture marks in the skin are the most obvious signs of animalistic predation. If you look closer, you can see gouges in the bone. Look at the symmetry of the scratches spaced about six inches apart."

"Could be a dog."

Raj shakes his head. "Given the spacing and depth, a lion would be more plausible."

I shrug. "OK, a lion then."

"Ah yes; the infamous yet elusive Brooklyn lion."

"Maybe it got away from Mike Tyson."

I can tell Raj is getting annoyed with me. "Mike Tyson has a tiger, not a lion."

"Whatever, it's still weird."

"I guess; not werewolf or vampire weird, but weird."

I give in to his logic. "What else do you have?"

I follow Raj back to his office. He sits behind his computer, clicks around with the mouse, and swivels the monitor toward me.

"These are images of the striations on the flesh and bones I showed you. These are of the crime scene before they bagged the bodies. Despite the rather shocking visuals, the most remarkable thing is this."

Raj pulls up an image of hair samples taken from the crime scene. They're thick and wiry-looking. I recognize them immediately.

"Shit."

"Officially, I'm leaning toward mastiff and Irish wolfhound mix, but I think we both know what it is."

"Shit!" I exclaim once more.

It's like being called to identify the body of a family member. You prepare yourself for the worst while praying the victim is not someone you know but, in the end, it is and you're still not ready for it.

"Can you get a copy of these for me?"

"Sure. Do you have a thumb drive?"

I stare at Raj as if he asked me if I have a tail.

"You do know what a thumb drive is?"

"Sure, it's how you pop a guy's eyeball out of the socket," I reply with a miming gesture of jabbing my thumb at Raj's head.

"I'm afraid to ask, but do you have an email address?"

"I don't think I even have a mailbox."

"Jesus, Leo, what planet are you from? I would burn them onto a disk, but something tells me you don't own a computer. Do you even have electricity?"

"Off and on," I reply with a shrug.

"Fine, I'll print them out," Raj says in resignation.

A few clicks and Raj's printer starts spewing out high-resolution color images. He slides them into a large manila envelope and hands them to me.

"So what do you do now? Start hunting it down?"

"The problem with hunting weres is it's real easy for them to start hunting you, which is not healthy," I tell him.

"If you are not going to hunt it down then what are you going to do?"

"Oh, I'm going to hunt him down, but first I need to make sure I'm after the right werewolf. It's bad enough hunting the right one, but if you jump the wrong one it creates another level of pain in the ass best avoided."

Raj gives me a grin. "You ever hunt the wrong one before?"

"Once, and it was unpleasant. It left me even more unpopular with the weres than the rest of my kind."

"What are you going to do when you find it?"

I sigh and shake my head. "I have no idea."

"Can't you just kill him, like a rabid dog?"

"Not only is that terribly insensitive of you, Raj, it's a political goat screw. There are other complications attached as well.

It is just now dawning on me that there is no way I'm going to get paid enough for this."

"You told me you put people down before. Why's this so different?"

"If it was a vampire it would be easy. He's in my ward breaking the law. Since it's a werewolf, there's sort of a jurisdiction thing involved. When one kind kills the other, you can expect a huge shitstorm, and that's when it's justified."

Raj furrows his brow as he asks me, "Can't you just hand it off to whatever werewolves handle this sort of thing?"

"It's complicated. Werewolves are not subtle, and they tend to act first and think later, if at all. I also have a client who has a vested interest in concluding this without folks getting torn to pieces."

If I go to the weres and tell them about the bodies and my interest in Mr. Goldstein, the wolves might also start looking for him, which has a high probability of not turning out well for him or my paycheck. Unfortunately, weres are a close-knit bunch of furballs, and if I hope to find out anything about Martin, I have no other option but to talk to them.

By the time I leave Raj's office I know where I need to go, and it does not thrill me at all. I will need to pick up a few things from my office before walking into a wolf den. The cab I called pulls up to the front of the medical examiner's office, and I take a seat amongst the stench of a thousand ass cracks. It's still better than the subway.

It's a short ride, and within a few minutes I'm home. I disable the alarms, heave open the steel security door, and step into the cavernous chamber I call home. They say a man's home is his castle. Anyone looking at mine would think I got the dungeon, which is fine with me. No one ever tries to rob a dungeon.

I enter my hidden arms room once more and begin transferring a few tools of my trade into the various pockets and straps of my custom-made Miguel Caballero bullet resistant trench coat. At over three grand a pop, it reminds me of one of the reasons I'm perpetually broke.

The first thing I grab is my sword, and I slide it into the sheath built into the inside left breast of the jacket. Next is a can of bear spray, and not the kind you pick up at your local sporting goods store. Federal regulations limit the maximum CRC to two percent; mine is custom-made at five.

I drop a few small explosives with remote detonators into my right pocket, because you never know when you might need to blow something up. Like the old saying goes: better to have explosives and not need them, than need them and not have them.

I save my favorite for last. Opening the padded plastic case and looking upon the beauty inside is the closest thing to a sexual experience I've had in a long time.

I cannot help but smile as I hold the Smith and Wesson .500 magnum. The barrel is a svelte four inches and takes two hands just to prevent the shooter from burying the front sight in his forehead. Thanks to my superhuman strength, I can pop off all five rounds one-handed with balls-on accuracy and little more than a twitch of the wrist.

In the movies, cowboys always have names for their favorite guns, usually something stupid like Betsy. I named my gun Shalonda because she is big, black, and when she shoots her mouth off, someone is going to have their day ruined. I named her after an unfortunate encounter with a woman at the Department of Motor Vehicles. I had been standing in line for the better part of the morning to renew my driver's license. Sometimes my job requires me to play chauffeur in addition to bodyguard, and getting in trouble for something stupid like an expired license is plain dumb.

After finally reaching the front of the line, Shalonda none too politely informed me my license had expired and I needed to take a retest. Given my already prickly disposition, my lack of patience, and being forced to stand nuts to butt with what I feel are cattle, I told Shalonda what she could do with her test.

She proceeded to open a verbal can of whoop-ass the likes of which I had never seen, much less been the target of. She reduced me to a pile of my elemental components right there in the lobby of the DMV. When she finished berating me like a vile child, she proclaimed she was going on a break and wouldn't be back until "that Matrix-looking, cracker motherfucker in the trench coat was gone."

It did not help my damaged ego getting the stink eye from

everyone who now either had to slide over to another line or wait for her to come back. The incident left me so traumatized it was three years before I went back and renewed my license. I'm not sure what kind of masochist resides inside of me, but I think I could have married her.

The gun slides comfortably into the holster built into my left coat pocket. The special construction of the pocket makes it almost undetectable to the naked eye. Given where I have to go, nothing less than a howitzer would make me feel truly safe, but I have to talk to people to find out about Martin; unfortunately, those people are werewolves.

Another thirty-minute taxi ride takes me to an alley bar on east Tremont. I step out of the cab near the end of the alley, navigate my way past the refuse lining the tall brick walls to either side, and stride confidently toward the huge, leather-clad man guarding the door.

He does not even try to hide the sneer carved onto his face as he watches me stroll down the alley. As I reach for the handle of the steel door, he stops me with an open palm that nearly covers my entire chest.

"Where do you think you're going, leech?"

I really hate being touched.

"Inside," I growl as politely as I can, which means with unsuppressed hostility.

The man shakes his big, shaggy, greasy, reddish-brown head. "Not gonna happen."

"Fine, maybe you can help, Mr...?" I ask him with a sigh.

"Meat."

"Meat? How charming. Is that short for dead meat or something?"

"Ain't short for nothing."

I sigh again. "Fine, Meat, do you know Martin Goldstein?"

"Why the hell would I tell the likes of you if I do?"

I'm not the least surprised at his contrariness. Weres are an unpleasant lot at the best of times, and me being a vampire does not bring out their best behavior. And me being me tends to bring out outright hostility with a high probability of violence, so I need to tread with care.

"Meat, it is important I speak to someone about Mr. Goldstein. Now, if you don't want to talk to me, I will need to talk to someone inside. So you can A. Answer my question, B. Let me inside so I can ask someone in there, or C. Continue to be an enormous pain in the ass, in which case I will go through you and talk to someone inside."

Meat gets the type of grin on his face that says he really wants to go with option C, but he surprises me by answering my question.

"Yeah, I know Marty."

"Now we are making progress. When was the last time you saw him?"

"Yesterday, getting his dick sucked by your mother on the corner of Fuck You Street and Kiss My Ass Avenue."

Son of a bitch, I walked into that one. I don't know what pisses me off more: getting slapped with a "your mother" joke, or the fact I got outsmart-assed by a talking dog. I have to work very hard to suppress my mounting irritation.

Meat is playing me, but I'm confident I can get him to tell me about Martin or let me inside. All I need to do is show restraint and patience. Unfortunately, I have neither of those things, so I shoot him dead in the face with my bear spray.

Meat begins howling and clawing at his face. I step away from his wild thrashing and move around to the door he is no longer doing a good job of guarding. I see he is shifting, so I point my arm behind me and give him another long blast as if I'm trying to put out a fire before stepping into the dim hallway of the werewolf bar.

I turn and throw the thick bolts of the door, locking it in hopes of keeping the pissed-off werewolf outside while I ask my questions. The gloomy entry hall opens into a well-lit interior. There are not many patrons, being only mid-afternoon, but they all cease their talking and shoot me full of hostile glares as I enter.

"Don't worry, fellas," I tell the small crowd, "I won't be staying long, no need for everyone to start pissing on the furniture."

Several of the patrons do stand up and are about to do more than glare at me, but the man behind the bar restores asmall measure of peace in the room.

"Calm down, guys. Drinks are on the house as long as the bloodsucker is here—beer only.How'd you get past Meat?" he asks me.

The owner and bartender is Rick, one of the more decent weres I've met. I did a job for him a few years ago, so I figure that gives me a shot at not being torn to shreds like a cat tossed into a dog kennel. I also hope it will get me a little information.

"I snuck past while he wasn't looking. I think he had something in his eye—or eyes."

"Leo, what the hell are you doing in here? You have a death wish?"

"I'm hoping you can tell me about Martin Goldstein."

"Martin?" Rick echoes. "Something happen to Martin?"

"I never said there was anything wrong. Why, do you think there is something wrong?"

"You only climb out from under your rock when something's wrong. Since you're asking about Martin, I assume something's happened to him."

I ponder how much I want to tell him and realize I will have to let slip a bit of my paltry hoard of information if I am going to get any in return.

"He didn't come home the other night, and his family asked me to look into it, that's all."

"I see; so you aren't looking to pin those killings on him then? I won't give you one of ours no matter what he's done. If there's a problem, we'll take care of it."

I should have known they would already be aware of the alley killings. Their information network may not be as sophisticated as ours, but it works.

Rick continues, "Did Katherine come to you? Why didn't she come to us if she was worried about her dad?"

"Maybe she wanted him found and not simply taken care of. It wouldn't be the first time someone overreacted and made a mistake."

Rick shakes his head. "Not Martin, no way he was involved."

"So you know Martin pretty well then?"

"Not really. His daughter comes in here more than he does, andusually on business. He's not big into the werewolf scene.

He's a pretty antisocial sort, but not in the dangerous kind of way."

"So he's not much of a brawler and bar hound kind of guy like most of you?"

Rick gives a snort of amusement. "Marty ain't much of a werewolf. I've never seen him at a shifter party, never seen him mad, and never seen him as anything other than a little book-worm accountant. Like I said, no way Marty did those losers. Not that anyone should really care."

Shifter parties are where a bunch of werewolves gather around a big fire in the country, howl at the moon, fight, drink, and screw all night. It's like a hairy, disgusting Burning Man.

I was going to ask Rick a few more questions, but what sounds like someone repeatedly driving a truck into the bar's steel door interrupts me.

I look from the direction of the door back to the bartender. "Rick, you wouldn't happen to have another way out of here, would you?"

"Sorry, only for people I like."

"You wound me, Rick, you really do," I reply in a voice full of false hurt.

"Not as much as Meat's going to hurt you when he gets hold of you. I don't know what you did, but he sounds pissed. Knowing you, it was something way out of line."

I ignore Rick's accusation. "That's a really strong door, isn't it?"

Whatever answer Rick is going to give me is cut short by the sound of the thick portal being bashed in and thudding to the floor, after leaving a rather big crater in the brick wall. It would not have mattered if it had been the side of a battleship. Meat is tough even for his kind, and nothing is going to stop him from tearing me apart.

I shoot Rick something resembling a pleading look, and I think for a moment he is going to have mercy on me.

"Leo," he says, "do me a favor and step away from the bar. Cleaning you up off the floor is a whole lot easier than having to rewash all the glasses. Plus there's a lot less to break over there."

"Sure, wouldn't want my death to inconvenience you,"

I reply, then step near the middle of the room to give myself space to battle my way past the furious werewolf and make my escape.

Contrary to popular belief, or at least sappy teen movies, vampires and werewolves don't fight often. We tend to avoid each other out of a mutual grudging respect and our own self-preservation. It's this unfamiliarity that makes me forget how incredibly fast they are compared to humans.

As Meat launches himself across the room, I have a brief second to realize how serious a tactical mistake I made in bullying my way inside a brick building with only one way out accessible to me.

Most werewolves are like a light switch. They are either on or off, human or big ugly wolf. However, a rare few, like Meat, have the depth of control to maintain a partial shift; the quintessential wolfman like you used to see in the movies. This is the most dangerous kind, especially in an enclosed environment. They have all the freakish strength of a werewolf, with the dexterity, opposable thumbs, and most of the intelligence and cunning of a human being. In short, I'm screwed.

Meat smashes into me before I can bring my bear spray up for another blast to his furry face. I can hear my ribs break from the punch he lands, and I fly back half the length of the bar to slam up against the wall with a sound like a wet pillow thrown against the bricks. Where my bear spray lands, I have no clue.

I am almost tempted to pull out Shalonda, but shooting Meat will turn every wolf in the place on me, so my only option is to try to talk my way out, or at least distract him long enough to get past. I doubt he will chase me out into the streets of New York.

I stand back on my feet, holding one hand out before me while I use the other to brace myself against the wall.

"Meat, I realize shooting you in the face with pepper spray was not a diplomatic way to get inside. I should not have done that." That is the closest thing anyone will ever hear from me in the way of an apology, and I only say it to try to save my life, so it doesn't count. "I was just trying to get information on a job I was hired to do, and you were being difficult. I overreacted. You broke most of my ribs, so I think we're good now. How about you let me leave?"

Meat responds with a barely intelligible snarl. "We are not good! I'm going to tear your arms off, you bloodsucking bastard!"

Despite the uselessness of the effort, I reach for a chair to hurl at him as he is readying himself to spring at me again. Right before he is about to pounce, I catch a blur out of the corner of my eye and a beer mug shatters against the back of Meat's head.

Meat spins on his new attacker with a roar of fury and stops with a look of shock and confusion on his face as Katherine winds up for a second throw.

"Calm down, Meat. You know me, and I have helped keep you out of prison many times," she reminds him in a calm voice, all the while keeping her right arm cocked back.

It is all I can do to keep from laughing at the ridiculousness of the entire scene. Here I am, the tough-guy vampire who fills even most of my own kind with fear, with my ribs crushed, and a monstrous werewolf who is about to make me his bitch is being held off by a pretty little blonde girl with a one hundred mile per hour beer mug pitch.

To my surprise, Meat shifts back to his disgusting, naked human form and presses his hand against the already healing gash in his head.

"Kate, what did you go and do that for?" the big werewolf asks. The pain of betrayal is evident in his voice.

"Because he is here helping me find my dad, and he can't do that if you kill him," she replies, seemingly oblivious to his nakedness. I wish I was.

"Oh, meat, now I get the reference."

He turns back toward me. "If she hadn't shown up, you *really* would have gotten the reference."

He shakes his hips at me and makes it dance like a kid playing with a garden hose. I swear to God, if he helicopters that thing, I'm going to puke right here and now. Thankfully, he turns back to Katherine, which does little to make me feel better.

"Sorry, Kate, he didn't say anything about working for you."

Rick calls out from behind his bar. "Katherine, be a dear and get him out of here while he and my bar are still in one piece."

"Sure thing, Rick. Let's go, Leo, I think you wore out your welcome."

"I'm pretty sure I did that before the cab dropped me off."

I cast my eyes about in search of my bear spray. "Anyone see where my dog spray rolled off to?"

"I think you should leave it here and go," Rick answers.

I shrug and try to shoulder my way past Meat in an act of defiance that says I'm not intimidated by him, but that image is ruined as I jump away when he swings his junk at me like a horse swatting a fly with its tail. He and the rest of his pack think this is the funniest thing they've ever seen and laugh uproariously. Weres are disgusting creatures.

Katherine and I step out of the gloomy bar and into the dreary grey light of a cloud-covered New York afternoon.

"You parked close by?" I ask her as we hasten past the ruined doorframe and into the alley.

She looks up at me quizzically and answers, "Yeah, right at the end of the alley. Why?"

I pull a small remote out of my pocket, similar to those used for car alarms, and press the little red button. A muffled pop responds from inside the bar, which is followed by a chorus of shouted cursing.

"Leo, what did you do?" Katherine asks in a mix of concern and amusement as I take her by the elbow and hustle her toward her waiting car.

Another little customization to my bear spray. Other than being two and a half times as potent, I place a tiny bit of C4 inside the can with a blasting cap and receiver in case I ever need a CS grenade effect—like now.

"What did you do?" she demands as she yanks her arm from my grasp.

I look over my shoulder and see the patrons of the bar come spewing out, wiping their eyes and coughing up great globs of phlegm.

"I'll tell you in the car. Speed is really of the essence right now."

Thank God for remote locks on cars these days. I can

imagine Katherine fumbling about with her keys while she tries to unlock the door as a pissed-off pack of gassed werewolves starts tearing down the alley toward us.

Thankfully, none of them shifts into wolf form. Not only would they be unlikely to have the sense not to chase us like dogs after a delivery truck, Katherine would have a hard time explaining to her insurance company how her door was ripped off its hinges. They'd probably piss on the seats out of spite too, and she'd never get that smell out.

"Now tell me what happened," she demands as we drive back toward Brooklyn.

"How should I know? One of them probably got bit on the ass by a flea and went into a fit." The scowl she gives me makes it quite clear she does not find me amusing or believable. "Fine, I think my can of bear spray may have exploded."

"And why would it have exploded?"

"I don't know; the heat? It felt pretty warm in there to me." Again the scowl. "Fine, I may have triggered a small explosive built into the can."

"Why would you do that? We were outside! There was no reason to do that."

"Hey, I asked for my spray back and they wanted to be dick-heads about it."

"Oh please, this has nothing to do with your stupid pepper spray."

"Then you tell me what it is about, Nancy Drew-Freud," I respond hotly.

"It's about you picking a fight and not being used to being on the receiving end of an ass kicking!"

Well damn it all to hell, a friggin' bullseye.

I cross my arms defensively. "What are you, a freaking lawyer?"

"Assistant prosecuting attorney," Katherine answers with an annoying, self-satisfied smile.

I decide to change the subject to one not involving me or my motivations. "You seemed awfully chummy in there consider-ing the fact you're a mutt."

If she was offended, she didn't show it. "I've kept a lot of them out of jail many times, especially Meat. Lucky for you, he owes me."

"It must be nice having a guardian angel in the prosecutor's office when you're an uncontrollable freak of nature."

"Hey, I've kept you out of jail almost as much as all of them put together!" she responds, showing true annoyance for the first time.

"Then I guess my point is proven, isn't it?"

"At least those uncontrollable freaks know how to say thank you."

"Yeah, how does Meat give his thanks, by the inch or by the pound?"

Katherine glares at me as she white-knuckles the steering wheel. "Why are you always a disagreeable asshole?"

"Decades of practice, honey."

Try as I might, I cannot keep Katherine off balance and annoyed with me. I must be losing my touch. I'll have to work harder. Her smile is already returning to her pretty face, a smile made from her perfect, full lips. Jesus, what is wrong with me! I force my eyes straight ahead as she starts to speak again.

"What were you asking about in the bar? Did you find anything out?"

"I asked about your father: what kind of a man he was, what kind of a werewolf he was, had anyone seen him lately, that sort of thing. Speaking of which, why were you in the bar?"

"I was going to do the same thing. My dad never went there, but I hoped maybe someone had seen him, or if not, I was going to ask them to keep an eye out for him. So what did they tell you?"

"That he rarely showed himself there and wasn't much of a werewolf."

"I could have told you that. I think I saw him shift one time in my life, and that was only after Roger and I showed signs of the trait. Mom knows about him, of course, but he tried to keep it from Roger and me."

"Let me guess. You started cluing in when you hit puberty at nine and could pitch a softball that made even the lesbians jealous."

Katherine's smile grows wider. "You saw that, huh? I went to NYU on a full softball scholarship, not that I'm a slouch in the academic area either. The hardest part was holding back. I maintained the second-fastest pitch in the world, but I can break a hundred if I really let loose."

"Yeah, it looked like you let loose on Meat's head all right."

"He can take it, and anything less wouldn't have gotten his attention. Have you found anything else out?"

"I went to the coroner's office and took a look at the crime scene photos of a triple slaughter that happened near your father's office."

Her smile vanishes. "What makes you think that has anything to do with my father?"

"I looked at photos of hair found at the scene, and it was definitely werewolf."

Katherine shakes her head. "No, no my father would never hurt anyone. He hates his condition."

"Even if his life was threatened?"

"I—I'm not sure. He would defend himself, but it would have to be very serious. He would run first. Who would want to hurt him or kill him?"

"Someone who is either stupid or didn't know who he was. I need to make a few calls and find out who those guys were, but I already know they were not innocent bystanders in the wrong place at the wrong time."

"I can't believe my dad could do that even then. You don't know him like I do."

"I don't suppose you could identify the hair sample by sight or smell, or know anyone who could?"

She shakes her head. "No, dad never shifted; just the one time I know of, and I wouldn't be surprised if that was the only time he changed around anyone. OK, a couple thugs jumped him and he shifted because he thought they were going to hurt or kill him. Then where is he? Why hasn't he come back?"

"That's the part that has me confused. Maybe he feels so horrified at what he did, he can't come home. Maybe, since he is so unused to shifting, he simply lost control during the rage and hasn't been able to shift back."

Katherine looks worried because she knows my supposition is the most likely explanation.

"What do we do now?"

"Follow the bodies and hope we find him before the wolves get involved."

CHAPTER SIX

Katherine drops me off at my place, and I tell her I'll let her know if I get any more information. I watch her drive away before I duck inside. Maybe it is just my ego talking, but I can't shake the feeling she was flirting with me, and I really don't know how to deal with that. It's never good to get involved with a client, especially when she's half werewolf.

I decide it is best to keep my mind on my work, so I call Angel's office phone. It rings five times before someone answers.

"Detective Sergeant Castillo."

Oh shit. How the hell did I dial Satan? That has to be outside my calling plan.

"Uh, Angel please."

"He's on another line. Can I help you?"

Yeah, you can shoot yourself in the face. "No, I'll hold for Angel."

"Who is this?" she asks with a profound pause. "Malone, is that you?"

"Uh, no this is his cousin—Vlad."

Vlad? Jesus Christ, my improv sucks.

"Detective Lopez," Angel says into the phone.

Oh, thank God. "Angel, are you alone on this line?"

"Yeah, who is this? Leo?"

"Yeah. I need information on those bodies you scraped up the other night."

"Leo, that's an ongoing investigation. I can't give out that kind of information."

"It's important. Besides, it's a dog attack so there's no need for all the hush-hush."

Angel sighs and pauses to think. "Why are you interested in this case?"

"I don't care about the case. I'm just curious about who the stiffs are."

"Bullshit. You ain't curious about anything. Why are you getting your nose in this?"

It's my turn to sigh. I hate the way information tends to require two-way communication.

"I have a client who has me looking for someone. I want to make sure none of the vics are my guy."

"You know, Leo, bullshit answers from you make my good answers cost more, which just serves to pay off the debt I have to you that much faster."

"Yeah, but until then stop busting my balls and make with the info, law monkey."

"You are such a prick, Leo." Angel laughs as he starts typing at his console.

"Yeah, that's the general consensus."

Angel comes back a minute later with my answers. "I have one Rocco Kilcuddy, Michael Rizzo, and Jeffery Sanders."

"What kind of priors are we looking at?"

"The usual: burglaries, possession, strong-arm robbery, assault. Rizzo was up for attempted murder once but pleaded out to a lesser assault charge."

"Any involvement with any crime families?" I ask Angel.

"Nothing is showing on my profile sheet. I'd have to check with the organized crimes task force to make sure, but I don't think so. They were all just your basic street hoods."

"All right. Thanks, Angel."

I hang up the phone. Angel's input doesn't make me feel any better or bring me any closer to solving this case. I already had a pretty good idea of the victims' identity.

I didn't know them by name, but I knew them by reputation. Like Angel said, they were toughs, thugs, and a general waste of space, but they weren't murderers. So why did they go after Martin? These guys knew the streets well enough to know who was a made man and not to screw with, so why go after such a high-profile target? It doesn't make sense.

That means I'll be pounding the pavement looking for clues, and those kinds of clues are probably going to be bodies. Vincent will have to get the Sheriffs involved if the body count goes up, assuming they aren't already. He said they had other duties, but that doesn't mean they aren't operating parallel to this.

I begin running the streets and jumping rooftops well after the sun goes down. Of course, the odds of me stumbling upon an attack are pretty slim. It's a big city after all, but I figure if there are going to be more attacks, they will likely happen close to the first one. It's not like a two- or three-hundred-pound werewolf can take the subway or run down the Brooklyn Queens Expressway on his way to Manhattan.

I am perched atop a roof overlooking Fort Greene Park near the first attack when I get a call on my cell.

"Yeah," I say into my phone.

"We got a call for a cleanup on 8th and Cumberland. Vincent wanted us to let you know."

"Got it, thanks."

The location is at the naval yard a few blocks from where I am now. It takes me less than five minutes to run there. When I arrive, I find the cleanup crew already at work along with a couple of my favorite Sheriffs.

Quinn accosts me the moment I drop down to street level. "What the hell are you doing here, Malone?"

I ignore his rudeness. Right now, I have better things to do than play who can piss the highest up the flagpole. When I'm on a job, I like to consider myself something of a professional. But when this is over, well, we'll just see what happens.

"I got a call. Thought I would look around and see if this is my guy."

"Yeah, well, you can go fuck off somewhere else. We got this, and we don't need any help from a washout PI," Quinn sneers, goading for a fight.

It takes significant willpower and calming techniques my shrink gave me, but I manage to keep my cool. It wasn't that long ago I would have made paste out of this kid, but since I got thrown out of the Sheriffs and started paying for my own therapy, I decided to do my best to make my time and money count for something.

"Vincent wants me to take a look, and the last I saw he was your boss, so shut your trap and get out of my way before I tear off one of your arms and bitch-slap you all the way back to Manhattan with it."

Nailed it. Textbook anger management. I can tell by the look on his face he is ready to throw down but, once again, Wyatt ruins what could have been the highlight of my day.

"Quinn! Go help them clean that mess up," Wyatt orders his minion.

Quinn smiles at me and sneers, "He might be the boss today, Malone, but things change."

"Quinn!" Wyatt shouts again, and Quinn stomps over to where the others are tossing body parts into thick, waterproof bags.

I find Wyatt poking around and presumably gathering clues. "Any idea who this was?"

Wyatt shakes his head. "We found a wallet and ID. Looks like some guy going home after his shift at the shipyard. Nothing more than that right now."

"Wolf attack?"

"Looks like it, given the scattering and wound marks."

This is good for me but sucks for Martin. I pull out my small but bright flashlight and begin scanning the ground. I take pictures of the body parts and surrounding area with my phone. It takes almost half an hour, but I finally find what I am looking for. I drop the tufts of rough hair into a small plastic bag.

I will have to wait until I get home to compare them to the photos I got from Raj, but I am certain they match. It is not looking good for Katherine's father.

I spend another hour looking for any clues that will tell me the direction the attack came from or where he went afterward, but I come up empty. The cleanup crew departed with a one-fingered wave from Quinn nearly an hour ago.

It is getting late, or early depending on your perspective, and I figure there is little if anything else I will find here, so I hightail it back to my place for a closer look at the evidence.

The first thing I do is pull out the close-ups of the hair samples Raj supplied. I don't need the lighted magnifying glass on my desk to tell they are a perfect match, but I will run them by Raj anyway just to be certain.

I'm looking over the photos and about to toss them all back into the envelope when something catches my eye. I stick the picture of the first crime scene under my magnifying glass and take a closer look. Next to one of the body parts from the three thugs in the alley is a small, silver object. If I wasn't familiar with it, I never would have been able to pick out what it was and, more importantly, to whom it belongs.

The object is a tiny silver blade designed to slip over the finger like a ring. It serves two purposes: chopping up cocaine and making a small cut to drink blood. Knowing the owner and the time of night, I am almost certain where I can find its previous wearer.

Once again, I cross the borough in the not so dead of night. Much to my displeasure, I enter a club so shitty and decadent it makes the Perestroika look like the Vatican without as many pedophiles. Looking around at the general clientele, I amend my opinion and call it a draw.

My target, Nicky, will be in whatever passes as a VIP section in this shithole. Nicky is what we call a bloodling and the closest thing to a half-vampire as you can get. Bloodlings are rare, since they are almost always created by accident and considered a fluke.

Bloodlings are usually created by being the victim of a non-lethal feeding but somehow get a bit of vampire DNA into their system. Maybe the feeder had gingivitis and his gums were bleeding or something, I don't know. The minor infection is not enough to turn the victim into a vampire, but it does imbue them with some pretty nice abilities if they survive.

They are stronger and faster than most humans, but not quite as strong as a half-were. Freak and Tiny would both make a good fight, but the smart money is on either of those hulking brutes. Bloodlings do not need to feed on human blood and never need to kill to survive, but consuming small amounts of blood does keep them strong and healthy.

Unfortunately, Nicky is an outright piece of garbage, and he uses his accidental abilities to be a tough guy and push around the humans. He likes to be the big fish in this cesspool of a pond, but he's really only a big fish amongst the lowest of the bottom feeders.

I find him in the back, surrounded by a group of whores and toadies all doing blow and drinking what they think is quality booze. Nicky is loudly proclaiming his greatness and mocking anyone who catches his eye, in hopes of provoking a fight. People know him here and they don't take the bait.

I approach him from the side and tap him on the shoulder. "Nicky, I need to talk to you."

"Fuck off, I'm busy," Nicky replies, then flips me the bird without bothering to look at who it is.

I grab the raised digit and snap it like a breadstick in two places. Nicky cries out, jumps to his feet, and cocks back a fist, ready to destroy whoever was foolish enough to attack him. His coked-out eyes take in my face and he goes so white he practically glows under the club's black lights.

"Oh fuck me, Leo, I didn't know it was you!"

I grab him by the ear like a mother scolding a child and drag him through the club in the most humiliating way I can think of. Guys like him need an occasional reality check.

"Ow, come on, Leo, I'm sorry!" Nicky cries as I lead him to a back entrance by his ear.

We step out into the dank alley and I toss him into the wall of the neighboring building.

Nicky stands in a half crouch with his hands held defensively over his head. "What'd I do, Leo? I ain't done nothin', I swear! I been straight, I know the rules!"

I know he knows the rules. I made them very clear to him after he changed and began acting stupid. Well, stupider, which given his general level of intelligence was quite a remarkable feat.

"Where's your little razor ring, Nicky?"

Nicky makes a show of patting his pockets. "I don't know. I guess I lost it."

"Where do you think you lost it?"

"I don't know. If I knew that, it wouldn't be lost, would it?"

I raise a hand and Nicky ducks and covers himself again. "I'm sorry. I don't know!"

"Then let me refresh your memory. How about an alley near 123rd? Does that sound familiar?"

Nicky stands up straight and extends his arms toward me. "Whoa, I did not do those guys! No way could I have done that even if I wanted to. You know that."

"But I know you like to skulk around that area, and I bet you saw something."

Nicky starts looking a whole lot more nervous. "You're testing me, aren't you? This is a test to see if I'll spill! I know the rules. I don't say nothin'. You ain't gotta worry about me."

Now this is very curious. "What rules, Nicky? What rules make you think you can't tell me what you saw?"

"The rules, man! You know, like Vegas! What happens in Vegas stays in Vegas. What you guys do stays with you. I'm no snitch, Leo."

I grab Nicky by his ear once again and twist it. "New rules, Nicky; what Leo wants Leo gets, and if you think leaving the club was embarrassing, think about how it will feel going back in with one fucking ear. Now you tell me what you saw, or I'm going to start pulling off parts of your body, starting at the top and working my way down. I suggest you spill before your new name becomes Nicholas the Dickless."

"Ow! It was you guys! I saw you guys!"

"What do you mean, 'you guys'?" I ask, my gut churning with the words I know are coming next.

"You guys, with the black coats and van!"

I let go of Nicky's ear. "Are you telling me Sheriffs were at the scene? What were they doing? Not cleaning up, apparently."

Nicky shakes his head. "No, man, they took down that werewolf. They shot him full of tasers and tranq darts, and then they loaded him up in the van and drove off. I climbed down from the roof I was on to check it out. I didn't find nothin' but a hundred bucks and a couple knives. I kept the money; the knives were shit."

"How do you know they were Sheriffs? Did you recognize

any of them? Would you be able to identify them if you saw them again?"

"Naw, man, they had the hoods of their jackets up like they didn't want to be seen."

I need to go home and process all this. Nicky isn't the most reliable of witnesses, but he believes what he saw. The question is whether I believe what he believes he saw.

"All right, Nicky, go back inside," I tell him, then start walking out of the alley.

"How can I go back in there after you disrespected me in front of my crew?" Nicky whines at my back.

"The way nature intended," I call over my shoulder, "with humility and a profound sense of shame."

"You're a real asshole, Malone, you know that?"

"That's what everyone tells me."

CHAPTER SEVEN

I am back to the rooftops the next night, looking and listening for anything out of the ordinary. Showing up to slaughter scenes after the fact is getting me no closer to finding Martin, and it's starting to piss me off.

Nicky says he saw what he thought were Sheriffs taking Martin away, but if it was them, why doesn't Vincent know about it? If Wyatt and his crew did take Martin, why didn't he tell me, and why are people still being torn up by a werewolf I assume is the same one Vincent has me looking for? Is it the same one? Could there be another and they are holding Martin to pin the murder on him?

Then there are the reports of unlawful vampire predation. Maybe it's more than one. A gang of young vampires stupid enough to think they can make their own little enclave, and they took Martin as a way to keep attention on a werewolf instead of themselves.

A bunch of younglings taking on a full werewolf? Not very likely, even if they did get enough information on how to do it and who to pick off. No, there are too many factors, too much inside knowledge needed to be plausible.

OK, a group of mature vamps carving out their own little niche, having the same agenda, motives, and with more strength and knowledge. That at least is possible if still improbable, but right now, I have nothing else to go on.

I need to verify any Sheriff involvement to find out if Vincent is sending me on a wild goose chase. If he is purposefully keeping me occupied by chasing a werewolf he already has in custody, what is he trying to keep me away from? Why bring me in at all? If you don't want someone to know you have an elephant, don't call them and tell them not to look for an elephant. It makes people start asking questions.

Out of all the Sheriffs present on my last visit, there was only one I trusted. Fortunately, I have a good idea where to find him. Greg has spent most of his nights in an Irish pub during his time off for as long as I've known him.

I make my way across town and find him at his usual bar, sitting in his usual seat, and if it weren't for the properties of evaporation, it could even be the same drink. Unable to get drunk, Greg spends most of the night staring into the glass's amber depths thinking thoughts known only to himself.

"Thought I might be seeing you soon," Greg says as I occupy the bar stool next to him.

"You don't sound happy to see me."

"No one is ever happy to see you unless you're walking away."

"Next time I'll walk in backward," I say.

Greg grins and chuckles into his drink. "Man, we need you back. These new guys…" He wags his head.

"Where the hell did they come from? Where's the old crew?"

"Retired, transferred, gone. You know where Linda is?"

"No."

Greg's shoulders slump. "Me neither, and she was almost as zealous in her job as you. She didn't like what she was seeing and had no problem taking Wyatt to task over it."

"What did she see? What's going on?"

"You know I can't talk to you about enclave business," Greg says with a slight shake of his head.

"Come on, it will be just between the three of us," I press.

"Three?"

"Yeah. You, me, and your aching vagina."

Greg laughs aloud now, erasing a little of the tension gripping his body. "What the hell. It's not as though I know much anyway."

"Vincent has me looking for a rampaging werewolf, but ordered me to steer clear of any rogue vampires. I got a guy who says he watched several Sheriffs load a werewolf in a van right after he tore those three thugs apart. Do they have my guy, and why does Vincent have me chasing a ghost if they do?"

"I don't know, Leo. I haven't done anything except house-sitting, paperwork, and playing the occasional driver in more than a year. If Wyatt and his crew grabbed that dog, I don't know about it."

"Do you think Wyatt is running his own agenda? Do you think he's involved in Linda and the other Sheriffs' disappearance?"

Greg scrubs at his beard and releases a long sigh. "I don't know. I just don't know. I hate to think Wyatt would turn on his own. We've been friends a long time, and I've always known him as a decent sort, if unimaginative. I don't know, and I'm not going to start asking like Linda did, which is why I am officially retired as of tonight. I'm leaving New York in the morning and not coming back. I wish I could help, but I've been kept in the dark. I can only hope Wyatt has been too. Here—" he scribbles an address on a napkin and slides it to me "—there's been a lot of activity around that area but few reports coming in through official channels. Might be you can find something around there."

I look at the address and find it is in the heart of my ward. I realize I have been slacking in my duties if there is unlawful predation going on so close to home. I hate patrolling, but it looks like I need to be more attentive to my territory. As much as I hate the responsibility, I would hate to lose my district even more. I'm not good at asking permission for anything.

I nod and clap him on the shoulder as I stand. "Thanks, Greg. Make sure you stop by the pharmacy and get something for that vagina. Those long flights are uncomfortable enough as it is."

Greg belts out another boisterous laugh. "You are a world-class prick, Malone."

"I should be. Been training most my life."

I leave Greg to his drink and pay a cab to drop me off in my territory a few blocks away from the address Greg gave me. Greg is as stable a man as I have ever known, but whatever is going on with the Sheriffs and in the enclave has him shaken. I too share the hope Wyatt is not neck-deep in some shady dealings that will put me in the position to end him. But if he killed Linda and the other MIA Sheriffs, I'll take his head and not shed a tear. My rules about friendship and loyalty are rather inflexible.

It is a little after two in the morning, and I decide I have wasted enough time for one night. I drop to street level and start walking toward home. I am on Hawthorne near Prospect Park when I hear the scream.

My ears pick out the direction and I am off at a dead run. Most likely, it's just a home invasion robbery, but just maybe it's my guy, or guys. A second cry lets me lock onto a single family house and I pull my hood over my head.

The first thing I notice as I bound up the front steps is the splintered doorframe, the door it held now in two pieces lying on the floor halfway down the entry hall. This is no robbery. This is good for me, but bad for whoever lives here.

Even so, I am unprepared for what awaits me as I burst into the living room. Cowering in the corner behind a couch is a woman holding two middle school-aged children. All are crying and in hysterics, but that is not what shocks me.

In the center of the living room are three vampires: two white, and one Jamaican-looking, whose face is buried in the open throat of a man I assume is the father. All three turn toward me and smile as the Jamaican drops the lifeless body to the ground.

"Hey, mon," the Jamaican says to me, "this house is taken. Best you go find your own. We ain't for sharin'."

"Yeah, go find your own," one of the white guys warns me.

"You stupid sons of bitches. What the hell do you think you're doing?" I demand.

"Whatever we damn well please," the third one arrogantly informs me. "Who's to stop us?"

All three are new, but unfortunately for them, they won't be getting any wiser with age. Maybe they don't know the rules, but I'm in a foul mood thanks to my lack of progress in my case and Greg's ill tidings, and I don't feel like taking the time to educate them.

"Me," I tell them as I reach into my jacket and start to pull my blade.

All three charge at me with blinding speed the moment they see my sword slide from its sheath, but they aren't as fast as I am. I am a trained fighter; these guys are hoodlums and newbie vampires.

I bury my sword into the Jamaican's gut just below the sternum, but a slight dodge at the last second causes me to miss the spine I am aiming for. He flails about and pulls my sword from my grip as he goes screeching and flapping around the room in panic.

The first white guy swings at me with a wild haymaker. I catch his wrist with my left hand in a vise-like grip hard enough to pulverize the bones of a human. I pull him toward me and pivot us both around as if I'm leading him in a tango. The third vamp tries to clobber me from behind, but I lash out with my right leg and send him flying through the wall, shattering several studs, and laying him out inside one of the bedrooms.

I spin back toward the one caught in my grip before he can take a swing at me with his free hand, grab him by the waist of his jeans with my right hand, and heave him into a roof beam before body slamming him onto the hardwood floor with the force of a pile driver.

The Jamaican calms down enough to pull my blade free from his chest and charges me with it raised over his head, ready to split my skull like a piece of firewood. Shalonda leaps into my hand and the look on his face is almost comical as he stares into the gaping black cavern of her barrel. I squeeze the trigger and his head vanishes in the flash of the discharge.

I snatch my sword from his limp grasp before his body hits the ground. I don't need to look as I pirouette and take off the head of the guy I slammed into the floor just as he is rising back to his feet. This is the part in the movies where the vampire spontaneously combusts into a pile of ash easily swept up with a Dustbuster. Unfortunately, this is reality, and reality is far messier.

A sound from the bedroom causes me to turn. I see the last vamp shaking the drywall dust from his face as he ponders his next move. We both come to the same conclusion at the same time.

"Don't you dare…" I begin to warn him, but I'm too late, and he isn't going to listen anyway, "…run. Damn it!"

He dives through a window before I can get a clean shot off and I give chase. I pull out my phone and hit the speed dial.

"Cleanup," I shout as soon as the other end picks up, and I rattle out the address. "Two rogue vamps and three human witnesses!"

I don't wait for a reply before flipping the phone shut and pouring on the speed after the fleeing vampire. He's young but he's fast, and I am barely able to keep pace with him.

Buildings fly by in a blur, but I'm getting no closer to my quarry. I need to bring this chase to an end as we begin nearing an area with a more active nightlife. It would be bad to have multiple humans witness two guys tearing down the streets at speeds upwards of forty miles per hour. This is not the way I want to become a YouTube sensation.

As we burst out of an alley, I snatch up a discarded tire rim and hurl it like a discus. Even I'm impressed with myself as the steel projectile catches the runner in the back of his head and sends him tumbling. I don't even break stride as I tear a parking meter out of the ground and advance with malicious intent.

He is already climbing back to his feet as I reach him, but a swing from my parking meter, worthy of the major leagues, sends him flying into the unyielding brick wall of a building amidst the chiming of flying nickels, dimes, and quarters.

The young vamp is persistent and tries to get back up, but I double him over with a hit to the gut from my makeshift baseball bat, and then send him back down to the sidewalk with a club to the back of his head.

I toss aside my parking meter, roll him over, and grab him by his jacket collar. "What the fuck was all that about? Are you all that damn stupid?"

It takes a moment for his eyes to stop rolling around and focus on me. When he does, he laughs in my face. "We're vampires, dude. We do what we want!"

I shake him and bounce his head off the concrete a couple

times. "Shit like that will bring heat on us, you stupid bastard! That's why it's against the law! Didn't anyone ever tell you that, or are you all just so damn stupid you don't care?"

He laughs again and his reply sends a chill down my spine. "Not for long, Malone. Things are changing, and they're changing real fast."

That sounded eerily familiar to me, and I wrack my brain trying to place it, but I don't have time to process it. I can already hear sirens in the distance. If the woman's screams didn't prompt the neighbors to call the cops, the near artillery blast from Shalonda certainly did.

"On your feet, asshole. I'm taking you downtown."

Again, Mr. Chuckles laughs at me. "I don't think so, cowboy."

The kid bites down on something in his mouth, and within seconds, a bloody froth is running down his face as he convulses. I step away, not wanting to get whatever he took onto me, and cast about looking for something with which to take a sample.

I find a small, glass vial, probably discarded by a crackhead, and carefully scoop some of the bloody drool into it, then seat the stopper in place before wiping it clean on the kid's shirt.

I fish around in his pockets. He's not carrying ID, but he does have a cell phone. Everyone has a cell phone. I drop the phone in my pocket, drag the body into the alley, toss it into a dumpster, and call in a cleanup with a quick warning of severe biohazard. The guy on duty gives me shit about it, but I tell him to quit his bitching and send a team. I have a good idea of what the toxic pill was and I'm furious, certain I have been played this entire time.

Not only do I know what this poison is, I know the only place on the planet it is found: Vtech Pharmaceuticals, owned by Vincent Van Graff, who just happens to sit in the president's chair of the enclave and hates my guts.

My friend, Dr. Wallis, the one who tried to find a cure and burned himself to death when he failed, inadvertently developed the most effective means of killing his own kind ever devised. In the very small circle of people who know of its existence, it is simply known as the Cure. Upon being informed of Dr. Wallis's disastrous failure, Vincent had all samples and every piece of data placed under biosafety level four in his top research lab.

Whether this is related to my werewolf hunt or not, I don't care. All I care about right now is putting a boot up someone's ass for jerking me around, and I have a good idea whose ass is a prime candidate and where it is currently planted.

I find a payphone and call the security desk. "Mr. Van Graff," I say as soon as the front desk picks up.

"One moment, I'll transfer you."

I hang up. If Vincent hadn't been there they wouldn't have bothered transferring me to his office phone. I figured he was in despite the late hour. The man is almost always at the office, despite owning a spectacular home upstate.

A short jog gets me to a street where cabs are running and I flag one down. It drives me into Manhattan and drops me off in front of the massive office building. I don't ask the driver to wait.

The murderous look in my eyes makes the solitary security guard stand up and come around the desk to intercept me the moment I barge through the doors. He pulls out a taser but is far too slow. I whip Shalonda up and put a round through his kneecap. Had he not been a vampire it might have taken the lower limb completely off. As it is, he drops and hurls expletives at me while he grabs at his ruined leg.

I roll him onto his stomach, cuff his hands behind his back, and take his elevator key to the upper floors.Despite being one of the fastest elevator designs in use, it takes far too long for me to reach the top.

When the doors open, I storm down the hall and kick in the decorative yet solid double doors leading into Vincent's palatial office suite. Although expected, I am still disappointed by his lack of reaction to my violent intrusion.

"Mr. Malone, I see the years have done nothing to improve your subtlety or tact. If you have information about the case you need to share with me, warranting more than a phone call, you can schedule an appointment and I will grant you an audience at my convenience. There is no need to shoot the help and ruin my doors."

I toss the vial of frothy pink poison on his desk. "Like you gave permission to your minion to ingest this?"

"And what might this be?" the senior vampire asks as he reaches toward the vial.

"Just a sample of the Cure I scooped out of a dead vamp's mouth a few minutes ago."

Again, I am impressed with the old vamp's composure as he casually withdraws his reaching hand. Most vampires would have leapt halfway across the room when faced with the most deadly poison to their kind in the world.

"I see."

"Do you? Because I sure as fuck don't! I don't see how a dirtbag vampire so new he still has teeth marks in his neck got a hold of the Cure when you are supposed to be the only person with access to it! Can you explain it to me? Can you explain why you have me chasing after a single werewolf when it seems we have an influx of rogue vampires running around fucking shit up in my neighborhood?"

Vincent scoops the vial into his trash can with a sheet of paper and regards me intently before answering. "In regards to the poison, I will perform an internal audit of our samples and security. Any unlawful vampire predation is being dealt with by the appropriate authorities, of which you are no longer a member. Continue your search for Mr. Goldstein as I directed you. Neither the Cure nor vampires are your concern."

"Not my concern!I have vampires packing poison and murdering people without regard for secrecy right in my ward. How is that not my concern?"

I finally crack his stony façade and get some emotion out of him. "Because I told you it is not your concern, you little prick! Now follow your orders, and get the hell out of my office! And you will be paying for my door."

I turn my head at a sound behind me and find Wyatt with his hand on his sword, waiting to escort me out. I can tell when I am being asked to leave. Damn it. Vincent was supposed to give himself away, a facial gesture, any kind of reaction to give me a clue as to what is going on inside that too-intelligent head of his, but he gave me nothing.

"I know my way out," I growl, then slap Wyatt's hand away as I stalk back to the elevator.

"Leo, tell me what's going on. Maybe I can help," he calls at my back, but I ignore him. "Leo, why won't you let me help?"

"Because I haven't decided whether or not you're part of the problem," I shout back as the doors slide open and I step into the elevator.

Out of pure spite, I snap the key off in the lock before flinging the chain and remaining piece of key to the guard already posted to replace the one I shot. Wyatt probably gave him the rest of the night off despite having recovered from his wound already.

I pace around my loft in frustration. Vincent has me looking for a werewolf who is probably not involved, at least not willingly, in several killings but he gets bent out of shape and forbids me to investigate known vampire attacks.

Add in the vampire equivalent of cyanide mixed with Ebola and this whole thing goes from confusing to outright bizarre. Vincent has the Cure on lockdown, but my gut is telling me he is unaware of it having walked out of his lab—maybe. For fuck's sake, I could wallpaper the Empire State Building with all the maybes I have. One thing I am sure of; there is a lot more going on than a nerdy werewolf and a few idiot vampires running amok in Brooklyn.

I fiddle with the phone I took off the vamp's body but it's no good. It's locked and I don't know how to crack it, but I know someone who can. I'll have to stop by for a visit and employ him. I have a few other tasks his technical genius can handle for me as well. I need information, and if anyone can get it, it's Marvin.

A very loud banging on my ground-level door interrupts my contemplations. Given the construction of my door and building, the fact it is loud means someone is either hammering it with a battering ram or repeatedly backing a truck into it.

I double-check Shalonda is in my pocket holster before springing up the steel steps to a narrow, barred window set about twenty feet above the street in front of my building.

Sure enough, a squad of cops in full assault gear is abusing my door with a handheld ram. I wonder how long they will continue their futile attempts before realizing nothing short of one of their battering ram tanks will bust my door off the one-foot-thick reinforced concrete wall.

"Castillo, is that you knocking?" I call down to the mass of cops.

Several cops train their weapons on me as Castillo backs up to get a better look. "Get your ass out here, Malone. I have a warrant for your arrest."

"Is there a search clause in that warrant?"

"No," Castillo calls up in obvious annoyance.

"Then stop banging on my fucking door and I'll come out."

Castillo motions her squad back and I climb down the stairs. I take my time emptying my pockets of their assorted weapons, if for no other reason than to deny Castillo the plea-sure of an excuse to shoot me. With a sigh of regret, I toss my Miguel Caballero with its incriminating blood spatters into the furnace. You can bet it's going on my bill. I grab another trench coat from my closet, a regular one, not the bulletproof variety, and put it on.

Lastly, I call my lawyer. I have stuff to do and would rather not spend any more time twiddling my thumbs in jail than I have to.

I push the door open and step into the morning gloom. Before Castillo can order her men to jump me, I slam my door shut with an audible click of its lock. Gotta keep the cops honest.

Castillo surprises me by simply cuffing me and reading me my rights. I really expected her to have me roughed up a bit.

"What's this about, Castillo?" I ask her as she pins my hands behind my back. "You got me on camera jaywalking?"

"Even better, Malone. I have three witnesses placing you at the scene of a home invasion and murder."

"Really? Three people said, 'Yeah, that guy Leo Malone was here.' Or did they say a white guy of average height and aver-age build wearing a black coat, and you just naturally pegged me for it?"

"Doesn't matter. As soon as I get you in front of a lineup and they pick you out, I'm sending you up for the rest of your life,"

Castillo answers as she starts patting me down. "I know you're packing, so where is it?"

"Front right pocket," I reply, glad she can't see my smirk from her vantage point.

"Where? I don't feel anything."

"Sorry, I tried, but I guess no amount of fondling from you is going to do it for me."

"No wonder I couldn't find anything."

"You know, you're a really mean person, Castillo, and coming from me that's saying something."

Castillo shoves me into the back of her unmarked cruiser and hauls me off to the precinct. I have to slog through the typical mountain of paperwork before she tosses me into an interrogation room and gets around to cluing me in on what has her even more fired up than usual.

"I know you were at that house, Malone, and I know you killed at least two of the three men who broke in. How many people in this city carry around a goddamn sword?" she shouts.

I return her wrath with a smile. "You would be surprised at how many. So, you haul me in, give me the third degree, and threaten to send me to prison for allegedly saving people from a group of murderous thugs? That seems petty even for you, Castillo."

"No, I want to know why you just happened to be there too. I want to know what happened to the perp you chased out of the house. But most of all, I want to know who the hell those people were who chased off my men claiming to be feds! I called every federal agency in the state and not one claims to have been involved. And when my guys do get access, the bodies are gone and no one knows who they were or where they went. The only thing left behind is a woman and two kids who say one of the men tore out the throat of their father and drank his blood. Then a guy fitting your description steps in and acts like he just caught a couple kids playing hooky right before he kicks one through a wall, blows the head off another, and decapitates the third. Now you tell me what's going on!"

"You really want to know what's going on?"

Anna leans on the small table I'm sitting behind and gets in my face. "Yeah, I want to know what's going on."

"What's going on is you look like you shop at the Cagney and Lacey outlet store and your breath smells like cigarettes, old coffee, and hooker vagina. Now, get out of my face and call me when my lawyer gets here."

I needed to piss off Castillo to get her to stop asking me questions, and that certainly worked. I didn't expect her to hit me though. Two more detectives rush in after she punches me in the face, and pull her off. One calls for a uniform to take me to holding while they try to calm down their coworker.

"Take him to cell six!" Castillo shouts as the uniform leads me away from the interrogation room.

"Man, Castillo must really hate you," the uniformed cop says as he leads me to a holding cell.

"Why do you say that? Doesn't she punch everyone in the face?"

"Cell six is where the really nasty guys go, and the camera's broken."

"I see," I reply, and can't help but smile at Castillo's level of vindictiveness.

The officer puts me in a cell with six of the meanest-looking thugs you ever saw outside the Gulag. One white guy, two black guys, two Mexicans, and a Native American make the cell look like the UN Assembly room for the criminally insane.

I barely have time to assess my surroundings before I hear Castillo's voice outside the door.

"Jones, go take a break," she says just before her face appears in the small window of the cell's solid steel door. "Malone, I see you met your new roommates. You boys make Mr. Malone feel real welcome and I'll see to it you each get an extra dessert and a smoke break."

Wow, that is low even for her. Anna leaves me with my new friends, who are looking at me as if I am a porterhouse steak tossed into a pen full of starving pit bulls. It is only a matter of time before Will springs me, so I just need to play nice and wait it out. No need to create any unnecessary trouble.

I look at the group of hoodlums. "What the fuck are you bitches looking at?"

Shit. I really need to get my brain and my mouth on the same page. Same page? Hell, they're not even reading the same book. I hear Castillo a short time later as I'm lying on the steel bench, plowing over my case in my head.

"Why the fuck is it that all three of my witnesses put your client at the scene, then five minutes after talking to you, they come up with three totally different descriptions? I swear, if you have threatened them in any way, I will bury your slimy little ass beneath this precinct. You won't even get to a trial!"

"I don't know, Detective. Maybe you coerced them or fed them information so you could get back what you wanted to hear," Will answered just as adamantly. "What I do know is you pissed away whatever favors you called in to get that bullshit warrant issued. And you put him in cell six? You better pray to God nothing has happened to my client or you just made us two of the richest men in the city!"

The heavy door opens with a squeal and Castillo cries out, "What the hell happened in here?"

Spots of blood dot the floor, walls, and ceiling, and all six thugs are crammed into the corner as if they're trying to set the world record for the most convicts stuffed into an invisible phone booth.

"Leo, are you all right?" Will asks me as he looks back and forth between the battered hoodlums and me.

"Other than having my morning wasted, yeah, I'm great. Let's get out of here."

"Christ, Leo, what did you do?"

"Hey, no means no," I answer with a smile.

I thank Will for getting me out so quickly, and Castillo escorts me to Property to pick up the few possessions confiscated when I was booked in.

"What the hell happened in that house, and what did you do in the cell?" she demands just before we reach the front doors.

I turn and look her in the eyes. "There are things in this world that if you even got a hint of their existence, you would curl up in a corner hugging your knees and cry yourself to sleep at night."

"And you're telling me you're one of those things?" she responds defiantly.

"No, I'm what gives those things nightmares."

Castillo senses a measure of truth in my warning, and I realize my mistake as soon as the words escape my mouth, but I am pissed and I've lost my patience with her meddling. You see, there are two kinds of people in this world. One kind, when faced with something truly terrifying, will run and keep running or collapse in fear and let the scary thing devour them. The other kind, when faced with the same thing, will stop at nothing to destroy it or die trying, and Castillo is one of the latter. It is that very attitude which makes a small part of me respect her.

Will has his car waiting out front and is good enough to give me a ride back home. He damn well should. I practically paid for the BMW by myself.

"I heard Castillo hit you. We can make good money off that if we can get the tape."

"I had it coming."

Will rolls his eyes at me. "That's completely irrelevant in a court of law."

"Guess that's why it's called the court of law and not the court of justice. If you ask me, this country would be better off with more people getting punched in the face and a whole lot less getting paid for the privilege."

"You call getting punched a privilege?"

I shrug. "Costs a lot less than therapy and is usually more effective."

CHAPTER EIGHT

Katherine is leaning against her car in front of my loft as we pull up. I can't say I'm disappointed to see her, and I hope Will doesn't see the corner of my lip twitch up in what on me is almost a shit-eating grin.

"Looks like your guardian angel is here to see you," Will says, somehow making the simple statement sound lewd. "So, are you doing...?"

"Some work for her," I interrupt.

"That explains the help I got from the DA's office in springing you so quickly. I gotta tell you, I wouldn't mind doing some work for her, or on her, myself."

"She's young enough to be your daughter."

"Yet older than my average date. Sounds like a happy medium to me."

"Stick to your hookers."

"Call girls! And at three grand a night, still cheaper than what that one's gonna cost you."

I get out of the car and shoot Will the finger. He returns the gesture, and then tops it by sliding it in and out of the joined thumb and index finger of his other hand.

"Ms. Goldstein, what brings you out on this unexpected visit? Not the view," I say as I look around at the decaying industrial buildings making up the majority of the local structures.

"I just wanted to see how you were doing since you were arrested and assaulted several unpleasant detainees."

"They snitch me out?"

"Hardly," she replies. "They refuse to say what happened,

which is unusual since almost everyone who gets arrested looks for a reason to sue the city."

"Yeah, well, I hope Castillo had a good time trying to explain locking me up with a bunch of scumbags in a cell with a broken camera," I say as I unlock and pull open the heavy door displaying almost no sign of the abuse the cops inflicted on it. "You know she sent the guard on a 'break' too?"

"You don't look to have suffered overmuch."

"Only because I'm a nasty son of a bitch, which she did not know; although she may have a clue now.What if I had been human? We might have been having this conversation in the hospital—weeks from now—when I woke up from my coma."

She ignores my whining. "When I heard what Castillo brought you in for, I thought maybe you had more information about my dad. Do you want talk about it over lunch?"

"I doubt they serve anything I like, and what I've learned wouldn't cover a conversation over coffee."

"Have you found out anything at all?"

I know Katherine isn't really part of the pack, but I'm still reluctant to tell her about the Sheriffs' suspicious activity. If even a rumor of that gets back to the local dog pack, this case will take on another realm of difficulty none of us want to contemplate.

"I think there's something happening that goes a lot deeper than a simple werewolf's nervous breakdown. I think your father may have gotten caught up in someone else's conspiracy, and they're using him to deflect attention away from whatever it is they are doing."

Katherine's delicate hand flies to her mouth. "Oh my God. Who's doing this, and what are they doing? Why bring my father into it?"

"I don't know, to all three," which is only a partial lie. "I have some leads I need someone to follow up for me."

"Do you think it will take you to my father?"

"The best these kinds of things usually give me is more breadcrumbs to follow. Get enough breadcrumbs and you eventually find the witch's candy house."

"All right," Katherine says, then gets in her car. "You know,

the offer for lunch was more about social convention than eating," she tells me through the open window.

"Sorry, never been much on the social graces."

She smiles, shakes her head, and drives away. I stand in front
of my door for several minutes trying to come to terms with the
foreign emotions tingling in my chest. The ones tingling in my
crotch I get, but these others are harder to comprehend. Maybe
I would be a bit more well-adjusted if I took a page from Will's
playbook and hired a high-class prostitute once in a while. I definitely need a distraction.

I replace the jacket Castillo confiscated, holster my sword and
hand cannon, and slip the phone I took from the runner into my
pocket. My first piece of real evidence is the phone, but I need
someone to crack it and get me the call logs and contacts.

Marvin doesn't live far away and, when it comes to anything
involving computers and electronics, he is my go-to guy. Marvin
is a certified genius. He also annoys the hell out of me, but then so
does everyone else on the planet, so I try to keep an open mind.

He lives in a shitty apartment in an even shittier neighborhood because he claims that having a real job is selling out. In a
way, I can understand the notion since I am self-employed myself.
However, one cannot put enough emphasis on the employed part.

Marvin isn't home when I knock, so I skulk around across
the street and wait for him to return. I don't have to wait long.
The lean, young black man comes strolling up the walk carrying
a pizza, wearing the most ridiculous clothes I've seen outside a
circus, and walking as though he suffers from an old gunshot
wound to the leg.

I don't know what new phase of weird Marvin is going
through, but I know he'll use it to annoy the crap out of me. I take
a deep breath, knock on his door, and am promptly ignored.

I knock harder. "Marvin, it's Leo, open up. I know you're
here. I watched you come in with a pizza, wearing a clown suit."

"How do I know you ain't the cops?" comes the reply from
the other side of the door.

"Because the cops won't shoot you through the door if you
don't open it in the next three seconds!"

"Only white people believe that, and I only know one white

boy dumb enough to walk this neighborhood alone." The door swings open and Marvin does a good job of looking pleased to see me. "My man Leo! You must have a job for me. I know it's not a social visit on account of the fact that you are the most antisocial motherfucker I ever met."

"You know me too well, Marvin."

The young man opens the door wider to let me in. "Information is my game but I don't go by Marvin anymore. My crew calls me Mo' Money."

"What crew, your World of Warcraft playmates? And what's with the ridiculous clothes and stupid nickname?"

Marvin throws his hands up as if I am going to arrest him. "Whoa, whoa! First off, it's called a guild, and online social networks are vastly exceeding the archaic concepts of flesh and blood interactions. Secondly, my gear shows I'm a man of the streets and a straight-up gangsta. Thirdly, Mo' Money says I'm a man of means and class."

"Firstly, it's called being a social reject and the prime factor in the success of Chris Hansen's career. Secondly, your clothes would look ridiculous on a clown even if they fit properly. Thirdly, going by Mo' Money when you're flat broke not only makes it an oxymoron, it makes you sound like you have a stutter."

"You are a very hurtful person, Leo Malone. No wonder nobody likes you. Besides, what does a white boy like you know about being street?" Marvin asks, sulking a bit.

"Your father is the dean of Medicine at Mount Sinai, your mother is a world-renowned biologist and Nobel nominee, and you attended MIT at age sixteen. You were tossed out at nineteen just before getting your master's degree in computer science for hacking into the SAT database and selling that year's answers. Then you were accepted to NYU, only after your parents pulled more strings than a harpist, where they threw you out for hijacking several pornography sites, hosting them on the campus servers, and selling access to other students. In street terms, you're whiter than me."

"Have you looked in a mirror lately? You're so white you make Michael Jackson, may God rest his soul, look like Flavor Flav," Marvin fires back.

"As much as I enjoy discussing your cultural identity crisis, I need you to do something for me." I pull out the phone and hand it him. "I need you to crack that and get me the contact information and call logs."

"Done," Marvin declares after tapping on the keypad for about three seconds.

"Done? How are you done?"

"Easy; most cells have a default security code and almost nobody changes it."

"And you have them all memorized?"

Marvin shrugs. "It's a common phone."

"Let me give you a word of advice. When someone gives you a job, don't be overeager to show off your skills. You'll make more money that way."

"Oh, so how much you gonna give me for this?"

"Well, let's see. I usually pay you twenty an hour and it took you about two seconds to crack the phone. Let's round up to an even dime," I tell him.

"Aw, damn."

"Fortunately for you, I have another job. I need you to hack into Vtech Pharmaceuticals and find any reference to break-ins, lost samples, or security breaches. Once you're in, I may have you look for something specific."

I need Marvin to find any records of the Cure and the names of anyone who has accessed them since Vincent had them interred over a decade ago.

"Vtech, that's a whole world beyond cracking a phone," Marvin replies.

"Think you can do it?"

The young hacker scoffs. "Of course I can, but it will take time. If I go in chopping at their system like a lumberjack, I'll have feds up my black ass with a quickness."

"Do what you gotta do. And Marvin…"

"Yeah?"

"Despite what I said earlier, if you milk this, I'll make that limping walk of yours legit."

CHAPTER NINE

It will take Marvin a bit longer to track down the call logs and a great deal longer to investigate Vtech's records and security logs, so I don't have much to go on right now.

Katherine is once again outside my loft when I return a short time later. I find the tingling has resurged, and it both annoys and pleases the hell out of me. I can't remember a case with more confusing components than this one.

"Back already? One visit usually suffices for a month, or a lifetime, for most people."

"I'm not most people. I figured since you skipped lunch maybe you wanted to tell me more over dinner?" she says as she pulls out two cartons of Chinese food.

"Sorry, I can't eat it."

"Social convention, Leo, remember?"

"Antisocial, remember?"

She kicks me in the shin and orders me to open the door. She takes a seat at my tiny table and starts popping bits of sweet and sour pork in her mouth with expert use of a pair of chopsticks. I sit across from her but choose not to grab a drink from my blood supply. It would ruin most people's appetite, but she's not most people and it probably wouldn't bother her. It bothers me though.

"So, did your man find any breadcrumbs?" Katherine asks between bites.

"Not yet, but it won't take long. I'll have some information soon despite Castillo's bullshit arrest."

"Technically she was right, so it wasn't bullshit."

"It was a hunch with almost no evidence to support it. She

would hang every crime in the city on me if she could."

She tilts her head to the side and smiles at me. "What would you have me do, talk to the commissioner and have her fired?"

"No. She doesn't deserve to be fired. Despite being a huge pain in my pasty white ass, I actually..." I sigh and choke on the word.

"Respect her?"

"I know she hates me and, being a cop, I give her plenty of reasons. It would just make my life a whole lot easier if she could show me even the slightest bit of respect in return."

"Maybe if you were a little more pleasant and put on a real jacket instead of looking like a post-apocalyptic road warrior she would. You could also do with a haircut. You're getting rather shaggy," she suggests, twirling her finger in an errant lock of my hair.

I'm almost struck blind by the light bulb flashing inside my brain.

I grab her by the wrist and pull her hand away. "Haircut!"

"It was only a suggestion," Katherine calls out to my back as I cross the room to my desk.

I nearly yank the drawer of my desk out getting to the pictures inside. I empty the large envelopes on the desktop, flip on the big, lighted magnifying glass clamped to one edge, and start shuffling through the photos.

I compare the pictures of the hair samples I got from Raj and the ones I took myself. I already know the answer, but I want Raj's professional opinion before I get Katherine's hopes up.

Pulling open another drawer, I take out the actual samples, put them under the magnifying glass, and take more pictures with my phone. It isn't ideal, but the magnifying glass helps me get the details I want to capture.

"Leo, what is it, what are you looking at?" she asks, feeding off my agitated state.

"Crime scene photos, particularly pictures of the hair collected at them."

"You were sure they belonged to my father. Do you think they aren't now?"

I shake my head. "I'm still sure they're your father's. I'm just not sure he left them."

"I don't understand."

"Give me just a minute." I'm already dialing Raj's number and find him still at his office. "Raj, it's Leo. I need you to bring the hair samples up on your computer. Let me send you the ones I took as well."

It takes only a few key presses to send Raj the pictures from my phone to his email and even less time for him to bring them up on his screen.

"I got them, Leo. What am I looking at—other than hair obviously?"

"Look at the ends and compare them with each crime scene photo and tell me what you see."

"Oh my God, I can't believe I missed that," Raj says after a moment of studying the pictures.

"I'm sure I already know, but tell me what you make of it. I want to be sure."

"OK, most of the hair from the first crime scene has a clean, rounded end which is characteristic of naturally shed hair. The samples taken from the other crime scenes have bits of skin still attached showing that they were ripped out, or have clean ends indicating they were cut."

My head is nodding along with Raj's explanation. "That's what I thought. Thanks, Raj."

"Damn it, Leo, what's going on?" Katherine demands.

I explain the difference in the hair samples to her.

"So what does that all mean?"

I run my hand through my hair as I try to put it all together. She's right, I do need a haircut.

"OK. Your dad was jumped by three guys with questionable reputations and even less intelligence, but it wasn't random. Someone sent them after Martin but declined to provide them with a critical piece of information, which I am positive the leaders of this conspiracy were aware of. These people wanted your dad to shift and tear those idiots apart."

"But why, and why my dad?"

"It's like the weres at the bar said. Your dad isn't much of a werewolf. They needed to catch a werewolf alive after he killed to give the crime scene some legitimacy. Can you imagine trying to catch a werewolf like Meat or another monster while he's in a blood rage? There would be way too much collateral damage and too much interest in finding him. Your dad kept himself apart and wasn't considered part of the pack. His disappearance is a low priority as far as the wolves are concerned. Now someone else is killing people and making it appear as though it's more werewolf attacks by leaving Martin's hair at the scene."

Katherine's eyes are shining with excitement and she squeezes my hand tightly. "That's good, right? It means my dad is not killing people!"

"No, it's not good, not good for anyone."

"But it means he hasn't lost control and is killing people."

"It means someone has him and all signs are pointing toward vampire involvement. Outside the pack or not, he's still kin, and if the weres get wind of it, there will be war. I have a guy who says he saw several vampires load Martin into a van, and worse yet, he thought they were Sheriffs."

So much for keeping this from Katherine, but this new revelation makes it impossible. Whatever is happening to Martin, he is an unwilling participant in something unpleasant. And when whoever has him is done, it's going to get a lot more unpleasant for him. I just hope he has enough time left for me to find him.

"Oh God. But why would someone do this, especially the Sheriffs? Do you think my father is still alive?" Katherine asks as the full weight of the situation becomes clear.

"It could be people wanting us to believe they were Sheriffs. I have rumors and suspicions, but no evidence supporting that theory. These things are always about money, power, or both. I can't see any kind of revenge angle, so money or power is the most probable motive, although I have yet to see how. I would bet money Martin is still alive. They'll want to keep him alive until it's time for the 'murderer' to turn up. That means I need to find him before that happens."

She looks up at me, eyes full of concern and asks, "How are you going to do that?"

"I have a guy getting me names. As soon as he gets those,

I'm going to start stepping on some toes and see who yells the loudest."

Katherine nods then catches me completely off guard as she embraces me tightly. "Please be careful, Leo."

"Not being careful has worked out for me pretty well so far," I reply, hoping to defuse the emotional bomb Katherine set at my feet.

I think I succeed as she unwraps her arms from my body, but then the bomb goes off as she pulls my head down and kisses me fully and deeply. I don't return the kiss, thinking she is emotionally compromised by the change in her father's situation, but she is unrelenting and my resistance evaporates like a shallow puddle under the blazing sun.

Her passion is raw and demanding. In that kiss, she releases a sea of pent-up emotions and overwhelms the walls I have spent decades erecting. I return her kiss, tentatively at first, then with a passion matching her own.

In moments, our clothes are scattered about the floor and I am so lost in our ardor I am unaware of when or how the transition came about. The flames of her passion burn so bright they illuminate the blackest recesses of my heart, a heart so shrouded in darkness I never thought it would see light again.

Our lovemaking is zealous and almost animalistic in its aggressiveness. We roll around on the floor, embracing, kissing, scratching, and biting. I can tell she is holding nothing back, releasing the animal side of her being she works so hard to control and deny every bit as much as I am embracing the humanity within myself butwhich I have denied for so long.

After what seems an eternity that ends too soon, we lie in an embrace on my bed, which is little more than a cot. Now that our zeal has abated, I am rebuking myself for getting involved with a client.

"You were very resistant at first," Katherine says, breaking the silence and my own thoughts. "Are you not attracted to me?"

"No, it's just that it's been a long time, and you being a client and all..."

"How long has it been for you?"

"What is this, March?" I ask as I do a mental count. "Fifteen years and four months, give or take a few weeks."

"Why so long?"

"It's complicated. After a while, it just didn't seem impor-tant. You may find this hard to believe, but some people find me unapproachable.If you really want to know, you should talk to my shrink. He seems to have a bunch of opinions on the subject. But that begs the question: why do you like me?"

"I find your brutal honesty refreshing. I'm a lawyer, and I work with nothing but lawyers, criminals, and politicians all day long. I have known you a lot longer than you think. I read your file many times and followed a few of your cases. This is not something I did without a lot of thought, Leo. I hope you don't think this is something I do often or on a whim."

"I just hope you don't expect any sort of discount when it comes time to pay my bill."

She punches me in the chest several times. "You are an ass, Leo Malone!"

"I'm sorry. That fact is usually well established the first time people meet me. Either I'm slipping, or you are the queen of obliviousness."

"Go ahead and keep being a shithead. It's one of the rea-sons I am attracted to you—no pretensions. Moreover, I'm not an emotionally weak little girl you can scare off with your rot-ten attitude so you can keep yourself all nice, safe, and alone. Shithead," she finishes, giving me another hard punch in the shoulder before snuggling deeper against me.

"It sounds like you've been talking to my shrink. I need to have a word with him about doctor-patient confidentiality."

"I don't need a therapist to tell me you're a shithead."

I stay awake pondering the full implications of what is hap-pening. It doesn't take long for the pressing warmth of her body against mine to lull me into a slumber. It feels so natural, so human, I don't even fight it.

A distraught keening wakes me from my sleep. It is dark, but I can see everything clearly. Pressed against the far wall of the hut are a dozen children all screaming, many covered in the blood of the adults who made a futile attempt to protect them. The last remaining adult is barely past girlhood herself.

She is cursing me in the rapid chatter of her native Vietnamese. I spent years in this country, but I have only a passing comprehension. She calls me rừng quỷ, or jungle demon, and renounces me. Rage replaces her terror as she comprehends her imminent death and she spits in my face.

I wrap my hands around her slender throat and lift her from the ground, and yet she continues to curse me and claws at the exposed flesh of my arms and begins plunging a small knife into my forearms.

I laugh at the futility of her struggles, but my laughter is cut off as I watch her face begin to shift and transform. Her long, black hair turns a golden blond, and her almond-shaped brown eyes enlarge and take on a brilliant blue.

I don't understand what kind of trickery the little squint is using on me, but it enrages me and I squeeze harder. I return her shouts with equal amounts of anger, hate, and fear.

However, she is no longer screaming at me. Her voice has softened and the gentle pleading is in English. She stops clawing and stabbing me and is instead grasping my wrists.

"Leo, please, it's Katherine," she gasps out. "You have to wake up; you're hurting me."

The last few words are a squeak, but they penetrate the dark recesses of my confused mind. Katherine crumples to the floor as I loosen my grip and stagger away, staring at my hands in shock at what I have done.

"I'm sorry, I'm so sorry," I cry out in anguish and rush around grabbing my clothes so I can flee, as if I can outrun my shame.

As I pick up my jacket, I'm hit hard from behind. Katherine climbs on my back as I take a face-first dive to the floor.

"Don't you dare think about leaving! You almost choked me to death, so it's not your turn to play victim!"

She relaxes enough to let me roll on my back and look up at her. "Katherine, I am so sorry. I didn't mean to hurt you, I swear."

"I know, you dumbass," she says as she lets me up and starts grabbing her clothes.

"I should have known better. I should never have let this

happen. This is exactly why I need to be alone!"

"Oh boohoo. Poor Leo has some issues so let's give the world the finger and keep everyone away. Well suck it up, buttercup, you're stuck with me. I'm not the kind of girl who hops in bed with a guy without some kind of commitment."

"Damn it, if you were a normal human I would have killed you! I damn near did anyway!"

She stalks over and looks me in the eye. "Well I'm not and you didn't, so stop being a baby. All it means is I won't be staying the night for a while. You have the kind of girl that most men can only dream of—the kind that doesn't stick around after sex."

I still have a dumbfounded look on my face when she kisses me. "It's morning, and I need to get ready for work. I don't suppose you have anything to eat in here, do you?"

"Just you," I reply, still in a daze.

She waves goodbye to me as she steps out the door. I'm still standing amazed as I listen to her car drive away. The woman either loves me, or she's more fucked up than I am. Honestly, I'm OK with either one.

CHAPTER TEN

I try to distract myself from what happened by considering the revelations of my new evidence, but it isn't working very well. Even when I can divert enough of my attention from dwelling on the fact I almost killed my client, the cementing of the fact vampires are at the heart of most of the killings only serves to confound me even more.

No matter how hard I try, I keep thinking about last night and my near fatal flashback, and I know I will continue to do so until I deal with what has happened. That means I need to go visit my shrink. That's always fun.

My mind is often stimulated by physical activity, so I decide to walk the three miles to his office. It's still early in the morning, so I need to burn some time anyway.

The air is cool and crisp this time of year, which I prefer. It suits my disposition. I can make the trek in minutes if I want, but I'm in no hurry so I take it at a leisurely stroll. I arrive at the front of the brick building and open the primarily decorative white door, with its three triangular glass panes set in the top forming a half circle. I can't help but scoff at the uselessness of the portal from a security standpoint.

Dr. Morison's clinic is on the ground floor of a three-story residential home. His office is past the reception room, which is the first door on the left. I see his receptionist, a wrinkled old crone who shares the consensus of the general populace regarding my personality, talking to a small man who jumps when I step into the room.

"I need to see the doc," I interrupt as I push past the flighty little man, who backs himself up against the far wall.

The receptionist's face turns sour at my abruptness. "Do you have an appointment, Mr. Malone?"

Her question annoys me even more since she has the appointment book right in front of her and knows damn well I don't.

"No, but I need to see him now," I reply, then give her my best intimidating look.

That glare and the power of my predatory presence have sent some of the biggest and meanest men in New York cowering and fighting to control their bladder. It doesn't faze her in the least. It's like trying to set a rock on fire—or a fossil.

She returns my gaze with equal venom. "Dr. Morison has a patient now. I can schedule you in at his next available time. If it is an emergency, I suggest you go to the emergency room."

My keen eyesight has no problem picking out the scared little man's name on her appointment ledger. "Ronald needs to reschedule," I growl.

"He most certainly does not!" she fires back.

Ronald finds the courage to speak, although with great trepidation. "Maybe it's best if I reschedule."

"Ronald, you do *not* have to reschedule," she assures him.

"Yes you do, Ronald," I snarl as I direct my scary glare at him.

He nearly pisses his pants, which makes me feel a lot better. I was afraid I was slipping.

"I'm sorry," he sputters, then bolts from the room before the old woman can respond.

"It seems the doc has an opening in his schedule," I tell her smugly.

She raises herself up from her chair, leans forward on her desk supported by her wrinkly old fists, and opens her mouth to unleash a bitter tirade upon me. The doctor interrupts her as he steps through the door separating his office from the reception room.

"It's all right, Jeanine, I'll see him."

I smile at her as she sits back down and I strut past her desk on my way into Stanley's office.

"Rancid little shit," she hisses as I pass.

My jaw drops in surprise at her vehemence, and it still registers on my face as I take a seat in the plush client chair in the doctor's immaculate office.

"Your secretary just called me a rancid little shit."

Dr. Morison sits in the chair in front of and slightly to the side of the one I'm occupying and pulls out a pad of paper and a pen.

"And you disagree with her assessment of your character?"

I purse my lips. "I don't disagree so much as find it unprofessional to vocalize it."

Stanley shrugs with a noncommittal grunt. It's obvious I'll get no sympathy from him.

"You failed to make an appointment after your last call, so I assume something else has happened that causes you to rudely barge into my office, frighten off my client, and demand immediate, special treatment."

"Yeah, I'm sorry about that, Doc."

"I am your psychiatrist and have been for years, so don't bother lying to me," he replies without looking up from the pad he is already scribbling notes on. "I don't think you've been sorry about anything since you left Vietnam."

"I had sex last night," I tell him, deciding to plunge right in.

He stops writing and looks up at me with arched eyebrows. Now I have his attention. Figures. I think all shrinks are closet perverts who get into the field to hear about other people's sexual happenings. Bunch of voyeurs, or whatever the auditory version of voyeurism is called.

"Now that *is* interesting. How did it go?"

"I almost killed her," I respond without emotion.

"Please explain."

"I had a flashback and woke up with my hands around her throat."

I am unable to make that statement without almost choking on it. Let him tell me I don't regret that!

"And where were you in your flashback, do you recall?"

"Vietnam, in the hut with the girl and the screaming kids."

"We have talked about this flashback before, haven't we? This is the same young woman you said broke you out of your feeding frenzy, from being rogue as you call it. Correct?"

I nod. "Yeah, that's the one."

"How did you feel going into this sexual encounter?"

"I don't know. Hesitant, resistant, but then I sort of gave in and let it happen. I stopped fighting."

"What kind of relationship do you have with this woman? I get the feeling it is more than a simple momentary physical desire on your part. You have not expressed any such impulses in previous sessions."

I think and shake my head. "I don't know, Doc. She's—different. I didn't think I could feel this way anymore. It's been so long. I don't even know what it is I'm feeling or how to deal with it."

"You care for her, and it makes you feel vulnerable," he tells me matter-of-factly. "The last time you allowed yourself to feel true emotions or some kind of mutual empathy was in that hut in Vietnam. The girl or the situation in which you found yourself broke through the walls you had erected to shield your own sanity. The fact this woman was able to get inside your defenses last night made you feel vulnerable, even though it is best for your own mental welfare. Your moment of emotional exposure saved you from yourself in Vietnam, but it also made you face the horror of your own existence and terrified you. Once again, you are feeling vulnerable; this may also force life-changing behaviors and it frightens you in much the same way. You spent so many years building these barriers against everything and everyone around you, not just to keep yourself safe from them but also to keep them safe from you, and here comes a woman who, with a single act, tears them all down. For once in a very long time, you are not in complete control of your little sphere of life. That's scary stuff."

What he says makes sense, but I'm not sure how it's going to help me. "So how do I deal with it so I don't hurt her again?"

"I suggest you embrace what she is willing to offer you. Accept that change can be a good thing, and you can share yourself with another and still be safe. The feeling of safety and control you think you have through avoidance is an illusion. How did she react after your episode?"

I smile ruefully. "She told me to stop being a big baby and that I couldn't chase her away so easily."

"She sounds like a remarkable woman. I hope you will consider building on this relationship. Maybe you won't be such a rancid little shit to everyone."

"Don't hold your breath, Doc. If a little sex cured crazy, you'd be running a whorehouse on the second floor. Costs about the same," I tell him as I stand up to leave.

"Are you leaving already? I'm sure we have plenty more to talk about. You're paying for the full hour, you know."

I turn around. "What? I've been here like fifteen minutes!"

"I bill for the hour and you ran off my other appointment," he replies unabashedly.

"I guess you don't need a whorehouse upstairs, you do fine screwing people right in your office," I mumble as I step out of the room.

I'm not actually mad. I know the score, but we both like to play our little word games. I give Jeanine a fake smile as I step out and feign a look of shock when she raises her bony old digit and flips me the bird.

As I step onto the sidewalk, a nervous voice speaks to me from behind. "You're not like other people. You're different."

My reaction is instantaneous. I spin around and catch the speaker by his throat, lifting him from the ground. It is the scared little man, Ronald, from the office.

"What do you mean, I'm different? How am I different?" I demand, thinking he somehow knows I'm a vampire, which may well mean the end of Ronald and all his troubles.

"You're different; you're not scared of anything. I can tell," he gasps out as he clutches my wrist with both his hands.

I release my grip and he falls on his ass. "Most people don't walk around in fear."

"But you're not afraid of anything," he reiterates as he scrambles back to his feet. "Me, I'm afraid of everything. I can barely leave my apartment to come to this appointment, and it's only a block away! How do I be like you?"

I'm impressed the little worm has the spine to approach me given what he said of his problems. He must be desperate or crazy.

"Dying helps. What is it that made you so afraid to begin with? I can't imagine you were always a complete chickenshit."

Ronald gulps audibly then relates his story. "A few years ago, I was mugged by a man with a knife. He took my money and my driver's license and said he now knew where I lived, and if the cops ever came after him, he would kill me. Ever since then, I haven't left my apartment except to see Dr. Morison. I lost my job, my wife, everything. Please tell me how to be like you."

I pause to think for a moment. I motion to the narrow alley next to the doc's office with my head. "Let's get off the street, and I'll see if I can explain."

Ronald hesitantly steps into the gap between the buildings as I follow close behind.

"I can't go on like this anymore. I'm losing what little grip I have on my remaining sanity," he babbles.

He holds his hands with clenched fists against his chest, his fingers twitching about as if he is using a subtle form of sign language. When he turns to face me, the end of his nose disappears inside Shalonda's massive bore. Every muscle in his body goes so stiff he cannot even fall down or release the piss trying to escape his bladder.

"This gun has a stock trigger pull of less than four pounds. I've modified it to half that. From your vantage point, you could set it off just by breathing too hard." There's no real threat of that since he hasn't taken a breath and probably won't until he passes out. "Look at me, Ronald. Look in my eyes."

Ronald's eyes uncross as he stops focusing on Shalonda's heavy black barrel and looks at me.

"Tell me, what will happen if I decide to pull the trigger now?" The terrified man's lips begin to quiver but no sound escapes them. "Come on, Ronald, stay with me. I need you to use your words. What will happen if I pull the trigger?"

"I-it w-would go off."

"And?"

"A-and I would die," he wails in a whisper.

"And?" I continue to press.

The man is confused as much as terrified as he answers. "I-I don't know. Nothing, I would be dead and then there would be nothing!"

"That's right. There would be nothing," I affirm as I ride the hammer back down and slip the big gun back into my coat pocket. "There would be no more fear, no more shrinks, and no more bad memories. There would be nothing. Now, what is so terrifying about nothing?"

"I don't know. Nothing, I suppose. What are you saying, that I should kill myself?"

"I'm saying death is going to come to you. It comes for every one of us whether it's today if a man stabs you and takes your money, tomorrow if a bus hits you as you step off the curb, or fifty years from now in your sleep. Death is the peaceful oblivion we are all rewarded with for suffering through all the bullshit we put up with in life. When you accept it as an inevitability, just like the sun rising and setting every day, when you can say 'fuck you, death,' only then can you actually live and enjoy your life."

Ronald's entire countenance changes right before my eyes. He relaxes his arms and stands up straighter.

"I think I understand. I thought I was afraid of death, but what I'm really afraid of is life!"

"You got it. Now repeat after me: fuck death!"

"Fuck death!"

"Fuck death!"

Fuck death!" Ronald cries out enthusiastically.

"Now what are you going to do, Ronald?"

He pauses and thinks. "I think I'll go to the zoo. I haven't been there in so long. Thank you, thank you so much!"

I flip open my phone as I begin walking back home. "Hey, Doc, we need to discuss your fee. This psychiatry shit is a piece of cake."

"Leo? What do you mean? Leo, what have you done?" I hear him shout before I end the call and drop my cell back into my pocket.

I think this counts as my one good deed of the year. Karma can kiss my ass now; we're even as far as I'm concerned. I feel rather good having helped Ronald out, but mostly I like to screw with the doc. My real reward is knowing Ronald won't be mak-ingas many appointments now, and that will hit Dr. Morison right in his wallet. That's what he gets for charging me a full hour.

CHAPTER ELEVEN

I'm cutting through Forest Park on my way home when my phone starts to vibrate. Caller ID says it's Marvin.

"What do you have for me, Marvin?"

"Everything, of course," the young hacker scoffs. "I pulled up all his contacts and cross-referenced the numbers with service providers. I then hacked into those and got their addresses. A couple of these fools actually have contract phones, so those addresses are probably good. Even the prepays have registrations, so I pulled those email addresses and snooped through them until I found a couple physical addresses to go with them."

"Good job, Marvin. I need you to send whatever information you have along with the phone to me. Use a courier and tell him there's a twenty-dollar tip in it if he can get it to me in the next thirty minutes."

"A'ight, I can do that, but you need to call me by my street name, Mo' Money."

"Yeah, that's not gonna happen, Marvin." I give him a nearby address for the courier to meet me at.

I cut off Marvin's reply in mid-expletive. Just as I flip my phone shut, something hits me hard from behind and we both go tumbling to the grass. I leap up just a fraction of a second faster than my attacker, who launches a flurry of strikes and kicks at my head and body.

I'm caught by surprise, not just at the attack but by the attacker as well; I still manage to block most of his swings, although a few get through and land with enough force to rock me back.

"I saw the bruises, you son of a bitch!" Katherine's little

brother rages and dives at me once more.

Prepared for his attack, I stop him in his tracks as he collides linebacker style into my midriff. I easily lift and flip him over my hip as I pivot and toss him several yards.

The angry pup lands hard and rolls to a stop, glaring hatred at me as he readies himself to throw down again. I can't help but sympathize with him as my anger at attacking Katherine deeply resembles his own.

"Roger, stop! It was an accident, and this is not going to help Katherine or your father."

His rage is still evident as he glowers at me, breathing hard, his fists clenched and held before him, but he does not continue to press his attack. He stands like this for a full minute before relaxing and dropping his hands to his side.

"Fuck!" he screams as he kicks a metal barrel used as a trash can chained to a park bench, deeply denting in the side of it. "I hate it when she does this!"

"Does what?"

"Falls for some asshole who always ends up hurting her," he replies.

"I didn't mean to hurt her, Roger. I tried to keep her at a distance, but she's rather persistent."

Roger sits heavily on the bench, and I take a seat next to him. "I know. That's what she said. She doesn't let herself get close to people very often. I don't want you to think she's a slut or something, who just hopped into bed with you out of boredom. It's just that when she does choose to get involved with someone, she goes all in, holds nothing back, and it almost always ends with her getting hurt, although not usually bruised up and this soon."

"If it makes you feel any better, I don't get close to people either. I think it's that passion she has that got to me. Look, I'm not about to get all girly and talk about my feelings for your sister and shit with you. I'm as surprised and appalled about what happened as you are, maybe even more so."

Roger nods in mutual agreement. "Kat tells me you don't think my father is killing all these people."

"I'm not sure what to think, but one thing is for sure, it goes a lot deeper than just a werewolf getting in a frenzy. Vampires are involved and may have set up the entire thing, including your father. I just don't know who or why.I'm expecting a courier a few blocks from here with some information that should serve to shed a little light on things or at least get me closer to the truth. So, if you don't mind, time is really not on our side right now."

Roger takes the hint and stands to leave but gives me a parting warning. "If you hurt her, I swear, somehow I'll kill you."

"If I hurt her, I might just let you," I reply, then stalk off at a brisk walk to meet my courier.

The courier and I reach the coffee shop at almost the same time. He's a typical bike rider, sporting spandex shorts, a plastic helmet, and a windbreaker with his company logo emblazoned across the back. I acknowledge him with a wave and he pedals over to me.

"Mr. Malone?"

I reply a curt, "Yeah," as I show my ID and pay him the COD and promised tip.

He thanks me and smiles appreciatively as he hands over a large envelope with the evident bulge of the cell phone in the middle of it before pedaling off to whatever delivery is next on his list.

I take a seat at one of the outdoor tables of the coffee shop and begin examining the contents of the envelope. I'm looking through the call logs when a young man in an apron and sporting numerous facial piercings interrupts me.

"Good morning, sir, welcome to Perk Place coffee house. What can I get for you?"

"Some fucking privacy," I growl in response without looking up from my stack of papers.

"Sir, I am obliged to tell you these tables are for customers only, and if you want to sit here you need to buy something," he counters in a voice showing how much he has to force himself to be polite.

"And I am obliged to inform you that if you speak one more word, I will tear your arms off and beat you to death with them."

I glance up and see he is actually stupid enough to ignore

my warning, so I grab the stainless- steel cocoa shaker off the table and crush it like a beer can. The idiot squeaks in appreciable fear and seeks safety indoors.

I have finished flipping through the papers and have started looking through the cell's contacts, putting names, numbers, and addresses with the entries on the pages when I am once again interrupted, this time by the manager with Shrapnel-face standing several paces behind him.

The scrawny man clears his throat, both to get my attention and to try to get his words past the obvious fear he is trying to hide. "Sir, threatening my employees and destroying Perk Place property is unacceptable."

"Not nearly as unacceptable as your comb-over," I fire back as I continue to scroll through the Contacts screen.

"I must insist you pay for that shaker and vacate the premises, or I will be forced to call the police!"

I look away from the phone and up at the sweating manager. "How much does that tin can cost?"

Assuming I am actually cooperating, he stands a little straighter and replies, "$9.99 plus tax."

"And how much do you think a skull fracture costs, calculating in the time lost from work and the perpetual drooling resulting from brain damage?"

"I don't understand," his words say, but his body language shows he knows exactly what I mean.

"It's not a complicated question. It's based on the basic business acumen of cutting one's losses. If that is also too difficult for your community-college-educated brain to comprehend, let me break it down for you even further. Fuck off before I add you to what may be a rather long list of people I need to kill today. Do you understand that?" I ask him nonchalantly.

I think the matter-of-fact tone more than the actual threat sends him and his moronic lackey running away. Whatever the reason, I am glad for the moment of peace. I pick a name with frequent calls and texts, and begin typing.

Yo, Mikey, U feed lately?

I despise the concept of texting so much I feel dirty, but a phone call is out of the question. I need to ascertain two things right now: is Mikey a vampire, and where can I find him?

Fortunately, I do not wait long before getting a response.

T-dog, what up? Yeah, ate some *prosti* near the docks last night but down 4 w/e. Where u been?

Problems, bro. U at home? Meet u there in a few.

I slip the phone into my pocket after Mikey confirms he is home and is waiting there for me. Thanks to Marvin getting me the billing and registration information from the various phone accounts, I know right where to go.

"I smell donuts and an undeserved sense of importance," I remark as I stand, turn around, and face the two uniformed cops standing behind me.

"The manager says you're threatening his staff and destroying property. What's that about?" Barney Fife number one asks.

"A simple misunderstanding, I think. I was simply giving Captain Comb-Over a lesson in business sense."

"Did you break the canister?" Barney number two asks, indicating the crushed shaker.

I look from the cops to the manager and pull out a twenty, deciding I have better things to do than continue picking fights at a coffee shop.

"You know," Barney one remarks as I drop the double sawbuck on the table, "it would have been a lot less hassle and a good deal cheaper if you had just bought a cup of coffee."

"Yeah, but not as much fun," I reply with a smile and tip of an imaginary hat.

Fortunately, the cops also have better things to do with their time than pursue a verbal threat, much to the manager's protests. I hear them giving the manager the same advice I did about cutting his losses as I walk away.

I order a cab to drop me off a few blocks from Mikey's apartment in the Bronx. I wonder why Mikey and his crew are operating out of the Bronx but hunting in my ward. Of course, I'm going on the assumption there is a grand conspiracy going on and not a few random vampires getting uppity.

It's a pretty shitty part of town, which is good because this is not likely to be a subtle interrogation, and the people around these parts are not prone to calling the cops unless the bullets start coming through their walls. Graffiti covers the walls and trash litters the stairs. Mikey lives on the fourth floor of the six-story complex. A few children, mostly black and Latino, are terrorizing the halls, but they disappear into their apartments when they see me. I'm not a regular, and people living in places like this have a sixth sense about impending danger.

I find the door I am looking for and give it a quick, soft rapping with my knuckles while standing to the side of the peephole.

"T-dog, that you?" a muffled voice inquires from inside.

I hit dial on my phone and hear the corresponding ring on the other side of the door. It's all the confirmation I need. A quick kick sends the door, a good portion of its frame, and Mikey tumbling into the center of the tiny, filthy apartment.

I leap through the ruined portal, sword in hand, and thrust it through the young man's chest and spine, pinning him to the floor like a bug in a collector's display case. Mikey looks up at me, his eyes wide and terror-filled, and begins crying out.

"Oh God, who are you? I can't feel my legs!"

"That's because I severed your spinal cord between the T2 and T3 vertebrae. If you were human, you'd probably have a hard time breathing. If you answer my questions, you'll probably get better; if you don't, you'll definitely get a whole lot worse."

"Who are you? What do you want?" Mikey wails.

I pick the door up off the floor and set it back into place as best I can while I answer the question. "I'm the guy who gets called when vampires get out of line. You and your friends have been getting out of line. Didn't anyone explain the rules to you?"

"Wait, you're a Sheriff? Andre told us the Sheriffs wouldn't bother us as long as we did what we were told! You're not supposed to touch us!"

"Oh, I'm not a Sheriff, not anymore," I reply as I cross the room and loom over him. "They fired me years ago. Seems they found me too violent, my tactics too heavy-handed. Can you believe it? Me, violent and heavy-handed? Do I seem violent or heavy-handed to you, Mikey?" I ask as I pull my blade free and plunge it back into his chest, intentionally missing the spine.

I give it a twist for good measure. Mikey lets out a scream, his spinal cord already healing enough to return the sense of pain thanks to what I assume to be rather gluttonous eating habits.

"Please, please tell me what you want to know, just stop stabbing me!"

"Who told you the Sheriffs are supposed to leave you alone and why?"

He shook his head rapidly. "Andre told all of us. He said we could feed all we wanted as long as we didn't draw too much attention to the humans and stayed near Brooklyn."

"Who's Andre?" I ask, but I already have a sneaking suspicion.

"He's in charge of our group. He got orders from someone else, but I don't know who, I swear."

"Was Andre a black guy with dreadlocks, from the islands?"

Mikey nodded enthusiastically. "Yeah, that's him! He knows more than me. I don't know nothing but what he tells me."

"No good. I killed Andre last night along with T-dog and another stupid-looking white kid. Who turned you?"

"Andre's dead? Oh man, oh man."

I give my sword a twist to get Mikey's attention again. "Let's focus on what's important here, Mikey. Who turned you and where was Andre getting his orders?"

My gentle prodding elicits another suppressed scream from the kid. "I don't know, I don't know!"

"You don't know what, who turned you or where the orders come from?"

"Neither, you fucker! I don't know who turned me; none of us do. It was the same with all of us. I was at a club talking to some smoking-hot Asian chick. She was asking me what I thought about stuff like power and money. She started asking me about weird shit like wanting to live forever and what I would do to get all that. I woke up in a room. Andre was there and T-dog and Street but I didn't know them. I got really sick for a couple days, they brought in this homeless guy or something, and told me I had to kill him and drink his blood. They told me I was a vampire now and to follow Andre and do what he said."

"Did they ever tell you who the woman was, or who brought you in?"

"No, just that it was the same with all of them: hooking up with someone, getting asked weird questions, and being brought in unconscious by a couple of dudes in long coats and masks."

As strange as all this sounds, it's starting to make sense to me now, but I am still lost on the motive. Someone is obviously creating their own little gang but why and, more importantly, how? The odds of creating a vampire are really low. Our condition simply isn't easily transferable. It's not like a damn cold. It's more like post-vaccine polio, but here are four who appear to have been created specifically to establish a power base. Does this mean there are hundreds or even thousands of failed attempts sunk in the bay, or has someone found a way to increase the likelihood of transmission? Call me dark, but I'm really hoping for the former.

"How many more little gangs are out there like yours?" I ask.

"I don't know. I'm pretty sure there's at least one in every borough, but there could be more. I don't know, I swear."

"Do you have contact with any of the other groups?"

Mikey shakes his head. "No, we aren't allowed to communicate even if we cross paths."

"What about Andre? He must have talked to someone outside the group, gotten his orders from a higher up."

"No. He had a phone, but the incoming number was always blocked when they called. Most of his orders came from a drop location on paper, usually saying to just stay put and hunt only in Brooklyn, and we didn't get many of those."

"Mikey, you caught me in a rare moment of compassion. You have been helpful and cooperative, so I'm going to let you live. If you happen to come across any more of your little gang members, you tell them Leo is coming for them."

I free my sword from the young vamp's chest and use the fire escape to make my exit. The kid is probably stupid enough to think I acted with mercy, but it's a tactical decision, not one involving any sort of emotion. The only thing his information revealed is whoever is behind all this is damn smart. These gangs he or she is setting up are built into small cells much like the more advanced terrorist cells are. No one cell knows the identity or locations of another until you get to the top, or real close to it.

The most disturbing thing was confirming that the Sheriffs were involved. The question now is how deep does it go, and how high? Is there a rogue operative or two inside Wyatt's squad, or is the entire thing rotten, with him part of it? My first inclination is to kick down Wyatt's door along with several of his teeth and find out, but I dismiss it as logic intrudes upon my urges. If the whole of the Sheriffs' organization is corrupt, I really do *not* want to go in guns blazing. That's a bit more than even my inflated ego and I are ready to take head on.

No, better to let Mikey go and hope he leads me to more of his gang. I don't know if Mikey is completely honest about not knowing anyone else outside his cell. T-dog's phone records hint there's more communication than he let on, but I am willing to bet after I took out Andre and his cronies last night, someone is watching these guys and they will certainly want to talk to Mikey and the others.

I don't have Andre's phone, but it isn't hard for Marvin to get his call logs from the provider's database since he has the information from the phone I gave him, and it definitely has numbers and addresses I need to check out tonight. I have a hunch there's a lot these guys are going to want to discuss once Mikey passes along my little message.

Another cab ride and I am home again. I grab a bag of blood from my refrigerator and sit down to call Marvin. If I keep getting into fights I'll need to hunt and take a life soon, but right now, I need to keep the inertia going on my case.

"Marvin, I need you to look at the guy named Andre's phone logs. Cross-reference them with the phone I gave you, along with Mikey's, and see if any calls show up more often than others. I also need you to watch Mikey's phone and track who he calls and see if those numbers correspond to the other most called numbers. Can you do that?"

"Marvin does not have that kind of mad skill, but Mo'

Money can do it without a problem. Maybe if you asked him real nice he would be happy to look into it."

It takes significant effort on my part not to crush my phone and hope it somehow reaches Marvin's skinny neck on the other end. "Marvin, do not toy with me. If I have to replace you, I will, and when I replace someone, I replace them permanently. Do not make me downsize our business. Do you understand me?"

"You know, you create a very hostile work environment, which is not conducive to maximum performance," Marvin replies, sulking from behind his easily bruised ego.

"How about broken legs, would that add or take away from your overall performance? For me, motivation through fear of impending pain is an excellent method for achieving maximum productivity from my employees."

"All right, don't get your BVDs in a bunch. Yeah, I can do it, no problem. I already have access to their accounts, so I can track the calls."

"Good. I have one more thing that may be a little harder. Can you triangulate the exact, current position of those cell phones?"

Marvin pauses to think. "Yeah! I can track the time differential of the signal as it reaches different cell towers. Then I can reverse plot those onto a satellite map of the towers back to the source of the signal. Where the lines intersect is where the phone is. Oh man, this is some straight-up James Bond, CIA shit here! Damn I love being a genius!"

"I'm glad you're a genius too, but don't think so much of yourself you start thinking you can't be replaced. There's seven billion people on this planet, and there's bound to be a few more geniuses amongst them."

"Yeah, but do you speak Chinese?" Marvin fires back, "because there's like a ninety percent chance that's who they'll be."

"Actually, I do speak passable Chinese."

"Oh. Well, don't you worry, I got this."

"Good work, Marvin. I never doubted you," I tell him. I figure it's always good policy to provide a little positive reinforcement, as long as the help remembers negative reinforcement is near at hand.

"By the way," Marvin says just as I'm about to hang up, "Mo' Money is no employee. Mo' Money is at least a valued partner."

"Yeah, but Marvin is my bitch, so you average that out any way you want so long as you do your job."

"You're a real asshole, Malone."

"That's what people keep telling me. I'll call you tonight when I need the locations of those phones."

A rapping at my door sounds as I hang up on Marvin. It's safe to assume anyone meaning me harm wouldn't bother to knock, so I don't check to see who it is, but I do keep a firm hold on Shalonda's grip inside my pocket as I open the door.

Katherine is standing in the doorway, illuminated in the golden aura of the sun like an angel sent down to save my soul—assuming I still have one. I almost let slip my façade and return the bright smile on her perfect lips. Fortunately, I am instantly aware of the poetic crap my brain is currently processing and it sufficiently sours my mood enough to prevent it.

"May I come in?"

I pause to respond, so she simply shoulders past me and takes a seat on the only other piece of furniture I own.

"How did your lead turn out?"

"I'm still seeing where it goes. I should have more information tonight. I did confirm that vampires are behind most of this."

"Hmm, that's not good."

"It gets worse. It looks like at least one or more Sheriffs are behind this, which means someone fairly high up the chain is also involved. I've never known any Sheriffs to have the imagination to attempt a power grab on their own."

"Do you have any idea who might be at the top of this and why they would involve my father?"

I shake my head but tell her my suspicions. "Right now, my lead suspect is Vincent."

Katherine looks appropriately shocked at my accusation. "Vincent, head of the council Vincent? Why would he risk so much on something so dangerous? Surely he doesn't want a war with the werewolves?"

"I'm not sure. Vincent is old, *really* old, and he's not fond of change. He comes from a time when vampires were feared and wielded enormous influence and power. It could be he wants to recapture those days. I also heard his influence is slipping amongst the council and voting vampires. He could simply be creating a crisis so he can resolve it and make himself look stronger."

"You think he would take such a big risk to get reelected?" Katherine asks, finding it hard to believe considering the high potential of disaster.

"It got Bush reelected after 9/11," I reply with a shrug. "People don't like to change leadership in the midst of a war. Look, Katherine, I need you to stay away from me. Don't even call me. It's for your own safety."

Katherine bolts from the couch and starts jabbing me in the chest with a finger as she speaks. "I told you before, Leo Malone, you're not going to scare me off easily. I'm a big girl, and I'll make my own decisions! I gave you my heart and more, and I won't be cast aside because you're scared!"

I gently grab her finger and hold her hand. "It's not about me, not really. If someone isn't watching me, they certainly will be after tonight, and the less they know about you the better. If they've seen you with me already, they probably assume you hired me to look for your father. But if they even think there's more to it, they can use you against me, use you to hurt me and to stop me from doing my job. I'll keep you informed whenever I get new information, but right now it's best we have as few connections as possible."

Katherine gives thought to my words and sees they make sense. "All right, but when this is over I'll be back. And Leo..."

"Yes?"

"If they hurt my father, I hope you kill every one of them," Katherine remarks with a vehemence that makes me proud.

"You can count on it. I won't even charge extra."

CHAPTER TWELVE

After Katherine leaves, I head into my armory to prepare for my date tonight. I go for the practical yet stylish Miguel Caballero bulletproof trench coat with custom-made weapon holders. It's my last one, and I hope it doesn't get ruined. An old saying leaps to mind: hope in one hand, shit in the other, and see which one fills first.

As housewarming gifts, I choose a wide assortment of explosives, my favorite amongst them being my high-tech triple whammy which I created by duct-taping smoke, concussion, and fragmentation grenades together. A few other explosives crafted for various functions round out my collection of party favors. I stash the smaller bombs amongst my many pockets and retaining straps, while the larger ones go into a black combat pack.

"All right, Mr. De Mille, I'm ready for my close-up," I jokingly say to my empty chamber. And people say I don't have a sense of humor. I crack me up sometimes.

I told Marvin to call me and report any increase in activity, but other than several calls being made, there's been no real physical movement yet, so I sit and wait. My gut tells me they'll meet tonight, and as the clock rolls over into the next day, I get the call I'm waiting for.

"Leo, I got several of those numbers all movingtoward the same spot. It looks like they're all heading to the docks on the northwest side of Brooklyn north of Conover Street. Two of the phones are already there and haven't moved for about thirty minutes, so I'm betting that's where they're all going. I can't say for sure, but Google maps show a huge brick warehouse near the water. That's as close as I can get you."

"I know the place. Good work, Marvin. I'm shutting my phone off, so I'll be out of touch until this is all over. Keep looking into Vtech's security logs and let me know what you find out."

I hang up and power down my phone so an errant call does not give me away. I need my surprise to be total. I am going to be outnumbered, but I figure I outclass them by a significant amount. So far, all these scum have been younglings and street thugs. None of the vampires I crossed have been well-trained or been a vampire long enough to come into their full strength. The entire physics of fighting changes when you can make a near twenty-foot vertical leap and have enough muscle to throw someone like a shot put.

It is this difference in skill and sheer meanness I hope will give me the deciding edge in this conflict. Everything could change depending on who else shows up to play. Even a couple of decently trained Sheriffs could cause my entire plan to go bad real fast, but I never let those small concerns keep me from doing what needs to be done.

Taking a cab is out of the question. I don't want any witnesses putting me anywhere near the scene, but I need to get there quick. It's time to dust off my trusty old 1981 Yamaha Maxim. It's unregistered, and I only use it on rare occasions. It is also common enough to give me plausible deniability of any witness sightings.

I take off in the opposite direction of my destination in case someone is already watching me. I weave in and out of the mild, late-night traffic, zip through several alleyways, and use streets with few or no nearby roofs to allow another vampire to follow by an elevated route. Once I am certain no one is tailing me, I make haste toward the suspected rendezvous point.

I park several blocks from the warehouse. There are no nearby structures to cross by rooftop, so I chance the open ground. I'm not too concerned. It's a cloudy, moonless night and I am decked out head to toe in black. The likelihood of posted guards is also slight. One of the vampires' greatest weaknesses is the confidence of their own immortality. This is especially true of the young ones who still remember how weak and frail human bodies are by comparison. They will likely be confident no lone vampire, regardless of his fearsome reputation, will attack an unknown number of enemies.

As I prefer to be, I am right and they are wrong. I spy no guards outside the building at all and I am prepared to deal an ass whooping of epic proportions upon the occupants of the building no matter how many of them there are. I think I've kept to the shadows for too long; people have forgotten what it means to cross Leo Malone. It's time to put the reality back into the legend and the fear that comes with it. The thought gives me shivers and a slight chubby. I need to focus.

I stick three small explosives to the steel door used to enter the building, place a hefty satchel charge in front of it, and attach a trip wire to the handle in case someone opens it before I'm ready. Locating a drainage pipe bolted to the wall, I shinny up the side and gain the roof where I set up a dozen shaped charges in a ring about ten feet across, not far from the door I booby-trapped a minute ago. I peer through the broken pane of a skylight and take stock of the goings-on below.

There are perhaps a dozen figures gathered near the center of the cavernous chamber, gesticulating and shouting in obvious agitation. The mob does not worry me as much as the lone figure most of them are addressing their concerns to.

He, or she, since whoever it is wears a mask and hood to conceal their features and identity, stands impassive at the fore of the crowd.

"I thought we were supposed to be protected!" one of the thugs shouts at the figure.

Another one pipes in, "I say we go kill this motherfucker and be done with it! It's one guy."

"You didn't meet him, Dirk. This guy is not playing around, and I for one don't ever want to meet him again."

Oh, Mikey, you poor dumb son of a bitch. You should have stayed home tonight.

"That's because you're a pussy, Mikey. You were a pussy in life and you're a pussy in death," Dirk shoots back with obvious derision.

"Look," the masked figure interrupts with a whisper, "Malone will be dealt with, but not yet and certainly not by the likes of you."

"Then what are we supposed to do? Just wait for him to hunt us all down one by one?"

"The situation is being dealt with as we speak. There are greater things at work here and more important people at risk right now than you. We are taking care of our loose end right now. We will deal with Leo Malone later. Until then, find a deep hole and hide in it until we call you in."

I don't know what loose end the masked man is talking about, but since I'm here I doubt he means me. Most likely, they're covering up a key piece of evidence like the fact the Cure apparently walked out of Vincent's secure laboratory. Whatever it is, there's nothing I can do about it right now, and it looks like my man in the mask is about to leave.

Pulling out a remote, I trigger the three small explosives attached to the door. They are too small to do any real damage, but that's not the intent. I want it to sound like someone try-ing to kick the door down in order to get everyone's attention focused in that direction, and it works. Knives and guns are pulled out and pointed at the door as they all stalk forward, huddling closer together as they do so.

I pull out all my triple whammies and hurl them through the small skylight so fast all four are in flight before the first one touches the ground. I sprint across the roof and leap into the air as my grenades explode, filling the room with thick white smoke, concussive blasts, and flesh-rending shrapnel.

At the apex of my leap, I trigger the ring of explosives on the rooftop, creating a perfect hole ten feet across like a giant cookie cutter. Gravity pulls me through the opening along with a slab of concrete the size of a large kitchen table, which I ride down like a surfboard right into the middle of sheer chaos and pandemonium.

A gory, red spray like a stomped-on packet of ketchup spurts out from beneath the slab upon reaching the ground, indicating it landed on one of the slower, less fortunate vampires. I hope it's the leader. With my blade in my right hand and Shalonda in my left, I begin dealing out death to everything in sight. The smoke is so thick it makes it difficult to distinguish friend from foe unless you're within a few feet of them. This is just one of many advantages of not having any friends.

I land hard, absorbing much of the impact by flexing my knees and rolling toward the nearest vampire. I lash out with my sword even before I stand up, taking out one of the vampire's legs above the knee. A lightning-fast strike as I spring to my feet takes his head off as he meets me halfway in his fall to the floor.

A pistol barks from about ten feet away, and I feel a bullet tug at the flap of my jacket. I point my hand cannon at the muzzle flash and squeeze off a round. I am already moving, not waiting to see if I scored a hit, but the scream of pain tells me my aim was true. Panicked voices ring out across the warehouse as the rogues try to pick out their friends and create a concerted defense. There is no way I am going to let up enough for that to happen.

More screams echo across the vast chamber, these ones of pain, most of which fall silent as I dance through the thick smoke, slashing and shooting at anything moving. True panic is starting to set in, and the vampires begin firing wildly into the pervasive screen without regard for friend or foe. Curses reply to several of the shots and allow me to home in on my prey.

I can barely make out the three forms running for the booby-trapped door. I throw myself to the ground as twenty pounds of high explosives and ball bearings go off, blasting and shredding all three fleeing vampires into something unrecognizable. I catch movement out of the corner of my eye and bring my sword up just in time to block a machete aimed for my neck. I force the lethal weapon wide and cut back in a swift slice, disemboweling its wielder. My equally fast return stroke succeeds in taking off my attacker's head where his had failed to take mine.

I feel the bullets slam into me the same instant as I hear the shots. Round after round punishes me even through my jacket as the shooter squeezes off his entire clip in mere seconds. A few of the wild shots find vulnerable spots in my Miguel Caballero jacket and manage to punch through into the flesh beneath. One even strikes my exposed lower left leg and staggers me. The shooter is a middle-aged Latino who runs out of bullets less than ten feet away from me. I swing Shalonda in his direction and squeeze off a round, striking him dead in the chest and making a hole big enough to see through. My second shot removes the greater portion of his skull.

The leader of this meeting of morons must have been counting my shots, because the instant I fire off my fifth round he comes flying out of nowhere, sword leading. The attack is swift and well-timed. I'm able to block it, but the force of the strike still sends me sprawling. I roll with the impact and regain my feet in time to fend off a flurry of the vampire's pressing attacks.

I come to the conclusion my attacker's skill is not on a par with my own. It takes me a moment to find my rhythm, and once I get into my attack routine, I put him on the defensive. I alternate my strikes from high to low, creating a pattern even an amateur should recognize. I pick my timing and make a feint. My foe anticipates my next strike based upon my previous routine and leaves himself open. My slashing blow cuts a deep line through his heavy leather coat and the softer tissue beneath. Dark blood wells from the wound, and he takes several retreating steps, clasping a hand over the gruesome but non-lethal injury.

Possibly taking a page from my own playbook, he reaches into a pocket and tosses a small flash grenade at my feet. I leap away as it explodes and start to pursue him as he runs as fast as he can out of the massive hole my satchel bomb made, but two lesser vampires foolishly seek to impede my progress.

I jump and turn a somersault over the head of the leading vampire. I come down between them, landing with a two-handed downward stroke, splitting the trailing vamp from crown to collar. I wrench my sword free, spin, and thrust it into the base of the other vamp's neck before he can even twist around. Another slash and I finish the job.

I want to chase after the masked man, but he has too much of a head start, and police sirens are already keening in the distance. Explosions tend to bring the cops pretty fast. A low moaning catches my attention as I survey the carnage around me.

"You should have stayed home, Mikey," I tell the young vampire as I stand over him.

"Please, please don't kill me. I'll talk. Whatever you want," he pleads.

"Can you tell me who the guy in the mask is?"

"No, but I can find out. I swear I will."

"It doesn't matter. I already know who it is."

"Please, I was following orders! I have nothing against you!"

"That defense was overused in the Nuremberg trials, and it didn't work for them either."

"What?"

"I weep for our education system. I let you off once. That was like a coupon—limit one per customer," I inform him before relieving him of the burden of a continued existence.

I am able to leap high enough to grab a hanging steel rafter and bound through the breach I made in the roof to recover my bag of goodies. I drop back down through the hole and pile up all the bodies before setting off three thermal grenades, also bearing my personal customization. They burn hot but create more fire by adding several ounces of fuel gel to the can. Even if I trusted the cleanup crew, which I don't since they too are part of the Sheriff corps, there isn't enough time for them to get here before the cops, so I do my best to destroy as much of the evidence as I can.

I want to head straight home, but I need to feed. I spent a lot of energy in the fight, and I'm not walking away unwounded. At least three bullets found their way to my softer bits and a couple of slashes have drawn blood, but they already closed up. If I end up fighting Sheriffs, I will need to be at the top of my game, which means a full feeding.

My old Yamaha gets me across town in short order without breaking any major traffic laws. The last thing I need is to be stopped tonight. I also don't want to do the deed anywhere near the battle, so I ride to the east side and find a bum near JFK. I prefer criminals when I take a life, but time is not a luxury I possess, and besides, no one will miss one more of New York's fifty thousand or so homeless people.

The battle is an hour or more in the past by the time I get home. I key my alarm system and am about to open the door when I catch a sound and strange scent from inside. As quietly as only a vampire can achieve, I ascend the stairs to my office and slip through the upstairs door. I jump from the upper landing to one of the steel beams making up the structural support of the roof.

My keen eyesight picks out my intruder from the surrounding darkness as he crosses below me. I should cut him in half, but I want to find out how he got past my security system before I do.

I drop from my perch, land in front of him, lift him an arm's length off the ground, and slam him against a support beam.

"What the hell are you doing in my house, Marvin?" I snarl in unfeigned fury.

Marvin tries to respond but can only clutch at his throat and mimic a landed fish due to inhaling whatever it is he was eating. I watch him for a moment, curious to see what colors a suffocating black kid turns. Seeing it's not as entertaining as watching a white guy choke, and still needing him to work for me, I punch him in the stomach with my free hand and drop him to the floor as the chunk of food becomes a projectile.

Marvin is still failing to take in air since I knocked out whatever wind he had in his lungs, so I lift him by his arms and make him touch his toes. I do this a few times and he begins to breathe again.

"Oh shit, Leo, you almost killed me," he gasps out. "Why'd you have to do that?"

"Why are you in my house? And how did you even find it?" I demand.

It's not as if I advertise my services in the Yellow Pages. You have to know people to find me.

"I found it by hacking the police records. They really don't like you. That Castillo woman has a serious hard-on for you, and not the fun kind. She put all kinds of disparaging remarks in your file. Oh my God, I can't believe you almost killed me."

"The night's still young. Why are you here?"

"Well, I figured you might be calling me, and it could be a late night, so I went out to that twenty-four-hour pizza joint nearby. Oh, you want some pizza? I looked in your fridge and saw you have no food in this place. It's a good thing I brought my pizza with me."

"You looked in my refrigerator?" I ask, concerned Marvin may have outlived his usefulness.

"Yeah. Why do you have blood in your fridge, man?"

"I have a medical condition. So, you got pizza and decided you would come over and share it with me?"

"No, it was because of the dudes in my apartment!"

"Who was in your apartment?"

"I don't know. I was coming up with my pizza and saw my door open, so I peeked in and these dudes were tearing up my stuff. I snapped a pic with my phone and got my black ass out of there."

"You got a picture?"

"Yeah, man," Marvin replies, then hands me his phone. "Check this shit out! I don't know if they're feds or mafia or what, but when I put this on Facebook, my street cred is going to go through the roof, boy!"

I study the picture, but I don't recognize anyone in the room. One is wearing a long, black coat and his back is to me, but I bet money it's a Sheriff with his lackeys.

"If I hadn't gone out for pizza, those guys would have found me and busted me up like my stuff. Do you realize the irony here? The very same pizza that saved my life back at my apartment damn near killed me in yours. I'm not superstitious or nothing, but that's gotta be a bad omen or something."

I erase the picture and hand the phone back to Marvin.

"Aw, man, why'd you delete my pics?"

"This is not a game, Marvin, and posting stuff like that is going to draw more attention. Now, how did you get in here?"

"Oh, it was easy. Your alarm system is made by LaRoche Security Corporation and it still has the old software. I can't believe it wasn't updated after the huge blowup and class action lawsuit two years ago."

"Wait a minute. Are you talking about Percy LaRoche's firm?"

"Yeah. Why, do you know him?"

"He's kind of a friend of mine."

Marvin looks surprised and exclaims, "Damn, how can you roll with rich cats like him and live in a shithole like this? There are Al-Qaeda terrorists living in caves who would consider this place primitive."

"What about this lawsuit?" I ask, ignoring his disparaging remark about my humble abode.

"There was a major flaw in his encryption and core coding. A bunch of Chinese hackers got into several DOD databases and corporate file servers. He lost his ass in court along with most of his contracts. They had to downsize like ninety percent of the company just to keep it limping along—corporate life support."

"Hmm. Now I understand why he is so intent on getting a citywide security camera contract," I muse aloud.

"So if you want me to keep working on this stuff, you need to set me up here."

"Here? Why do you need to stay here?" I ask, not liking the prospect in the least.

"One, I got nowhere else to go. Two, if bad-ass thugs want me dead, I need somewhere secure. And this place is like Fort Knox, if Fort Knox had a shitty alarm system."

I cannot deny his logic no matter how irrational I want to be right now. "Fine, but you fix my alarm, and if you think I made for a hostile work environment before, get on my nerves here and you will experience hostility of a biblical level. What do you need to start working again?"

"I can see this is going to be a real joy. A lamp would be a good start. It's darker than a BMA after-party in here. I also need a laptop, a server tower running dual Xeon processors with a hundred and twenty-eight gigabytes of RAM and five two-terabyte hard drives in a RAID configuration. And Internet, really, really fast Internet."

Marvin is already giving me a headache. "Make a list. I need to go make a call."

"About the blood in your refrigerator," Marvin calls out as I walk away. "You're not like some crazy Jeffery Dahmer guy

who's gonna rape me, kill me, and eat me, are you—or any vari-
ation thereof?"

"Not exactly," I answer.

"What do you mean 'not exactly'? What part is not exactly—
the killing part or raping part? I gotta tell you, I am not cool
with either of those. Leo? Leo!" I hear Marvin drop to his knees
and start praying as I step out to grab my bike. "Please, black
Jesus, watch over this young fool and protect him from crazy-
ass white people, amen."

CHAPTER THIRTEEN

Whenever I need something quick, I call Yuri. "Yuri, it's Leo. I need some stuff."

"What de fock is a Xeon processor?" Yuri asks as I read off Marvin's list to him. "Sounds like something from *Star Trek*."

"I don't know. I also need an Internet connection using multimode fiber optic cable to the ISP, and I don't know what that means either, but apparently it's important."

"I'm kingpin, not focking cable provider! You think I am Comcast or AT&T or something? Is this going to get my accountant back?"

"It's crucial in finding Martin."

Yuri blows out a long breath and makes his lips flap. "OK, I have guy. I send him over right now to do cable. I get you computers in morning."

"Thanks, Yuri."

"Leo, strange things are happening in my town. What you know about these strange things?"

"I'm not sure, Yuri. Just watch out for yourself."

Yuri's silence as he hangs up tells me he thinks I am not being entirely honest with him. I hate to lie to him. Yuri is one of the few people I respect and almost like, but some things I can't share unless absolutely necessary.

I step back inside. Marvin is sitting in my chair surfing the Internet on his oversized smartphone and eating pizza.

"How far have you gotten on cracking Vtech's systems?" I ask him as I grab his arm, propel him out of my chair, and sit down.

Marvin glares at me as he rubs his abused arm and takes a

chair from my small dining table. "Hostile work environment, Leo, remember?"

"Beating you to death with your own arms, remember?" I counter.

The night's combined revelations are putting me in a bad mood, and Marvin provides an easy outlet.

"I got into the on-site system and found the security logs. None of the records show any forced entry to the lab or anyone touching the samples you asked about in over five years, other than standard security checks. I decided to dig deeper into the files themselves and ran cyclical redundancy checks on every log file starting from today and working my way back."

"English, Marvin," I tell him.

"You want me to dumb it down?"

"I would choose a different description if continued health is anywhere near one of your priorities."

Marvin looks like he is going to launch a retort but chooses the more prudent course of action by continuing.

"I examined the file contents for tampering. Files are made up from packets of data. Each packet has what is called a header. These headers have tiny bits of code telling the receiving computer what to expect in each packet, how many packets are being sent, and the sending computer's ID. Each packet header also has a time stamp showing the date of creation and time sent. I found the contents of a few particular packets didn't match what the header said should be in them."

"So you're saying someone faked some log entries?"

"Exactly. It's like someone took an envelope, steamed open the seal, took out the letter inside, and replaced it with one of their own. You think you're getting the original letter with handwritten addresses, cancelation stamp and all, but in reality you're getting a fake, and unless you know what to look for, you'll never know the difference."

"Is there any way to get the original logs to see who changed them or accessed the sample?"

"That's what I was working on before my place got trashed. Vtech has an off-site storage facility for backing up all of their data including the security logs. Unless the person who changed the on-site logs is a real computer whiz, I bet he didn't check the backups and couldn't hack the storage site's systems even if he thought about it."

"I made a call and you should be back online by tomorrow afternoon," I inform him.

Marvin goes back to doing whatever he does on his phone while I go over current events in my mind. I have one confirmed Sheriff in on this and a strong assumption of a second one at Marvin's apartment. I suspect Quinn was the masked man I fought in the warehouse. Although his voice was distorted by the acoustics of the place as well as the mask he wore, his movements were similar to the ones used when he attacked me at headquarters. Maybe I want him to be my guy and just see what I want to see.

I wish I had been able to take a couple of them alive, particularly Quinn if that was him, but I doubt I would have gotten much information. The minions probably don't know much and Quinn wouldn't tell me who is in charge. Vampires have an ingrained sense of loyalty to their creator. It's tied up in the genes somehow, although it's in no way total. A familial bond is created, like a child to a parent, but the bond can be broken through abuse, and diminishes with time.

A hesitant knocking at my door interrupts my thinking. I open it after looking outside to see who's there. A bedraggled man who appears to have been recently roused from his bed looks nervous, and the scent of fear seeps out of his pores. I spy a white van across the street with the logo of a cable company emblazoned on the side.

"Marvin, it's for you," I call out, waking Marvin who is slumbering with his face pressed against my table.

Marvin informs me the job is finished less than two hours later. Now I need to get his computer equipment. I can give Marvin one thing now, however.

"Marvin, I want you to keep this at hand at all times," I tell him as I hand him a ten-gauge, double-barreled shotgun. "It's loaded, so all you have to do is pull the hammers back, aim, and squeeze the trigger."

The gun is an antique but in terrific condition. The weapon's ease of use, the massive bore firing three and a half inch 00 buckshot, and barrels sawed down to the length of my arm, make it a good weapon to have on hand.

"Damn! This is straight-up old-school gangster shit right here!" Marvin crows, then starts waving the gun around before I grab it out of his hands and cuff him in the side of his head.

"It's not a toy, Marvin! I don't even want you to touch this unless you need to shoot someone. You got it?"

"Hostile!" Marvin grumbles as he flops down on my bed and goes back to sleep.

I almost kick him out of my bed, but I won't be sleeping and he needs the rest if I expect him to be of any use to me tomorrow, so I let him be. I mentally add an air mattress to my shopping list. The masked man at the warehouse said his cohorts were taking care of a loose end. I assume the loose end was Marvin. They know Marvin is snooping into Vtech's computers and don't like it, so I must be on the right track. A phone call breaks me out of my contemplations a few hours later.

"Leo, it's Raj. If you have time, I think you may want to take a look at something."

"Another attack?"

"Yes, but this one has some interesting hallmarks that might make more sense to you than to me."

"I'm on my way," I inform Raj, then go to wake up Blackylocks who is still sleeping in my bed. "Marvin, get up. I'm stepping out. Don't open the door for anyone unless a guy shows up with your computer shit. He should tell you Molotov sent him or something to the effect. If anyone gets in, shoot them and run like hell."

Since I prefer to keep my bike out of the spotlight as much as possible, I elect to take a cab. Besides, I can add the fare to my list of expenses. I find Raj in his office, but he waves me to the exam room as soon as I enter.

Raj pulls a sheet off a body already laid out on the metal exam table. The body is less savaged than in most of the other attacks, but the wounds look similar. Raj begins pulling back the torn skin and muscle, pointing out the distinctive aspects of the gruesome injuries.

"At first I thought this was another attack like the others. You can see how the flesh was torn away as if by claws and teeth. But look here. See this clean line in the muscle tissue?"

"It looks cut."

"Exactly. Now, I'm not an expert on werewolves, but I assume a transformed wolf is not packing a knife and slicing up his meal into bite-size pieces. Now look at the bone of the humerus near the elbow and tell me what you think."

I peer into the massive gash Raj is holding open with a pair of retractors and examine the exposed bone. "It looks like another cut."

"And deep enough to almost sever the arm. Come look at the X-ray I took."

The medical examiner flips on the fluorescent light of the view box and illuminates the X-ray already in place. "Here's the cut. The injury is clean and almost shears through the entire bone. This means it was a large blade, wielded by a strong individual. But the most interesting part is the top-down image of the same injury."

Raj shifts my attention to another X-ray. "Here is the same cut taken from a top-down viewpoint. The dark line is the cut. You can see by the angle the victim probably had time to raise his arm in an attempt to ward off the blow. It cuts through the soft tissue, shears into the bone from the lateral side, and stops about three-quarters of the way through to the medial. But look at this nearly perfect triangular protuberance inside the bone."

"The blade had a notch in it," I respond.

"As good as a fingerprint. You find the sword or machete with the notch and you have your killer."

I already know who my killer is. At the very least, my list is narrowed down to two suspects. When Quinn jumped me, I used one of the Sheriff's blades to block his attack, which put an appreciable notch in both blades. This attack occurred a few blocks from the warehouse, which makes sense since I wounded the masked man and he would feed to repair his injury and maintain his strength. I doubt the vampire I fought in the warehouse was the nervous kid I borrowed the sword from, so that leaves Quinn.

As much as I am pleased to confirm Quinn as a bad guy, I don't know what to do with the information. Sure, I can track him down and kill him, but killing Quinn gets me no closer to finding out who the others are behind this entire fiasco. When I end him, I need to do it in a way to maximize the amount of damage I inflict on his organization as a whole. Still, I get a good feeling having at least one certainty about this case which I can follow.

"I hope this helps you."

"You're a big help, thanks, Raj. You should have been a real doctor."

"I like this job. My patients don't play me to get drugs, and I don't worry about getting sued," he replies, ignoring my playful insult.

I am about to call another cab when two Cadillacs pull up, disgorging six large men toting serious firepower. I recognize three of them as Yuri's men, which saves everyone a lot of trouble.

"Malone, Yuri wants to talk with you—now," a man named Yaakov informs me.

"Tell Yuri I'm a little busy right now. He can call me if it's important."

"Yuri says now. He said to say please. If still you do not come, we stop saying please. Please come now."

A powerful tension fills the air. I am surprised I failed to notice their anxiety. These men are very serious—and very afraid. Something must have happened for Yuri to take this heavy-handed approach with me, so I climb into the back of the lead Cadillac, sandwiched between Yaakov and a man I'm not familiar with. I don't bother asking questions, certain they are not likely to answer them.

My unease increases as we head into Queens. Yuri's territory stretches into Queens but not far. His operations are centered in Brooklyn, so I wonder why he isn't there now when I am fairly certain he was last night.

We come to a stop in front of a squat, three-story building that looks more like a bunker with urban camouflage. All the first-floor windows are bricked up and thick bars cover the few on the upper two floors. The only visible door looks like it was salvaged from a battleship.

No one stands guard outside, but once we go in, after having phoned ahead to gain entry, I find several men are posted inside and armed as though preparing for war. These men look weary, scared, and ready for violence. They are packing AK-47s, Uzis, and AA-12 automatic shotguns.

They take me to a reinforced room near the center of the building. The room is far too small for so many people, and the combined smell of sweat and vodka nearly bowls me over. Counting my escort, a dozen men pack into a room barely able to accommodate four. Of all the people in the room, only two really catch my interest.

Yuri sits behind a solid desk with several empty bottles of vodka and shot glasses randomly decorating its surface along with a Russian SP-12 probably loaded with non-standard ammunition. The figure who really takes me by surprise is Freak, balled up in a corner, rocking and silently weeping. This does not bode well at all, but since I'm not stripped of my weapons, I figure I'm not in too much trouble.

"What's going on, Yuri? It seems a little tense around here," I say to break the ice.

Yuri laughs but in a way that actually increases the tension instead of relieving it. It's the laugh of a man who's spitting in the face of his executioner.

"Tense, yes. Is very tense. Focking devils kill half my men, and I am very tense."

"Who killed half your men, Yuri? What devils? When? Tell me what happened."

Yuri throws back another shot of vodka and slams the glass on the table. "Early this morning, maybe two, three hours after you call me for focking *Star Trek* Xeon phaser or whatever de fock you call it. Focking devils come and start killing everybody! They shoot my men with guns, hack them with focking swords, and they tear my men apart with their bare focking hands like animals! We fight back hard. We shoot them, but they ignore bullets or get back up if we hit them enough to knock them down. They were so fast, so strong. We run and fight our way to the cars and drive away."

Yuri pours and slams back another shot of vodka, shatters the glass against the wall, snatches the pistol off his desk, and points it at my head. I refuse to flinch and meet his gaze dead on.

"I saw you. I saw you take bullet in my club. Focking vest my hairy Georgian ass! I know vests. I shoot people with vests, and you were no wearing no focking vest! You took that bullet, and didn't care. Just—like—them. I bet if I shoot you right now, you get back up just—like—them," Yuri says, punctuating his theory I am one of them.

"That's right, Yuri. I took a bullet. I took the bullet meant for you," I remind him.

"You work for me many years, Leo Malone. You tell me honestly. Whose side are you on?"

"I'm on the same side I'm always on—mine."

Yuri stares into my eyes a full ten seconds before slapping the pistol back onto the desk and sitting down. "My *bebia*—grandmother—she is Romani. She tells us children's stories her *deda* and her bebia tell her when she is little girl. She tells us of the night men—*strigoi*—who hunt in darkness, killing and feeding off blood of people. She tells us these strigoi are so fast and so strong they slaughter entire villages. We think they are just stories to frighten children to make them go to bed, but I see my men killed by these things, and I don't know what to think. You, Leo Malone, you tell me what to think."

"I think you should listen to your grandmother," I reply. "How did you end up with him?" I ask, inclining my head toward Freak.

"After we flee, we see him running so hard I think he is about to have heart attack. I think Hanako sends these things to kill me, so my men grab him up."

"And Hanako, what about him?"

"The big one says they are all dead. He and his brother were the last alive and, when his brother fell, he just ran. Been big pile of blubbering crap ever since. These things, more will come?"

I shake my head uncertainly. "I don't know, Yuri. I don't know why they even attacked you and Hanako."

"I send out a few of my men. They say Carletto got hit too in East Bronx. He did not do as good as me, but better than Hanako. This has to do with Martin?"

"Martin is a tool in someone's game. Why they're targeting local mafia is beyond me. Every time I think I am starting to put the puzzle together, someone throws in a bunch more pieces I'm not sure even go to the one I'm trying to figure out."

"How many are there? Do they all want to kill me? How much should I be afraid?" Yuri asks me. "You think maybe they decide to sell drugs, prostitutes, and push Yuri out?"

"I don't know why they attacked. There's something going on inside the—organization—but I don't exactly know what. Even if I think I know the what of it, I'm not sure of the why."

"So not all want me dead?"

"No," I respond, shaking my head.

Yuri looks thoughtful. "Ah, is power play. Yuri knows of power plays. Someone wants promotion, wants more power, more money."

"That's my thinking, but my main suspect has money and power."

"Never enough money and power for some people. Maybe he fears rival. Maybe he wants to make sure he stays in power or make another look bad so he cannot get more power. Whatever, I don't care. What I want to know is how to kill them. You know how to kill them, yes?"

I give Yuri an evil smile. "Oh yes, I have become quite adept at killing them."

"Now there's the Leo I know!" Yuri barks out with a laugh, a genuine laugh, not the gallows laughter from earlier. "Tell me how I kill them. If they come back for me, I will show them what it means to go to war with Molotov!"

"If you shoot them enough, they will go down, but they'll get up eventually. The best way to kill them is to take their head off. Take out their knees, then take off the head. Fire is also effective. They'll burn like any man, and when they die by fire they stay dead."

"Yes! Yuri knows all about fire. I will burn them, burn all who come for Molotov!"

I have to call a cab since once again no one is gracious enough to drive me home after shanghaiing me. I am starting to feel as unappreciated as an ugly girl the morning after prom night. Wham bam thank you, Leo, you can find your own way home.

I walk into my loft and stare in disbelief. It looks like a Radio Shack exploded in my house, or they relocated the war room at NORAD.

"Marvin, what the hell is all this?" I ask the hacker who is barely visible behind a wall of huge monitors.

"This is command and control right here! This is where I exercise my mad hacking skills."

"Why do you need so many monitors?"

Marvin points to the various displays and explains. "This one shows my botnet: second largest in the world. I set it to attack the datacenter using thousands of computers all over the world. Each system is unknowingly running code I wrote, looking for vulnerabilities in various parts of its system, and my bots exploit those weaknesses when they find them. Once inside, it writes a small code giving me backdoor access to the server. When it does that, it sends me a message letting me know I'm in. This monitor goes to my main system here. It's the one I actively work at when I need to get hands-on."

"So why does it look like you're not doing anything?"

"Oh I suppose you want to see me mash away on the keyboard like some retarded monkey like they show in the movies? Man, fuck Hollywood! Every time I see one of those morons pretending to be a hacker, typing away at a thousand words a minute with some 3D graphic floating around on screen, I want to slap someone. Hacking is about running scripts and commands from the command line. I write the automated routines then let my botnet run it. This ain't no Nintendo Wii game where the guy who waves his hands around the fastest wins. Please."

"OK, what about this monitor?" I ask.

"That's for watching YouTube. Look, the monkey is drinking his own pee. He's nasty!"

I can't prevent the sigh of annoyance from escaping. "How

are you coming along with getting into the system?"

"Look, he stuck his finger up his butt and is gonna smell it. Oh that's so nasty it knocked the little nigga out of the tree!"

"Marvin, focus!"

"Oh right. I'm getting close. I should have something pretty soon."

Sitting in my chair, I ponder the implications of vampires making a concerted attack against notable human figures. It violates all of the rules set by the council, rules largely recognized around the world amongst the various ruling enclaves.

No vampires in recent history have belonged to major crime organizations. There's too much risk of exposure in a high-profile career. Modern technology makes it too easy for law enforcement to track them. If this is a grab for underworld power, how do they expect the council to sanction it? The Sheriffs are obviously compromised, but surely not the entire department. If the council loses control of them, they can call in Sheriffs from other regions to clean house. It's happened before, where outside enclaves were forced to purge a rogue enclave for gross violation of the rules, which threatened exposure.

None of this makes sense, and I'm little closer to solving it now than I was before. At this point, all I can do is wait for Marvin to get those security logs and for whoever is behind this to make another move, which I am certain they will. Despite my lack of clarity, I know I am getting closer to the truth.

They probably assume I'm suspicious of the Sheriffs and suspect someone highly placed in the council. That means I'm a dangerous loose end; they'll have to move soon to silence me, and every time I force them to act, they risk revealing themselves.

I don't like the idea of being my own bait but, unless Marvin comes up with some particularly damning evidence, it's the only strategy I have. Fortunately, being a pain in the ass is what I do best, and the more I'm a pain in the ass, the more overt they'll have to get to deal with me. I just hope I live long enough to act on whatever they reveal when they do.

My phone starts buzzing in my pocket and I assume it's Yuri. I'm surprised when Angel's name is displayed on the screen. No way is this good news.

"Malone," I answer.

"Leo, you have to help me here," Angel says in obvious agitation.

"I sincerely doubt I *have* to help unless you want me to help you bury Castillo's body, then I certainly would *want* to help."

"Damn it! Don't screw with me right now!"

"Fine, what can I do for you?"

"When's the last time you saw Yuri Poplonovich?"

"What's going on?" I ask, intentionally evading the question.

The fear and frustration is evident in Angel's voice when he answers. "I got a goddamn warzone here, that's what's going on. I have nearly a dozen charred corpses in a warehouse and what looks like a massacre of three major organized crime families along with two dead feds who were staking out Poplonovich's primary hangout."

"Two dead feds, sounds like a rock band."

"Damn it, this isn't a joke, Leo!"

"Comedy is very subjective," I reply dryly.

"You work with Yuri. What can you tell me about his whereabouts or at least what's going on?"

"I am occasionally hired by Yuri, and that's as far as our relationship goes."

"Leo, I have the mayor, feds, and every head in the department climbing up homicide's ass demanding answers. You are on the front lines down there, and you talk to major players on both sides. Help me out."

"The only advice I have for you is to keep your head down, wait for the smoke to clear, then come clean up the bodies."

"You think there's going to be more?"

"I would almost count on it."

"You gotta give me something, Leo. We aren't gonna stand by and let some Mob feud turn Brooklyn into a goddamn warzone!"

"Tell the feds and your bosses it's terrorists," I tell him.

"Is it terrorists?"

"Everything is terrorists. If a bomb goes off, it's terrorists. If your milk goes sour, it's terrorists. If it burns when you piss, it's terrorists."

"Fine, be a prick and don't tell me."

"I'd still be a prick if I did tell you," I remind him.

Angel responds with a mirthless chortle of assent. "If you hear anything you can share, please call me. If you're in the middle of this, you better get out because the feds are ready to bring Homeland Security in if it really does start looking like terrorists."

Thankfully, Angel gives up trying to get specifics out of me. I just hope he takes my advice and stays out of the way. I can hear Marvin tapping away on his keyboard. Apparently, there is the occasional human interaction necessary to do what he does. I hate sitting around doing nothing, so I decide to pay Katherine a visit. I feel it's safer if I see her at her office than her coming here.

"Marvin, I'm stepping out. Don't let anyone in, and keep the shotgun close by."

Marvin gives me a thumbs up, too preoccupied with whatever is on his screen to give me any further recognition. I take a cab to the district attorney's office in Kings County. There's a small business a block away where I can rent a locker to stash my arsenal. Even so, I pack light. It's daylight and I'm not going far, and it's unlikely anyone will make a move against me in a public setting.

I manage to pass through security without a problem, but getting to Katherine's office proves problematic. Just as I round the corner, I run right into Castillo. She is so surprised to see me in the DA's offices it doesn't register in her brain when I cop a feel as we collide.

She suppresses her surprise and snarls, "What are you doing here? Coming to confess your crimes?"

"Actually, I came to file a complaint. I don't feel safe walking the streets anymore with the sudden increase in violence, and it doesn't seem to me the police are doing anything about it. The murders don't bother me so much, but someone lit a bag of shit on fire on my doorstep, which is just rude. It made it personal."

She leans in and sniffs me. "You smell funny, Malone."

"Funny how, like a clown fart? Sorry, I'm single and I probably don't shower nearly as often as I should."

"Explosives were used in a massacre in a warehouse last night. I think maybe you smell like residue. I bet you wouldn't know anything about that, would you? Wait a minute... I seem to recall you saying something about having a demolitions license once. Now, this is interesting. What do you think?"

"I think you smell like cats. I think I'll call you catwoman. Not Halle Berry Catwoman, but old lady catwoman; just a mess of cats shitting and pissing all over your apartment. You clean it up and think the neighbors don't notice the smell but they do. The whole hallway reeks, but you don't know it because you live with them—your cats. How many cats do you have? Is it like five or six, or are you a crazy hoarder with fifty cats?"

"I will end you, Leo Malone, if it's the last thing I do!"

"If it's the last thing you do, who will feed all your cats?" I ask, then hiss at her as she stomps away.

That was fun. I really did smell a cat, probably only one or two, but I needed to throw her off quick. I also need to burn these clothes as soon as I get home. Better make this a quick visit before she comes back with dogs.

Katherine smiles as I walk in. She gets up and, for a moment, I think she is going to embrace me, but she steps past me and closes the door—then wraps her arms around me and kisses me deeply.

"This is a nice surprise. I need it too, given everything that happened last night. You wouldn't know anything about it, would you?"

I roll my eyes, curl my lip, and give a sort of grunt.

"Oh dear. Tell me you weren't part of it."

"Just the warehouse," I reply with a shrug.

"Please be careful."

"I'm always careful."

She scoffs at my statement. "There were explosives and a fire. You do not sound careful to me."

"You're right, but it is damn exciting and a little fun, if I'm totally honest here."

"What have I gotten myself into?"

"I know what I got myself into the other night, and I wouldn't mind getting myself into it again."

She punches me in the chest hard enough to make me take a step back. "Pig."

She sits back behind her desk, and I take a seat in a chair across from it.

"I assume the disaster in the warehouse is about my father?"

"It certainly pertained to the case, but I think from a grand plan perspective your father is a minor part."

"Do you think the attacks on the mobsters are part of it?"

"Most definitely, but whether it is a big part, small part, or just something to distract me, I don't know. There were vampires in all three attacks, and at least two Sheriffs are involved. There's so much I don't understand. You know they hit my computer guy last night too?"

"Oh no!"

"He got away though. The reason I came here, other than to see you, is to find out if you have any word on how the wolves are taking the sudden increase in vampire violence."

"They're laying low but watching very closely. I don't know how long they'll stay on the sidelines if they think there's a threat to their identity, which means that there's a high probability of the vampires revealing themselves as well. The hunt for one kind could easily uncover the other, after all."

Werewolves going into pack mode would not be a good thing. "I hope they stay out of it. The last thing any of us need is for them to try to deal with it. Of course, I may welcome their help to clean up these new vamps afterward; I'm sure some of them would love to join the hunt."

Katherine looks at me quizzically. "What new vampires?"

"Someone has spent a lot of time and gone to a lot of trouble to make new vampires to serve them. The recently turned are the easiest to control. Plus, having large numbers is usually a benefit as well."

"How many do you think there are?"

"I don't know. I've killed at least a dozen already. I can't imagine there are many more out there, unless this has all been planned for a very long time."

"What makes you say that?"

"What do you know about making vampires?"

"Not much. You bite them, infect them, and they turn into a vampire."

"Contracting vampirism is unlikely even if you are trying. At best, the chances are maybe one out of a hundred, otherwise there would be a lot more of us."

"Are you saying a thousand people died to make just the vampires you've killed in the last few days?" Katherine asks incredulously.

"At least. And consider that group was maybe half the number that attacked Yuri, Hanako, and the Italian."

"How can thousands of people just die and no one know about it?"

I shrug. "It's a big city, and most of them are lowlifes with few people to notice and even fewer who care. Remember, too, most of the ones who become vamps go right on acting as though nothing happened."

"Will you have to kill them all?" she asks.

"If they register with the council and follow the rules, probably not. But from what I've seen, these guys were chosen because they are complete shitbags who revel in breaking rules and being a huge pain in the ass. Some of them may conform, and I have no problem leaving them be if they do. Contrary to popular belief, I don't take joy in killing—usually. There are exceptions, of course."

She rolls her eyes at me. "So what now?"

"I figure they're going to have to call in some skilled help to deal with me. I assume it'll be one or two of the dirty Sheriffs, considering how easily I laid waste to their younglings. I hope I can take at least one of them alive and extract some information to get me close enough to the boss to crack this case. The problem is getting them to talk. An experienced vampire can block most pain, so physical coercion is difficult, but I have my ways."

"So you're just going to wait for them to attack you and hope you can capture one, assuming they don't kill you?" Katherine exclaims.

"Pretty much. I have other leads too, or will as soon as Marvin gets me a name or two from his end."

Katherine comes around the desk, puts her arms around

my neck and kisses me. "Please be careful. I have a hard time replacing men once I decide to keep them."

"I am addictive. I better go just in case Castillo is serious about coming back with dogs."

"I was wondering what that smell was."

"Explosive residue and vampire bits. Cop dogs would look at me like a giant Snausage right now."

She tells me to be careful once more before I make a hasty exit. I really don't have anywhere else to go today, and I would rather not leave Marvin alone any longer than I have to, so I return to my loft. They've already tried to take him out once, and as secure as I think my home is, I would be a fool to think it is impregnable—especially after Marvin already broke in.

I watch Marvin pull his hand back from reaching for the shotgun propped against his desk as I come in. Good. It shows he's taking the danger he's in seriously, which is something I wasn't sure he was capable of until a vampire jammed a hand into his chest and showed him his own beating heart.

"How's it coming?"

"I'm getting real close. I'm in their gateway router, and that's half the battle. Unless something really unexpected happens, I should be in their server in a couple hours tops."

Now could not be soon enough. I am getting tired of this game of waiting for others to make a move. I begin stripping off my clothes and tossing them into the huge furnace.

"Yo, Leo, whatcha doing over there?" Marvin calls out over his monitors.

"I have explosives residue on my clothes. I have to burn them before Castillo sticks her nose in them again."

"What the heck have you been blowing up?"

"Just people who failed to meet my expectations. It's my idea of a motivational speech," I tell him, then deliberately look his way.

"Hostile work environment," Marvin reminds me.

I replace my jacket and clothes—I am going to have to do some major clothes shopping after this case—and decide to occupy my time in my armory. I find I do my best thinking breaking down my guns and designing explosives. I push the hidden button, and the section of the floor lifts and rolls back to expose my armory.

"Whoa!" Marvin exclaims, then darts over to the stairway. "What you got down there? Is that your bat cave?"

I grab Marvin by the shoulder and propel him several steps backward as I descend the steps. "It's a very quick and painful end to our business relationship, and possibly your life, if you ever go near it."

"Hostile work environment!" Marvin calls down the stairs after me, enunciating each word.

As I putter around my armory, I try to make sense of what is going on. The first thing I need to figure out is who gains from all this. Vincent is becoming increasingly unpopular with the council and the voting members of the enclave for a variety of reasons. He could have created this crisis and threat of exposure so he could resolve it. It would show to the enclave he was capable of acting with strength and decisiveness, and perhaps shore up his declining popularity.

It would not be the first time such a ploy has been used. But if he *is* behind it, why hire me? Vincent may hate me, but he knows I'm good at my job and could uncover the entire charade. Ahhh…motive. He calls me in *because* he hates me. He calls me in, gets me involved, then kills me or makes me a scapegoat.

Theory number two is someone else in the council smells Vincent's weakness and decides to hasten his removal. They create this disaster, run it until Vincent is removed, then sweep in, make it go away, and are hailed as a hero. They gain strength in the enclave, maybe enough to be elected to the head of the council.

I really don't care what the reason is at this point or who is behind it. My problem is every scenario I come up with ends up with me dead at its conclusion. I really need to be more choosey about what cases I take. Then again, Vincent didn't really give me a choice. If I die, at least I got laid first.

Marvin calls down to me several hours later, so I put away my toys and see what he wants. I have to assume he has the information I need. Either that or he wants to order another pizza. I can't imagine eating that much pizza can be healthy.

"You got something for me?"

"Of course. Mo' Money always delivers."

"Mo' Money takes his sweet time. What do you have?"

Marvin drops a stack of papers in front of me. "Dr. Sandra Johnston, senior biopharmaceutics researcher, all-level access. Records show her card was used not only to access the biosafety level four area but the secure storage system containing nothing else but that sample. Here is her picture, her address, and her work schedule. Give me another hour and I will have her hobbies, turn-ons, and turn-offs."

I grab the stack of papers and cross the room to close the access to my armory. I'm not sure what tips me off, a sudden shift in the air perhaps. A black form drops from the ceiling and nearly takes my head off. My split-second dodge saves my life, but I still end up with a slash from my right shoulder to my left hip.

I block the pain as best I can without hindering my ability to fight. His weapon is a vicious little thing. It has a punch knife handle but instead of a sharp blade for stabbing, it has a large, half-moon-shaped blade, perfect for popping off heads or cutting pizza. He does not look like a pizza guy.

The assassin forces me into a fighting retreat, fending off lightning-fast strikes and kicks with my bare hands. One mistake and I'll lose some fingers at the very least. My own blade is tucked inside my jacket, but it may as well be on the other side of the room. The assassin's attacks are so relentless I have no chance to draw it.

I don't recognize the face, but it's apparent he's a killer of exceptional quality and probably quite expensive to hire. His fighting skills are at least equal to mine. He also has a momentum he is not willingly going to relinquish.

He slashes again at my throat with his unusual blade. I duck it, then block the knee strike he launches at my face. I spin into a roundhouse kick and, in one fluid motion, pull Shalonda out of my pocket, but he kicks it out of my grasp before I can bring it to bear.

I earn several more slashes across my arms and chest as he forces me back across my loft. I need something to change the dynamics of this fight and quick. No sooner do I think this than it happens, but not in a good way. Something rolls under my heel and I slip, just a little, but enough to give my opponent the opening he needs.

A monstrous kick to my chest lifts me from the ground and slams me into one of the big support pillars. A new source of pain shoots through me. I don't have the chance to look at what it is, but I already know. It's a piece of rebar protruding from the concrete support. I don't know its original purpose; perhaps they hung tools or iron bars from it. I use it to hang my jacket up, and once again my jacket is hanging from it, only this time I'm still in it.

He uses his left arm to hold me against the pillar as well as pin my arms down. As my assassin cocks his strange weapon back and prepares to relieve me of my pretty head, I know I am well and truly screwed.

We both realize at the same moment we have made identical errors. We discounted the other occupant in the room, but for different reasons. I disregarded Marvin as being any help in a fight, and the killer apparently dismissed him as a threat. We are both mistaken.

From my left I hear Marvin shout, "Break yourself, fool!"

Partially blinded by the flash, I make out Marvin being blasted onto his skinny ass by the recoil of the shotgun as he fires both barrels into the intruder from just fifteen feet away.

Buckshot strikes the killer in the shoulder and neck. It doesn't drop him, but it staggers him. I kick him back even farther, launch myself off the pillar and the length of metal piercing my back, and draw my blade mid-flight. I come down with a hard chop to the arm holding the weird knife and sever it at the wrist. My backswing does the same to his head.

I would like to have taken him alive, but he was too dangerous, and he probably didn't know anything anyway. A professional assassin, as I have no doubt he was, rarely meets their contractor face to face. Nearly all correspondence is done electronically, through dead drops, or a third party at the very least. This hasn't been totally uninformative, however. The fact someone went to this kind of expense means they consider me a serious threat to their operation. He waited until I had a new lead, which suggests I am going down a route they do not want me to follow. It could have been coincidence, but I doubt it. I have a feeling he had been up there for quite a while.

"I take back what I said before, Leo. Now *this* is a hostile work environment," Marvin calls out as he picks himself off the floor and retrieves the shotgun from where it flew several feet farther back. "Daaaaamn, you see that shit? I just smoked that dude gangster style! Oh, man, his head is gone. What are you, some kind of Highlander or some shit? Who the hell carries a sword and cuts a nigga's head off with it?"

"The kind who's still alive," I reply as I search the intruder's clothing, even though I know he won't be carrying anything to identify himself or his employer.

"Dude, my street cred is gonna skyrocket when I post this!" Marvin crows, then starts taking pictures of the body with his phone.

I launch myself at Marvin, grab his phone, and shatter it against the wall. "Do you think this is a game, Marvin? This is a highly skilled assassin, and it's just dumb luck we aren't both dead right now!"

"My phone! Oh my God I can't believe you just destroyed my phone! Why would you disrespect me like that after I just saved your life?"

"You helped, but it does *not* change the fact that this is very serious, and advertising it is not going to help our position."

"Helped? Dude, I saved your life. That guy was two seconds away from popping your ugly head off. Do you thank me? No, you just wreck my phone! Phone didn't do nothing to you!"

"I'll get you a new phone."

"And are you going to get me back the hundreds of hours I put in to make my custom operating system and applications?"

"I bet a smart programmer like you has that kind of thing backed up somewhere."

Marvin still sulks. "Yeah, but it still don't make it right. You owe me a bonus and a new phone. I don't know how much a 'saving Leo's mean old ass' bonus is worth, probably not much, but you owe me."

As I carry the body to the furnace, I tell Marvin, "What you need to do is find out how he got in here without tripping my alarm. I thought you fixed it."

"I did. No way he got in like I did. Let me get on the system and check the logs," Marvin replies, then darts back to his workstation.

By the time I toss the assassin and his head into the furnace, Marvin has an answer. "He used an admin code, didn't hack it or bypass anything."

"How would he get a code?"

"Same way as me, hack their server or snatch a data packet with the password in it. Or someone gave it to him who already knew it."

"Disconnect me from their system and change the password. I want a standalone system from here on out. Someone knows you have been snooping into Vtech's computer system. How?"

"Not possible. I am like a ghost in there. No one can match my genius when it comes to being a cyber-ninja. My kung fu is unbeatable."

"First of all, kung fu is Chinese. Ninjas are Japanese and use ninjutsu. Secondly, what about three guys half as smart as you working together?"

"No one likes a know-it-all, Leo." Marvin looks pensive. "But your math is solid. I guess they could do it."

"I need to get to Sandra Johnston before someone can tell her to disappear. Lock up behind me, set the alarm, and drop the crossbars in place."

"Are you sure it's safe?"

"Yeah, she's just a scientist. Shouldn't pose too much of a danger."

"Not for you, for me! This dude just jumped from the roof, started kicking your ass, and now he and his head is a briquette in your giant stove!"

"Look, I overestimated my security and got lax. Whoever sent this guy, they went all in. If they decide to strike again, it won't be for a while, and I bet it'll be a lot more subtle," I assure him. "Keep the gun close, and call me if you even think there's trouble."

"Call you with what? You wrecked my phone!" Marvin rages, completely forgetting his earlier fear.

I give him an exasperated sigh, go back into my armory, and return with a cell phone. I toss him the old Nokia and watch his eyes widen in disbelief.

"Are you serious? Now I know what that room is. It's a time machine to 1992! You cannot seriously expect me to use this phone."

"It works," I reply.

I have newer phones, several in fact. I use them for long-distance remote detonators, but his constant whining about his phone is pissing me off, and I know giving him the ancient Nokia will irritate him to no end.

"Works as what, a hammer? Submarine ballast? I guess I don't even need the shotgun anymore. If anyone breaks in, I'll just hit them with this phone! Oh, hold on. I have a call. It's Fred Flintstone and he says he wants his phone back."

"I need you to look into the email records of Dr. Johnston and Vincent Van Graff, both home and office. I also want you to get a good layout of Vincent's security system at his house and figure out how to bypass it like our friendly assassin did mine."

"Yeah, I can also shop for a new phone while I'm at it, you mean, angry, phone-wrecking bastard," Marvin grumbles under his breath, thinking I can't hear him.

Marvin is still mumbling complaints as I push my motor-cycle out and roar off into the night. Dr. Johnston has an apartment in Manhattan, and I want to be gone as little as possible, so I take my bike. I meant what I told Marvin about the likelihood of another assault anytime soon, but I still want to be cautious. The stakes are getting higher, and my enemy has shown he's had enough of my meddling.

Dr. Johnston lives on the twelfth floor of her fifteen-story apartment building. A quick elevator ride to the roof and an easy drop has me standing on her balcony in minutes. My acute hearing picks up the sound of a running shower from inside. I try the door, and I'm not surprised to find it open. Few people expect an intruder to come in through the balcony door over a hundred feet above the street. People are foolish.

Just as I am about to slide open the glass door of the patio, my phone vibrates. The number tells me it's from Marvin so I answer it.

"Leo, did you get my text?" Marvin asks me.

"No, I didn't."

"A cat probably ate the little bird that flew out of this phone to deliver it," Marvin says without missing a beat.

I'm less mad about his inane phone call than I am about walking right into his bad joke. "Marvin, do you have something important to tell me? I'm a little busy."

"Yeah. I was watching this show on the Discovery Channel about these ancient cave drawings in France. They show these cavemen hunting mammoths and saber-toothed tigers and shit."

"I don't see what this has to do with what's going on right now."

"Just listen! So this one image shows a guy with a spear in one hand getting ready to stab a mammoth. This is the crazy part. In his other hand—was this phone!"

"Marvin..." I warn.

"I don't mean one like it. I mean this very phone! It's so big I can read the serial number off the cave painting!"

"Damn it, Marvin, don't call me unless it's important!" I hiss into the phone, nearly crushing it in my grip.

"You getting me a new phone is important! I need a new phone, Leo!"

I resist the urge to throw my phone over the balcony and settle for hanging up. The water is still running, so I sit in a leather club chair facing the bathroom. A few minutes later, the water stops and I hear her fussing around.

Sandra Johnston steps into the living room wearing a bathrobe and scrubbing furiously at her hair with a towel. I assume she doesn't even realize I'm here until she speaks.

"Buddy, you really picked the wrong apartment to break into," she tells me as she looks up and tosses her towel to the ground.

She's a vampire and probably thinks I'm a burglar or rapist who will make a very convenient snack.

She looks to be in her mid-thirties, with a fit but soft build and a bobbed haircut. It's still damp, so I can't tell how dark it is naturally. Her face is a little rounded, bordering on cute and plain. She looks every bit the academic type.

"Sandra Johnston?" I ask without rising from my seat.

"That's right. Who are you?" she asks a little warily.

She takes a sniff in my direction and her eyes widen in alarm when she realizes I too am a vampire.

"My name is Leo, and I need to ask you a few questions."

She gulps audibly and her face goes from nervous to outright terrified. "Leo Malone?"

"Oh good, you've heard of me. That will save me the time of convincing you of the sincerity of any threats regarding grievous bodily harm I will make if you are anything less than completely forthright."

"Wh-what do you want with me? I haven't done anything wrong. I haven't had a full feeding in almost two months, and I am always very clean."

"I'm not concerned with your feeding habits. I'm not a Sheriff anymore, and you aren't in my ward. Please have a seat and try to relax. Panic is terrible for the memory. I also don't want you to try to make a run for it; I get really unpleasant if I have to chase people."

Sandra takes a seat on a matching love seat, sits up perfectly straight, and places her hands on her lap. "I can't imagine why else you're here."

"Really? The level of your anxiety says otherwise."

"There have been rumors."

I arch my eyebrows. "Rumors? I love a good rumor, especially ones about me. It makes me feel like I'm still relevant."

Sandra nervously licks her lips before answering. "People are saying you've been killing a lot of vampires lately, that you're going rogue again."

"I see. Well, let me put that rumor to rest. I have indeed killed many vampires recently, probably a dozen or so in just the last few nights. Hell, I killed one just before coming over here to see you. But I assure you, they all had it coming."

"What did they do?"

"They irritated me. Some tried to kill me. Others were in front of me at the express checkout with more than fifteen items. Tell me what you know about the Cure."

"Not much. I'm afraid I'm not a fan of their music," she answers with forced levity.

"Dr. Johnston, now is not the time to be cute."

She loses her smile and nods. "I assume you know what it is. It's contained in our lab under strict security, and if you want me to get it for you, you'll have to kill me. I will die before I ever let it out on the streets."

Sandra is looking less appealing as a suspect. "Your access badge is considered a sensitive item, correct? Meaning it requires accountability at all times?"

"Yes, of course. All access badges must be accounted for and reported as missing immediately so the card can be invalidated."

"When did you notice yours was gone?"

The doctor looks very uneasy again. "What do you mean? I have my badge."

"Six weeks ago, you lost accountability of your card. How long was it missing, and how did you end up recovering it?"

"How do you know that?"

"Your card was used to access the secure storage system housing the Cure outside your normal schedule. I no longer think you are the one who took it, so someone else used your card, which means at some point it was missing."

Sandra lets out a long sigh and answers. "It was gone for less than an hour. I noticed it wasn't on my lab coat, so I searched frantically for it. I found it in my locker, where it had fallen behind some of my books and papers. I didn't think it was a big deal, not enough for me to report it missing and get a mark on my record. Is it important?"

"Not to me, but that bit of information may have saved your life. What if I told you the Cure is already out on the streets?"

"No, it's not possible. Only three people have direct access to it, and only five even have access to the level four bio ward. It's inventoried twice a month, and I personally checked it last week."

"Did you actually examine the contents, or has it become so

routine you simply saw the container and assumed what was inside was the Cure?" I'm no stranger to shortcuts in repetitive actions, thanks to my many years spent in the military. "What about the others who have access?"

Dr. Johnston looks at me quizzically. "What about them? They feel as strongly about the Cure as I do. None of them would ever take it out of the lab."

"How often did Vincent come down to the level four biosecurity ward?"

"Not often. He comes through maybe every few weeks, asks about our work, and does a cursory inspection of the lab, but he does it with all of the sections."

"Where's your phone?"

"My phone?"

"Yes, it's a little electronic device that sends your voice to a similar device over long distance."

She points to the small table in the dining room. I follow her gesture and locate the cell. I use it to dial my phone and store the number for future use.

"I think I have what I need. I recommend you check the sample and see if it's gone in its entirety, or simply diluted like I often did to my father's whiskey when I was a kid," I tell her as I head for the front door.

"Mr. Malone," she calls after me, "you have to get those samples back from whoever took them. If it falls into the wrong hands, it could be devastating."

"I can assure you, Ms. Johnston, it already has."

I use the stairs to make my exit from the building. I have no love of elevators. It's not a fear of them, it's just there are very few options once you get inside one; not to mention I can usually beat any elevator in a race, especially going down.

My phone starts buzzing just as I clear the outer doors of the apartment building. "Yeah."

"I'm in trouble, Leo," Marvin says, obviously agitated about something.

Anxiety courses through me and I fear I may have misjudged my enemy's tenacity and he has struck again. "What is it?"

"I put this phone in my back pocket, and when I went to the bathroom—I noticed all the hair had fallen out of my right butt cheek."

"Goddamn it, Marvin!" I scream at the phone.

"This is not healthy, Leo! I need a new phone! I can feel the tumor growing in my head right now. You need to find a twenty-four-hour Best Buy or something and bring me back a real phone."

"Forget the tumor in your head, Marvin. You're going to have a phone growing in your ass if you call me to complain again!"

"So is that a no on Best Buy?"

"No, I'm not going to fucking Best Buy!"

"Then can you stop and bring back a pizza? You still don't have anything to eat in this place."

I force myself to calm down. "I'm on my motorcycle. How do you expect me to bring back a pizza?"

"I've seen a Korean carry his whole family and the bulk of their personal belongings on a moped. I'm sure you can manage a pizza."

I think Marvin is actually trying to get me to kill him. It's like suicide by cop, only a lot more painful; suicide by vampire. All I can do is hang up, get on my bike, and wonder why in the hell I'm stopping for pizza.

Several minutes later, as I'm standing in a pizza parlor waiting for my order, I wonder if Marvin has driven me to some kind of mental breakdown. All I want to do is go home and beat Marvin to death with his phone, but instead I'm standing here waiting for a pizza. For Marvin.

It's the phone. I gave it to him to deliberately piss him off, but now I'm the one being punished for it. He beat me at my own game, and my mind simply cannot deal with the realization, so here I am waiting for a pizza. I'll be damned. This entire case has completely unraveled me. First I end up with a girlfriend, which is a tragic miracle all its own, and now I get beat in a 'who can be the biggest pain in the ass?' contest with Marvin.

Can it be I actually like Marvin? Impossible, I don't like anyone. I like Katherine. I like Katherine a lot. Has my relationship with Katherine opened me up to allow a friendship with another human being? God, I hope this is just an emotional breakdown. Dr. Morison is going to love this.

CHAPTER FOURTEEN

"Marvin," I shout as I pound on the door to be let in. I hear Marvin struggle with the steel crossbar securing the door against anything short of explosives or a multi-ton vehicle. He jumps away with his arms in front of him as I swing the door open.

"I have information, so don't kill me!"

I shove the pizza box into his hands. "I'm not going to kill you. I have your damn pizza. I can't have you passing out from hunger when you're supposed to be working."

"Ooh, pizza." Marvin smiles but then flashes me a disappointed look when he peers in the box. "It has mushrooms. I don't like mushrooms."

"You son of a…" I snarl, then grab for the pistol inside my jacket pocket.

"It's cool, I'll pick them off!" Marvin yelps, then seeks refuge behind his computer monitors.

His fear makes me feel a little better. It helps reestablish a semblance of balance to my universe. "What did you find out?"

"Johnston had nothing in her emails, but I did find a deleted message from Van Graff to Bryan Dawson telling him to get 'the sample' from the biosafety level four lab and to make sure no one saw him."

"Who is this Dawson guy?"

"Some security drone. He was hired a year ago, but the time sheets show he hasn't checked in to work for a couple of weeks. His termination is going through channels right now."

"I have a feeling Mr. Dawson has already been terminated—permanently."

"Hey, if they used a sword like you do, at least he got a severance package! Get it?"

Marvin enjoys a laugh over his own twisted joke. I have to admit, it was pretty good.

"What about Vincent's security system? Have you hacked that yet?"

"Too easy. His alarm had the same vulnerability as yours and a million other people who got LaRoche Security Corporation in so much hot water. I can't believe how many people don't understand the importance of installing software patches. I was able to grab the encryption key between his system and the corporate server. All your base are belong to us," he finishes in some weird voice.

"I don't get it."

"Resistance is futile?"

I respond with a blank stare.

"It's a nerd thing, never mind."

"Enjoy your pizza, and make sure you have that system locked down. I want to pay Vincent a visit soon."

I return to my armory to think and prepare for what I hope is my final assault in this case. As I work on the tools I'll need to accomplish my mission, I go back over everything I know about the case, my suspicions, and the evidence I have gathered putting Vincent right in the middle of everything.

A new realization hits me like a truck. The hit made on Yuri and Hanako that night in the club. I had dismissed it as a power play or a revenge killing by a rival family, but I now realize it too is part of this, except I stopped it. I cannot believe I didn't link the two hits. Vincent called me into the case the day after the failed assassination. That pulled me away from Yuri. A few days later he, Hanako, and the Italian are hit hard. But that's not what's bugging me. Something else is itching in my brain, and it takes me several minutes to figure out what it is.

"Marvin," I call out as I emerge from my armory, "I need you to do something else."

I explain what I want to Marvin.

"You sure like to challenge me, don't you?"

"Can you do it?"

"I don't know. The system is almost the same, but this one's been patched, and you know it's going to be top of the line, but I can try."

"What about using the encryption key you got from Vincent's system?"

"No, each key is unique." Marvin pauses to think. "But the algorithm used to encrypt the key was never the problem, it was how the keys were stored and exchanged that got LaRoche in so much trouble. They may still be using the same algorithm. That's a big part of the battle right there. I have a few ideas I can try. If I hadn't gotten into the vulnerable system at Vtech, this would be impossible. But since I have an inside look at nearly the same system, I'm pretty sure I can do it."

"Excellent. I need you to get me inside. I hate to leave you alone again, but I need to go out."

Whoever hit Yuri and the other mobsters made a serious attempt, and not one meant to fail. Whatever the criminal underground connection was, it was important to whoever was orchestrating this giant goat screw, and I'll bet my last Miguel Caballero they're gonna try again.

I'm not sure what I can do to help Yuri except warn him and maybe give him some tactical advice. The outside of his building looked reasonably secure. Maybe I can give him some pointers on mounting claymores in the walls or something.

I don't know what has my spider sense tingling, but I race my motorcycle across town, ignoring traffic lights when I think I can get away with it. When I reach Yuri's urban bunker, it looks the same except for the noticeable lack of outside guards. I look for cameras when the steel door clicks open at my approach but fail to see where they are hidden.

Men outfitted for war surround me the instant I step inside. I now see why there are no guards outside; they're all in here. Four hulking eastern Europeans escort me down the hall past dozens of equally armed men. The changes to the inside of the building in such a short amount of time are nothing short of amazing, and I doubt I'm seeing half of what has been done. Most of the doors are new and solid. The walls all look refinished, and I bet with more than just fresh plaster.

The goons deposit me in Yuri's office. Three of them step just outside the door while the fourth stands within the open doorframe, ready to gun me down with his AK-47 if I decide to be hostile.

Yuri Poplonovich, aka Molotov, Georgian Mob boss, sits at his desk and pours another shot of vodka. "You have found my accountant?"

"No."

"Then you should be out there looking for him, not in here."

"I realized the hit made on you, Hanako, and the Italian was part of whatever Martin got wrapped up in, and it started at the club."

"I wondered about that," Yuri says, then downs another shot. "I was also wondering when the strigoi will come to finish off me and my men. Entire day has been chaos. Everyone is scared, but these are tough men, and we will not go down without a fight."

I nod at Yuri. "That's why I wanted to come by. I thought maybe I could help. From what I can tell, most of the ones doing the active assaults are weak. They are new recruits and lack the experience of what I am hoping is just a few strong leaders."

"Weak?" Yuri exclaims. "These strigoi ignore my bullets and kill my men. I hate to see strong ones."

"They'll fall to bullets. Take out the legs, shoot them in the head, then decapitate and burn them. If you put them down like that, they'll stay down."

The Mob boss throws back another shot and looks at the empty bottle in disgust. "I listen to you, Leo. I have plan for strigoi. If they come, we are ready. My people spend all day making ready. Let them come. I will show them real face of war."

As if on cue, gunfire and shouts break the tense silence permeating the building. Yaakov, Yuri's lieutenant, bursts into his office.

"Yuri, the devils are here! Everyone's fighting a retreat to the safe room."

Yuri replies with a nod, grabs his pistol from the table, and follows Yaakov through the narrow hallways. Not knowing what else to do, I follow behind even though I'm not being paid as a bodyguard. I tell myself I'm protecting my investment. A dead Yuri means I don't get paid.

Smoke, shouts, and the rattle of automatic gunfire fill the air. The entire building shakes from small explosions caused by what sounds like grenades. The body of one of Yuri's men flies through a doorway followed by a young vampire in a leather motorcycle jacket.

I throw myself against the wall as Yuri raises his pistol and fires six shots into the vampire at the same time as Yaakov opens up with his automatic shotgun. The devastating combined attacks blast the vampire off his feet, but none of us has time to ensure he will not rise again. I drill him in the head with a single shot from Shalonda just so I can feel like I contributed. Even if he isn't dead, he isn't going anywhere soon.

The hall is getting crowded as Yuri's men file in front and behind, providing an escort for their leader as they all fight their way to what I assume is a defensible position. Dark shapes flit in and out of view down the smoke-laden passageways, darting between rooms and side corridors to avoid the hail of bullets trying to put them down. Occasional return shots reply, blasting holes in the walls or striking a human who is grabbed by one of his retreating comrades and carried or dragged along.

I feel almost useless as I am swept away in the increasing tide of humans fleeing from what I can only describe as a horde, or maybe an infestation, of vampires. They are all young, and I don't recognize any of the few faces I catch a glimpse of as we all shove down the passageway. I hate the feeling of not being behind the wheel in a battle, but in these narrow confines against so many foes, even these younglings would overwhelm me with sheer numbers.

The hallway opens into a larger room with an open door on the far end leading to what must be a panic room. Boxes of food, ammunition, water, and anything else needed to withstand a siege are already inside. I become the meat in a mafia sandwich as Yuri and his men pack themselves into the room. I have to fight against my claustrophobia and revulsion at the stink of humans. The latter is easy when I remind myself I don't have to breathe. Removed from battle for the moment, I no longer need the olfactory information.

When the last man jumps through the doorway, a heavy steel door drops into place, sealing us all inside a fraction of a second before the leading vampire slams into it with his body and begins beating on it with his fists and kicking it with his feet.

Yuri stands on the other side of the door, glaring through a tiny window made of tempered safety glass several inches thick and watches as over two dozen vampires pile into the room, searching for a way to get to the humans beyond the door. I watch them in one of the monitors in the room. Almost all of them sport numerous holes and tears in their clothing, but if any of the bullets put them down, it wasn't enough to keep them from rising again.

"Nice panic room, stupid human," the vampire who had slammed into the door hisses at the speaker built into the wall next to the door. "You have trapped yourself. Do you think we can't get explosives to blast you out of your hole?"

"Did you think I would let vermin like you trap me and my men?" Yuri replies.

Another steel door slides down from the ceiling, blocking the entrance into the outer chamber. Several of the vampires begin tearing at the walls with their fingers and pounding with their fists. Chunks of plaster and Sheetrock rain down under the assault only to reveal sheets of steel bolted to the concrete walls.

"Do you know who you are focking with?" Yuri shouts into the speaker. "I am Yuri Poplonovich! I am Molotov! Now burn, you motha fockers, burn!"

With the push of a button, gas-fueled jets built into the walls by what must have been an army of contractors working through the night and the rest of the day, erupt into flames, sending a fiery hell of flame into the room. In moments, the creatures trapped within turn into flailing, screaming masses of flaming dervishes futilely trying to claw their way through half an inch of steel and a foot of concrete. If I wasn't enjoying this so much, I might have felt sorry for them. Even as I smile, I can't help but wince as the fire consumes them.

It takes only a minute for the thrashing to cease as the temperature inside tops a thousand degrees. Plaster burns away to reveal the faintly glowing metal beneath. Yuri does not turn off the flames until nothing but ash and charred bones remain in the room that has become a huge crematorium.

Turning his eyes to the security monitors, Yuri pushes past me and barks some orders. His men must have been waiting only a few blocks away, because several vans screech to a halt all around the building. Men with automatic shotguns and rifles pour out of the vehicles and pump round after round into the legs of the few vampires positioned outside. A single man from each vehicle, armed with a flamethrower, steps forth as their targets drop to the ground, and incinerates the vampires right on the street.

"The strigoi caught me by surprise once before. They will never do so again."

I simply nod, knowing Yuri was not just talking about these rogues or whatever they are. It was a warning for me to take back to the council. Yuri knows about them now, and he is not going to let them intimidate him. I consider the implications as I'm shown the door. True, Yuri and his guys handled themselves amazingly well, but against a bunch of young morons. If the council felt forced to move, Yuri had better have some nukes tucked away, or even his bunker of death would not save him.

"Damn, Leo, you go to a rough party while I'm in here working?" Marvin asks.

"Something like that. You get what I need?"

"Not yet."

"Then you're not working that damn hard."

I hear him mutter "asshole" as I lie on my bed and stare at the ceiling. I really don't want Yuri and the council to go to war. Yuri is my best employer and doesn't complain when I shoot someone or blow them up. It's hard finding a good boss who appreciates your talents. I'll have to convince the council it's in their best interest to leave Yuri alone.

What's even more disturbing is the numbers sent against

him. I got a rough count of close to thirty vampires, and not one I recognized. Add those numbers to the ones I already put down and I'm looking at close to half the New York enclave, and ours is one of the largest, most well-established groups in the western hemisphere. How someone got so many new vampires to work for them is beyond me. It's possible most were brought in from outside, but such an active recruiting of so many would be extremely difficult to keep quiet. Great, more puzzle pieces. Screw trying to put this thing together. It's time to start cutting the pieces to make them fit.

It is nearly 3 a.m. when Marvin shouts, "Leo, I'm in!"

I emerge from my armory to see what he has for me. "You have control of their alarms and cameras?"

"I got it."

"I want to see everything regarding his finances. Log into his bank accounts and check his emails. I'm looking for one or two large withdrawals and several small ones occurring around the same date."

Marvin begins typing and clicking away on the computer, and it doesn't take him long to find what I am looking for.

"Damn, this dude had a lot of money, but he's bleeding Benjamins like crazy!" Marvin exclaims as we both scroll through the bank records. "Other than this guy being very broke really soon, is it telling you anything?"

"Yeah," I reply. "See these small withdrawals all at the end of the month? He's paying the bills for his minions. This large cash withdrawal was probably paid to get the sample out of Vtech."

"Sample of what?"

"A virus," I answer with a partial truth.

"So this guy is some kind of bioterrorist or something?"

"I don't think so. I think it's just something to use as leverage in what appears to be an extremely large and complicated corporate conspiracy."

I lay out my plan for Marvin and return to my armory to pack up the equipment I've been preparing. Katherine shows up right on time and is looking spectacular, despite the late-night call and short notice.

Marvin takes her hand and gives it a kiss as I introduce them. *"Enchanté de vous rencontrer ma jolie dame."*

"Oh, merci monsieur," Katherine replies with a small curtsy.

"I thought the only women in Leo's life would be chained down in the dungeon he disappears into," Marvin says, indicating the entrance to my armory. "To what do I owe the pleasure of such beautiful company?"

"What happened to your Ebonics, Marvin?" I ask snidely then answer, "She's here for protection while I'm gone."

Marvin shoots me a leering grin. "You leave her with me and the only protection she'll need is birth control."

"She's here to protect you, not the other way around," I reply darkly, not caring for Marvin's attempt at humor.

Marvin responds with a laugh, "This pretty little thing?"

Katherine moves with impressive speed, grabs Marvin by the front of his jacket with both hands, lifts him from the floor, and pins him to the wall.

"That's right, so you best keep your hands to yourself," Katherine says with a grin.

"Damn, Xena, I'm just playing!"

I give Katherine a smile as she sets Marvin back down. That's my girl. Marvin regains his composure and brushes the wrinkles out of the front of his coat.

"Now I see the attraction," he says, pointing back and forth between Katherine and myself. "You're both mean and violent people. Does it mean there's something wrong with me if I'm a little aroused at being dominated like that? I'm not gonna lie; there was something exciting in that—in a sexual way. Did you feel it?"

"Not in the least," Katherine answers.

"Are you sure? Because I know a white guy like Leo probably has a hard time satisfying a strong woman like you."

Katherine gets a mischievous smile on her face. "I assure you, Leo is quite—adequate."

"Hey, be nice," I tell her.

She wraps her arms around me. "I'm sorry, honey. I thought I was."

Marvin nearly drops to the ground laughing. "Oh, man, she burned you good, Leo! Oh my God, I like her."

"I am so glad you all can enjoy this levity while I go off and risk my life."

"I'm sorry," Katherine says, then kisses me on the cheek.

I look at Marvin who looks at me in confusion. "What? I'm not sorry, that shit was hilarious."

I show Katherine how to open and close the access to my armory. "If anyone comes, get yourselves inside. You can lock it shut from within, so even if someone finds out how to get into it, they won't be able to. A small access hole leads to an old storm drain. You can follow it to a street access cover."

"What's with all the computer equipment?" Katherine asks. "It wasn't here last time I visited. It looks like NASA mission control."

"I had to set Marvin up here after some—people—raided his apartment," I explain to her.

She looks at me skeptically. "I suppose all this is going to be on my bill?"

Marvin calls out, "And a phone!"

"And a phone," I confirm. "It will all be itemized."

"And the phone is because...?"

"Because your boyfriend is an angry, phone-hating bastard!" Marvin answers before I can respond.

"You must be close to finding my dad if you called me over to watch Marvin," she says.

"Yeah, I think this is it."

"You'll have to fight, won't you?"

I nod. "Yeah. I can't go attacking Sheriffs willy-nilly, so I need to lure them out and deal with them wholesale. I also can't have them at my back when I approach the one responsible for all this either."

"It sounds so dangerous. Are you strong enough to beat them all?" Katherine asks.

Her concern touches me and, for the first time in decades, I have a reason not to get myself killed. "Honestly, no."

"Then how can you win and bring my dad back?"

I smile evilly, "By being a sneaky son of a bitch."

I return to my armory and come back out with a laden rucksack.

"Do I even want to know what's in the bag?" Katherine asks.

I look at her innocently. "Just some library books I need to drop off."

We kiss passionately before I jump on my bike and speed northward upstate to what will be by far the toughest fight of my life. I meant what I told Ronald about not being afraid of death, but I'm now seeing my view was based largely on having very little to live for. I'm not so arrogant as to think my strength and fighting skills are so great I can ride in Rambo-style and proceed to kick ass. If I am to succeed, I need to pick my battleground and prepare it in my favor.

I'm counting on the crooked Sheriffs being new to the game. If they were the Sheriffs I worked with back when I was amongst their ranks, I would be in serious trouble. Fortunately, whoever decided to hatch this plot replaced good men and women with loyal ones, sacrificing quality for manipulability. Of the Sheriffs I've seen on duty, only Wyatt has any tenure.

Nearly an hour later, I hide my bike in the bushes near the wall surrounding the massive estate. The wall itself poses little in the way of an obstacle, but I need to deal with the cameras and other security systems. That's where Marvin comes in.

I talk to Marvin through my headset. "I'm at the spot."

"Let me know when you're ready to go."

We mapped out every camera and motion sensors on the property and assigned labels to them. When I call out the number, Marvin turns the camera or sensor off then back on in hopes anyone monitoring them will attribute it to simple anomalies and not sound the alarm.

I take a running leap and clear the ten-foot brick and wrought-iron wall. "One."

Marvin does not answer, as expected, and I can only hope he hears me and does his part. "On."

"Two." I speak into the headset as I sprint across the acres of manicured lawn, trees, and shrubbery.

"On. Three, on," I continue as I swiftly approach the enormous mansion.

I crouch and hide in the shadows of a hedge next to the

palatial home, listening for anything that would indicate some-one is aware of my presence.

"Damn, Leo," Marvin says into my earpiece, "maybe you are blacker than me. I have never seen a white boy move so fast! Jesse Owens has nothing on you!"

"Focus, Marvin. I'm making my way to the outer library doors. When I get there, I need you to turn off the outside cam-era and disable the inside motion sensors."

"I know what to do. You told me five times before you left. Part of being a genius is having a rather remarkable memory, after all."

"And part of not getting killed is making doubly sure every-thing goes exactly as planned and knowing my security guy isn't distracted by a pretty woman being in close proximity."

"She is distracting, I'll give you that, but I'm all over this," Marvin assures me. "But when you're done, you can bet I'll be all over her, yes sir."

Through my headset, I hear a slap followed by Marvin's curse. "Damn it, your woman hit me. You two are perfect for each other."

"She's just making sure you understand the boundaries."

"Yeah, well, you better hope she didn't knock any of the genius out of me."

I ignore Marvin's whining and edge along the wall toward the French doors that open into the library. I pause beyond the view of the camera and give Marvin the signal to shut it off. The door is not designed with security in mind, and I easily pop it open and step into the chamber.

The smell of hundreds of thousands of sheets of paper bound in various volumes filling shelves and lining walls welcomes me the instant I step through the door and secure it behind me. I tell Marvin to turn the outside camera back on and begin set-ting up my battlefield.

I position several heavy oak tables near the inner door, which should serve to funnel my opponents between the tall rows of bookshelves in the center of the room. I will be outnum-bered, and my greatest vulnerability is my foes outflanking and hitting me from multiple directions, so I need to do what I can to get them to attack me from one direction.

Their superiority of numbers, although advantageous for them, could also be their biggest weakness next to being a bunch of noobs.They will be overconfident and feel secure enough they'll probably forego any real tactics and seek to overwhelm me. At least I hope they do. If I misread them, I'm in a lot of trouble.

I order Marvin to cut the outside camera once more and turn it and the library motion sensors back on once I am about a hundred yards away from the library doors. I make my way back to the library in a hunched jog and reenter, taking almost a minute to "pick the lock."

If everything is going to plan, the traitorous Sheriffs should already have been waiting for me at the mansion and will take only moments to converge on the library.

Right on cue, nine trench-coated forms almost casually stroll into the library with swords and guns drawn to intercept me. I jump back as if startled, near the far end of the massive bookcases standing to my left and right. Quinn is of course leading the way, but I am disappointed to see Wyatt to his right as they all take several steps toward me.

"Who says the cops are never around when you need them?" I say to them. "You all having a slumber party? I'm almost hurt you didn't invite me. You know how much I love a good pillow fight."

"You fucked up, Malone," Quinn tells me. "We know your computer guy was snooping around in the system, and you tripped the alarm outside. Thanks for tipping us off. I knew the 'legend' of Leo Malone was bullshit."

"Is that what you think?" I ask, then turn my attention to Wyatt. "I am most disappointed in you, Wyatt. I thought better of you than this."

I can tell my words hurt him. He casts his eyes to the ground for an instant, which gives me hope I might be able to improve my odds diplomatically.

"I follow orders, Leo. You wouldn't understand anything about that. I took an oath to obey and so I obey. That's what soldiers do."

"Only weak soldiers blindly obey, Wyatt. That's always been your problem; you put the words of your oaths above the intent. The question is, how blind were you? Do you know about Martin Goldstein, or all the new vampires running amok? How about the fact your leader has let the Cure get out on the street? Did you kill Linda and the others yourself so you could replace them with these losers?"

The widening of his eyes tells me my last comment took him by surprise, but he buries his shame and shakes his head. I almost feel sorry for him, being caught between what he perceives as his duty and the corrupt intentions of someone he thinks he is supposed to obey without question. It doesn't mean I won't kill him if I have to, but if I can take him out of the fight, my odds improve significantly. Of the nine, only Wyatt comes close to being my equal. Weak-willed or not, he is a trained and formidable warrior.

Wyatt looks at me, his face full of remorse. "It doesn't matter now. I closed my eyes and asked to be left out of the details as much as possible, but I've chosen a side, whether I wanted to or not, and now I'm stuck with it. I'm sorry, Leo."

"You can still choose, Wyatt. I'm not asking you to turn or even help me in this fight. I can respect Switzerland. I'll tell you what, those who want to live, go stand over there" I point toward the far corner of the library. "Those who agree with Quinn and want to die in the next couple of minutes, just stay where you are."

After a moment of indecision, Wyatt turns, slips between two tables, and stands in the corner I indicated. Two others, the nervous kid and a young Asian woman, look to each other before following their leader.

"Are you fucking kidding me?" Quinn bursts out. "You're done, old man. It looks like I'll be taking your job sooner than planned. You two I'll kill later."

"I guess you all aren't as close-knit as you thought," I tell Quinn. "The odds are looking a whole lot better for me and a whole lot worse for you."

Quinn scoffs. "It's still six to one, which is twice as many as I need to deal with you."

"Really? Because when we fought in the warehouse you ran like a scared little bitch."

"I wasn't ready to deal with you then, and I was surrounded by weaklings!"

"You think you're ready now?"

"You're damn right I'm ready," Quinn answers confidently.

I shake my head. "No you're not, Quinn. You never were, and you never will be."

Wyatt can see me in the space between the two bookcases to my left and barely has time to comprehend the chaos I am about to unleash. Noticing the rubber plugs set deep in my ears and glimpsing the tiny remote in my hand, he grabs his two young charges and pulls them to the ground the same instant I press the button.

The bookshelves to either side of my foes explode in a mass of concussive force and flesh-rending steel balls. Leafs of paper and smoke fill the air as the half-dozen claymores I disguised as books destroy everything before them.

I drop the small remote, pull my sword with one hand, Shalonda with the other, and wade in before the remote even hits the ground. My first target is Quinn. As the second in charge of the Sheriffs, I have to assume he's the strongest amongst them. The blast staggers him, but he doesn't go down. One slug from my hand cannon changes that.

Even that massive amount of damage is no guarantee of permanently putting down one of our kind, but that's what my blade is for. I sweep it in a lethal arc as Quinn stumbles backward and down into those behind him, taking his head from his shoulders and ensuring he never rises to cause trouble again.

I catch movement out of the corner of my eye and duck a sword swing aimed for my head. Continuing the motion, I spin, sweeping my blade at the same time, and open the guts of the young black woman with the nearly shaved head. She leaps away before I can administer a finishing blow, holding her innards in with her left hand.

I come out of my spin and point Shalonda at the face of a man recovering from the blast and squeeze the trigger. A large section of his skull vanishes, exposing the grey matter beneath.

I don't follow up this attack either. The key thing in a battle like this is to never stop moving.

Pure instinct tells me to duck and spin once more as a blade goes whistling over my head.I come out of my one-eighty with a thrust, catching my attacker below the chin. The flat tip of my sword pierces the soft throat, slips between the two uppermost vertebrae, and erupts from the back of his neck.

I make a diving roll to my left as two vampires pick themselves up after I blasted them off their feet. A man and a woman, both firing automatic pistols, empty their clips at my dodging form. Bullets tug at my heavy trench coat, and I feel at least three rounds strike home in my shoulder, thigh, and calf.

I find momentary refuge behind a bookshelf half-tipped onto the one next to it as I come up. I lob a flash grenade toward the source of gunfire and come out the instant it goes off. The woman is already taking aim at me, so I unload two shots into her chest as I sprint at her and her comrade.

The massive slugs, each striking with almost three thousand pounds per square inch of force, rock her back, and she falls to the ground. I am standing over her before she can recover and mete out a swift end to her undead life.

The man who took the brunt of my grenade's blast is rising too slowly to stop me from giving the same to him, but he tries. From a semi-prone position, he fires off one more burst, grazing my right side before I drop him for good as well.

Another young vampire is getting to his feet, having been in the worst place when I triggered the claymores. He has a loose grip on his sword as he looks at me, and then at the carnage around him. He decides he wants no more to do with this. He drops his sword and raises his hands.

"I'm done, please don't kill me," he pleads, spitting flecks of blood.

"Sorry, kid, you joined a high-stakes game. You're either all in or all out. There's no folding," I inform him, then put the last bullet in Shalonda's chamber right between his eyes.

The young black woman has managed to close her gruesome wound and stop the worst of her bleeding. She takes one last look at me and sprints through the outside door in a spray of glass and wood. I follow her with my eyes for a second as she recedes into the darkness. I assume she's not going to come back. Only after all movement ceases do I go about ensuring none of my enemies can get back up again.

Wyatt and his remaining two soldiers are getting up and shaking off the dust, loose pages of books, and bits of wood blasted throughout the now ruined library.

The Asian girl looks around the room and then at me in disbelief. "My God, the stories about you were true."

"Oh yeah, baby, I'm larger than life," I reply with all the confidence and arrogance I can put in my voice. Image is everything, after all.

"You know you're still going to have to fight him," Wyatt tells me.

"Yeah. You know you're done no matter how this turns out, right?"

Wyatt nods. "I had a feeling my days were numbered no matter what happened this night. The problem with being on the fence is the first time you slip, you land on your nuts. Do you think you can beat him? You've lost the element of surprise, and he's waiting for you."

"I'll be honest. In a straight-up, toe to toe fight, the smart money bets against me. What about you? What are you going to do now? I don't suppose you all are ready to throw in with me?"

"I'm sorry, Leo, I still can't. I'll take these two back to the Tower and plead for mercy. They're young and following the orders of their maker. I know my life is forfeit, but maybe I can get some clemency for them on the off-chance you actually succeed."

I nod and Wyatt leads his charges through the shattered remnants of the outside doorway. I pick my way across the debris-strewn room and step over the bodies as I exit the library and enter the marbled hall of the mansion. The moment I do, a voice comes over a speaker hidden somewhere in the wall or ceiling.

"Ah, I wondered whom I would see emerging from the battlefield. As disappointed as I am, I cannot say I am terribly surprised. You always have been a massive pain the ass, Leonard," the disembodied voice says to me.

I look around and see the camera at the end of the hall. "If you thought I was a pain in the ass before, wait until you see what I do with this sword when I find you. Now, do I have to start blowing holes in the walls while we play hide and seek, or do you want to tell me where you are so we can get this over with?"

"I think you have done quite enough damage to my home for one night. I am in the study. Take the next hallway to your left. It is through the double doors at the end."

I reload my pistol as I make my way cautiously down the hall. I don't expect any subterfuge, but I haven't lived this long by being careless. The doors at the end of the hall are open, probably as a sign certain courtesies will be extended.

I can smell the blood, but I am still a bit surprised when I walk into the study and see a dead woman on the floor and another huddled in the corner. I imagine he dined on the first to ensure he is at the top of his game, and the second is there to help take care of any injuries he will undoubtedly suffer in our inevitable battle.

"I shouldn't be surprised you're here, but still, you are supposed to be at Vincent's house, not mine," Percy says, then takes a sip of what I think is Scotch.

"You certainly went to great lengths to make me think that."

"Not great enough apparently. Where did I misstep?"

"I won't lie to you, Percy. You didn't make it easy. I was ready to pounce on Vincent, but one thing kept nagging me. Too many times security came into play. Vtech security, my own security system, someone tracking Marvin's computer activities. A big tipoff was the email Vincent allegedly sent to the security guard to get the Cure out of the lab. It was too sloppy. He would never make such a tactical mistake. Then you practically gave Marvin the keys to Vtech's security system, and I *know* you aren't that sloppy either."

Percy takes another sip of his whiskey. "Hmm, yes, your pet negro did prove to be significantly more capable than I had expected. Another obvious error on my part, letting old prejudices cloud my judgment. It's hard adapting to new ways when your roots go so very deep. Forgive my manners. Care for some Scotch? It's quite well-aged. My father started the brew, and I continued to age it in the cask made from an oak tree cut from our plantation. I know, technically it's not Scotch since it spent most of its life in Georgia, but it's all the same stuff. It's a shame I can't properly enjoy it, given our nature. I truly would like to get good and drunk after this."

"So is this what this has all been about, restoring what you think are the 'good old days'?" I ask.

"My feelings are hurt that you think my motives are so shallow." He pauses a moment for thought. "Then again, I suppose there is a grain of truth to it, although it is really a lesser goal."

"So you want Vincent's position so you can railroad your citywide security camera initiative through the council, netting you a fat government contract you desperately need since losing almost everything after your debacle a while back."

Real anger clouds his face now. "I lost more than contracts. I lost my reputation! Do you think I did not see the other council members laughing at me behind my back? Well, they will not be laughing for much longer. After I expose Vincent's weakness for letting the Cure out on the street and allowing rogue vampires and werewolves to nearly expose us, they'll beg me to fix it, and I will."

"You kidnap a werewolf and create a fear of rogue vampires and other fearmongering situations, all to set yourself up as some kind of savior. I get it. What I don't get is why you attacked Yuri and the other Mob families."

"Simple economics. This economy is in the toilet, and Vincent's policies are strangling the financial life out of us all. We could be so much more than we are. Do you know the one recession-proof industry in the world?"

"Prostitution?"

Percy gives me a humorous grin. "Close; it's crime. Yet humans control all the major crime syndicates. Once I am elected as the council leader, I will have influence over not just the top of society, but the bottom as well. And once I have the top and bottom firmly in my grasp, everything in between will inevitably be mine, as well."

"There is a reason we're supposed to stay out of crime, Percy, or have you forgotten? The feds are always watching the Mob, and you know that. One misstep and you risk exposing what you are, and that risks all of us."

Percy waves off my statement. "Nonsense. I would leave men like Yuri and Hanako in charge. I'm a shadow figure, and not even they know who I am, only that I am ultimately the boss. They funnel their illicit gains to me, I make them rich, and we're all happy."

"It was quite a plan. Too bad I fucked it all up for you, but I think it's for the best. Had you actually succeeded, we all probably would have gotten bit in the ass eventually."

"I was surprised Vincent called you in. This would have all gone a lot smoother if he hadn't. I could have brought in the werewolf, declared the menace taken care of, and shown the council the dogs need to be put on a tighter leash. I had you to pin the rogue vampire attacks on. I still will of course, but I wouldn't be down as many men as I am now."

"You think you can still do this, don't you?" I ask.

"I don't see why not. The rogue, that's you, broke into my home and killed off several Sheriffs before I was able to put you down. I already have a plethora of evidence putting you at many of the scenes. Don't get me wrong, Leo, I always respected you, and I would much rather have had you replace that yes-man Wyatt than that idiot Quinn.His willful ignorance was useful for a while, but I think we both knew it could not be sustained. So that left me with Quinn, since your twisted sense of duty would pit you against me. But it's all moot. You're here, so I'll do what I have to do. I'll even drink a toast at your funeral."

"You still have to kill me," I remind him.

"A mere detail. I'm older, stronger, and faster than you. I have trained with the sword since I was a boy. I have recently fed, as I am sure you noticed. You don't have the element of surprise. Sure, you are a great fighter, but your greatest strength was always being a sneaky bastard. So, shall we do this like gentlemen, with swords and no guns or bombs?" he asks as he stands and draws what looks like a cavalry saber.

"Of course, Percy, you know me," I reply as I whip Shalonda

up and try to put a bullet in his brain.

Percy is a lot faster than I gave him credit for. He must have been packing away the blood for a while from the way he moves. Of course, he isn't faster than a bullet, but his eye registers my muscle movements and he reacts before I can even pull the trigger.

He dodges left and lunges straight for me, swinging his saber in an incredibly fast arc. I try to intercept it with my blade, but his strength forces my arm to the side. With equal speed and power, he reverses the cut and knocks Shalonda from my hand. With both arms forced wide from his strikes, I am open for the boot he puts into my chest, which sends me flying across the room to smash painfully into the wall. I hope the loud cracking I hear is from the oak paneling splitting and not my bones.

"Leo, I'm disappointed in you."

I struggle back to my feet, pull out a big survival knife like the one in Rambo, and get into a guard position. "Did you think I would limit my methods of winning a fight? You know me better than that."

Percy grins at me. "I said I was disappointed, not surprised."

We circle each other warily in the middle of the study. Well, I'm wary; Percy is just amused, which strikes my ego hard.I figure my best chance is to launch an all-out assault and keep him on the move so he can't put his full strength into his swings like he did with his opening attack.

I alternately slash high and low, then break the pattern at irregular intervals so I don't get into too much of a routine. When he parries my sword, I bring the big knife around to try to cut him. The more he bleeds, the weaker he gets. Of course, he can close off any wounds as easily as I can, but it's not instant even though the shallower ones seem that way. Still, each cut takes its toll.

Unfortunately, the same goes for me and, after less than ten minutes of fighting, I am suffering from far more numerous and severe wounds than he is. As we continue our deadly dance around the study, I realize if I don't do something soon to change the balance of power I'm not going to win this fight.

I hop backward over a table as Percy presses me across the

room. The moment my feet touch the carpeted floor, I kick the table at Percy, hoping to hit him and knock him off balance. But he leaps up and over, and the only casualty is the table and another section of paneling.

Percy continues to force me around the room in a fighting retreat. He's toying with me. He could have ended this fight when he first kicked me into the wall; this calls for desperate measures.

I fall into a defensive routine and Percy adjusts his attacks to match. I cut hard across his midsection and come back to block his counterattack. The height of the slashes varies, but the motions are the same. We do this for a solid minute, but the next time I parry his sword, I continue my spin instead of trying to intercept the inevitable return strike.

I turn and strike out almost blindly behind me with the survival knife and feel a certain satisfaction when I bury it to the hilt in Percy's chest. This also puts my back to my foe and leaves me wide open. Had we been normal humans, my strike would have been decisive.As it is, the wound is little more than an irritant, and I may have just paid for it with my life.

I feel Percy's saber slide into my back below my ribs and skip off my spine instead of severing it. I look down at the blade protruding from my stomach with a little disbelief and a lot of irritation. Even this horrible wound would be only minor cause for concern, but Percy is obviously tired of the game and decides to end it.

Instead of pulling the blade back out, he turns it edge out and tears it through my side, creating the most painful and horrible wound I have ever received. I drop my sword, press my arm against the gaping wound in hopes of keeping my guts inside, and stumble forward into the wall before sliding down to the floor. I focus all of my energy on trying to close the wound, unsure of the degree of success I might achieve. It does not occur to me my efforts are ultimately futile since there is no way I can continue the fight.

"Now this time you did surprise me, Leonard," Percy says as I lie helpless on the floor. "What on earth possessed you to use such a foolish maneuver? Surely you did not think this knife was going to cause me much harm?"

"No, and don't call my Shirley." I gasp out between bursts of agony. "I expect the plastic explosives packed into the handle to."

Percy looks from the small remote now visible in my hand to the knife buried in the center of his chest and hurriedly grabs the handle to pull it out. I trigger the explosive the instant he grips the hilt.

The effect is multiple and instantaneous. The blast tears his fingers from his hand and turns the blade into a projectile, which is propelled with enough force to drive it through his sternum and into his spine. It must have severed the spinal cord because Percy drops to the ground, his legs useless and unable to hold him upright.

"Not fair, Leonard," Percy says in shock as he looks at his ruined hand and cratered chest.

"The battle cry of the loser, Percy," I reply as I stumble to my feet and retrieve my sword. "You shouldn't be surprised. After all, you know I'm a sneaky bastard."

"Not surprised, Leonard, just disappointed."

I am barely able to muster the strength to swing my sword and take his head. The amount of my blood all over the floor is shocking. I look at the young woman huddled in the corner, eyes wide in panic and nearly in a terror-induced catatonic state. I can take enough blood from her to regain a small measure of functionality without killing her, but that is not a viable option given what she has witnessed.

I leave her lifeless body on the floor where I found her. Chalk up one more victim to Percy's delusions of grandeur. The only thing worse than cleaning up your mess is cleaning up someone else's. Even with a full feeding, my wound is horrible. It's closed, but my insides are still a mess and it hurts like hell. I could close off more pain receptors, but I would suffer a loss of movement. Subconsciously, I probably want to feel the pain for having killed the woman.

This is a huge house. I wish I had gotten Percy to tell me where he hid Martin; it could take forever to find him. I'm certain he is on the property, though. Percy would want to keep him close by and make sure no other weres got a whiff of him by moving him far out of the city. The room would need to be strong and very secure. If it were me, I would chain him in a basement or outbuilding. My gut, what's left of it, tells me basement.

I pull my phone out of my bag and call Marvin. "Marvin."

"Leo, you sound like shit. You OK?"

"I'm alive. Look at the security schematics and see if anything doesn't look right or jibe with the blueprints of the house."

It takes several minutes but Marvin finally replies, "There's an alarm sensor in the kitchen where there shouldn't be a door or window."

Marvin directs me toward the kitchen and I find it a couple of minutes later. It looks more like something for a restaurant than a home. I spy a door that looks like the kind for a walk-in freezer. I pull the large metal handle and find a walk-in freezer. Shit. Sometimes I hate being right. A closer inspection of the room reveals a second door similar to the one I just opened. I figure it goes to a giant refrigerator, but I had best check it out before I start taking down walls with explosives.

I try the handle, but it's locked. Rummaging through my bag, I pull out a small block of C4, press it onto the handle in close proximity to the locking mechanism, and blow it with a remote blasting cap. My small explosion blows off the handle and scorches the door, but fails to crack it open. I give the door a cursory kick and find it's built much more like a bank vault than a freezer door.

One of my favorite sayings is when in doubt, use more explosives. I follow my personal rule and shove a full one-pound brick of the plastic explosive onto the seam of the door and frame. After sticking another remote detonator onto it, I make my way into an adjacent room and blow the door.

The mansion trembles on its foundation and the air fills with dust and the acrid smell of explosives. I find the door and a good portion of the wall it was set in gone. Beyond the gaping hole is a set of stairs leading down, thankfully made of solid stone since the force of the explosion would have destroyed simple wooden ones. I am once again reminded of my weakness in thinking through my actions. I also smell gas. I think the explosion knocked a gas line loose from the stove.

Sword and gun in hand, I descend the steps and enter a chamber straight out of a medieval dungeon. Barred cells are visible along the length of the passageway that ends with a door about a hundred feet farther down from the stairs. The door could lead to a closet, but more likely leads to a tunnel to the outside.

A rack of cattle prods is mounted to the wall partway down, with four of the devices resting in the charging cradle. Across from it is another barred cell holding a small, naked man huddled in the far corner.

"Martin Goldstein?" I ask, as if I expect it could be someone else.

"What's happening?" he asks softly, his voice quavering with fear, or possibly the cold. "I heard gunshots and explosions. Are you here to get me out?"

"I am. Can I trust you not to shift on me if I open your cage?"

"Of course, I..." He stumbles forward then backs away when he gets a whiff of me. "You're a vampire! You're one of them!"

"Yes to the first part, hell no to the second part," I assure him.

Martin looks unsure whether to believe me or not. It's obvious he has been greatly mistreated. "Who are you? Why are you here? Who sent you?"

"My name is Leo. Yuri feels you've had a long enough vacation and wants to make sure you get his taxes filed on time."

"Yuri sent you? Does he know what you are?"

"He does now. Things have gotten problematic lately, your kidnapping being the least of many things needing to be unfucked."

"Please get me out. My family must be so worried."

I open the cage and Marty tentatively steps out. "Your daughter also sent me to find you."

"You know my Katherine?" he asks, pausing to look up at me.

I can't prevent the smile creeping onto my face. "Oh yes, I know her quite well."

"Leo, I don't know how I can ever repay you for this."

"Well, your daughter has already made sure I'm taken care of. But if you want to do something for me, wear my jacket," I tell him, then hand him my less than tidy coat. "We have to take my motorcycle, and the last thing I want is your hairy wolf balls on my back the entire way home. And if you get an erection for any reason, you're walking back to New York. I mean it: wind, vibration, whatever, off you go."

Martin blushes as he puts on my jacket, ignoring the blood, slashes, and bullet holes in it. I lead him back up through the kitchen.

"I smell gas," the werewolf says, sniffing the air.

"Yeah, I ate a Mexican for dinner. It happens every time."

I leave my bag of remaining explosives in the kitchen with the increasingly pervasive odor of gas. I help it along by kicking loose a few other gas-fueled appliances. The sun is less than an hour away from making its morning debut, so Martin and I hightail it back to New York. Luck is with me again, and I don't get pulled over for having a nearly naked man without a helmet on my bike.

By the time we get back, I figure the mansion has filled with enough gas, so I dial the number to the cell phone detonator attached to the explosives in my bag. I should have called for a cleanup before I blew the place up, but I am feeling particularly vandalistic and spiteful. I call in the cleanup crew and warn them they need to hurry and will need credentials to keep the cops and fire department out of the way.

CHAPTER FIFTEEN

I got Marvin another apartment and kicked him out. I get cranky when I don't feel well, and Marvin's ability to piss me off isn't healthy for either of us. He took the computer stuff as payment for his services, which was pretty stupid. If he were such a genius, he would have chalked up the stuff he lost in his old apartment as a business expense. It's definitely on my bill to Yuri and Vincent.

Yuri paid without question and even gave me a nice bonus, I assume as a consultation fee for vampire killing. He is now headquartered in the secure building where he set his trap for Percy's crew and has hinted at further improvements. I told him I would talk to the council about his knowledge of us. Yuri is familiar with meetings between Mob heads and treats it as one.

It takes me three days to get to the point where I am well enough to pay Vincent a visit and take a cab to the towering headquarters building. I get a dirty look from the guard on duty, and it takes me a minute to recognize that he's the one I shot last time I was here. I've shot, stabbed, and blown up so many people I can't keep the faces straight, and I don't even try. I have enough problems without dwelling on that stuff. He keys the elevator for me, and I arrive at the top in short order. One of Vincent's toadies instructs me to wait in a conference room. I stare at the walls for about fifteen minutes before Vincent enters flanked by two Sheriffs I've never seen before.

I look at Vincent's two bodyguards and say, "Seems like there are new faces every time I come here. You know, a high turnover rate is indicative of an unhappy work environment."

"Due to the pollution of our ranks, it was necessary to

contract outside security from other enclaves until ours can be reliably reestablished," Vincent answers.

"Speaking of polluted ranks, what's happening with Wyatt and the other Sheriffs who sided with Percy?"

"The two younglings retook their oaths and are on strict probation. I removed Wyatt from his position and assigned him to administrative duties in the Tower where he is under house arrest. I probably should take his head, but due to his decades of service and lack of active participation in Percy's schemes, I feel leniency is appropriate."

"What are you going to do about Yuri and his men? They know about us—and how to kill us."

"We came to a suitable agreement with Mr. Poplonovich. We each recognize that both of our organizations have positions of strength as well as vulnerabilities. He and his people will hold our existence secret as long as we stay out of his territory, both physically and in a business sense. He understands the vampires who attacked him were primarily younglings, and if the enclave is forced to move against him to protect itself, he and his men will be wiped out to a man in an instant."

I don't think Vincent has a full grasp of Yuri's cleverness, but neither do I think Yuri can withstand a full assault from the enclave no matter his preparations. The council members alone have enough strength to defeat a small army. But Yuri is smart and knows his place. He'll keep to the agreement and deal with the enclave as another power to be watched and respected.

"Mr. Malone, I trust you are feeling better?" Vincent asks, certainly not out of concern for my health.

"A fair bit. I'll feel a lot better when you take care of this," I reply as I hand him a folded slip of paper.

Vincent plucks it from my fingers and narrows his eyes as he reads it. "What is this?"

"It's a bill. I've itemized my charges and expenses."

"Ridiculous! As I told you before, you are a warder of your district and performed your duties as required to hold the position. I will not pay you, especially this ridiculous sum, simply for doing your duty."

"Doing my duty? My duty is to deal with sloppy, unlawful

predations and the general stupidity of individual vampires. You called me in to solve a highly complex problem you knew was endemic to your organization. You knew you had corrupt Sheriffs and at least one dirty council member. That kind of duty falls on the Sheriffs, which I am not one of since you fired me for doing my job. Calling me in to deal with this large an issue puts me firmly in the realm of private contractor, and that is my bill."

I'm proud of myself for not jabbing my finger into Vincent's bony chest to punctuate each of my points. I needed to appeal to his logic, and the finger thing would have made him defensive. And he probably would have ripped my finger off. I watch his jaw muscles convulse as he mentally chews on my argument.

"Very well, Mr. Malone, but the sum is still grossly inflated. I will pay you half, which is more than fair compensation for the work you did outside your duties as a warder. I suppose you desire an apology from me as well?"

Oh, glory days! This is going to be the best part yet. I would waive my entire fee to see the old bastard humble himself and admit he was wrong for firing me. I wish it were more public. My kingdom for a tape recorder.

I beam as Vincent continues, "Well, you won't get one! I still think you are a miserable little shit and hope you die a slow and painful death."

I feel my smile verbally slapped off my face.

Vincent pauses to take a deep breath. "That being said, your continued loyalty and willingness to risk your own safety for the sake of the enclave makes me realize I may have acted hastily in removing you from the Sheriffs. I need a new captain and extend to you that position."

I actually feel my heart leap with joy, which is quite a feat considering it hasn't beat for more than eighty years. Not for the invitation, but for watching Vincent wipe the flecks of spittle spraying out of my mouth from his face as I erupt in laughter. I can hear his teeth grinding in fury when I push past him and his guards and give him the finger over my right shoulder as I walk away, still laughing like a madman. It isn't an apology, but this is just as good and far more to my liking.

EPILOGUE

I got a call earlier in the day from someone needing heavy protection, so I'm in my office with my feet kicked up on my desk waiting. It's not long before I hear the sound of feet clomping up my stairs—too many feet. And I think I smell a cat.

With a sigh, I pull out my phone and hit the speed dial for my lawyer just before Castillo bursts through the door with half a dozen cops, all with their guns drawn.

"Don't move, Malone!" Castillo orders. "I have a warrant for your arrest."

"What for now?"

"We have a missing persons report and a witness who saw you assault him just before he was last seen alive. I already have a videotaped witness report positively identifying you. Let your shitbag lawyer tamper with this one."

It takes me a minute to connect the dots, a problem when you assault so many people on a regular basis. She's referring to that kid I ended on the way to Yuri's club, the one who was going to rape the girl.

Will picks up. "Will, it's Leo. Yeah, Castillo is taking me in now."

"Move it, Malone," Castillo orders as she pulls out her cuffs. "I have your ass this time."

Kurt and Danny are best friends and celebrating their recent high school graduation by having a few beers in the bar of the Marriott, thanks to their fake IDs.

"I can't believe we're finally done with high school," Kurt says to his friend.

Danny raises his glass of beer. "Here's to no more wedgies!"

"Here's to NYU and hot college chicks desperate for math tutors!" Kurt adds, then takes a deep drink from his glass. "I can't believe we'll be in college in the fall."

"I can't believe that gorgeous woman at the bar has been checking you out for the past ten minutes."

"What woman?" Kurt follows his gaze to the bar. "Her? No way, dude. She's like forty."

"Yeah, but a Courteney Cox forty. That is one hot cougar, and she's totally checking you out."

"You're crazy. Women like that don't look at guys like us."

Nevertheless, the woman is looking right at him and gives him a wink. Kurt points at his chest with a quizzical look. The stunning, raven-haired woman smiles, nods her head, and beckons him with a crook of her finger.

Kurt whips his head back to face his best friend. "Oh my God, she's a hooker!"

Danny shakes his head. "No way, dude. If she's a hooker, she's one of those high-class ones costing like ten grand a night, and she would know we don't have that kind of dough just by looking at us."

"What, you're now an expert on prostitutes?"

"Actually, yes. I realized by my junior year that if I want to get laid before I am thirty, my best bet is to pay for it, so I've done my homework. Now, get over there before she sobers up and realizes you're a total dork!"

Kurt looks at his friend, back at the seductress, then back to his friend before standing up and walking over to the bar.

"Um...hi. My name's Kurt."

"Hello, Kurt," the woman says with a faint accent, then demurely extends her hand.

Kurt takes her hand, gives it a small shake, and starts to bow to kiss it before he realizes what he's doing and shakes it once more.

"You are amusing. Do I make you nervous, Kurt?"

"A little. Women like you don't usually talk to guys like me, and the girls who do only want help with their schoolwork. You don't look like you need me to do your math homework."

"That is the difference between being a girl and a woman. Girls are foolish and cannot appreciate the quality of a good man."

"That's an interesting accent. Where are you from?"

She takes a sip from her glass and gives him a slow, almost predatory blink. "Quebec. I like to come to New York when I'm feeling especially playful. There is so much life in this city. It is unlike anywhere else in the world. Are you feeling playful, Kurt?"

Kurt feels an electric tingling course through his entire body. It is so strong he has to set his beer down on the bar before it falls from his nerveless fingers.

"Playful? Did you want to go to Coney Island or something?"

The woman gives him a laugh that nearly buckles his already trembling knees. "You are so cute. I have a room upstairs. Come with me."

She takes him by the hand and leads him to the elevators before he can respond—not that he could. Kurt's blood is pounding in his head, and the whole world takes on something akin to a dream state. He is also aware of the blood pounding almost uncomfortably in another part of his body as well.

Once the elevator reaches the desired floor, she continues to lead him by the hand until they get to her room. Digging into her small, expensive bag, she swipes the keycard in the reader and steps into a lavish suite.

Kurt pauses outside the door, taking everything in, and praying he does not wake up from what must be a dream.

"Aren't you coming in?"

"Sorry, I'm new at this sort of thing. I don't even know your name."

"Lesile," the seductive woman whispers as she gently takes him by the tie and pulls him inside.

LOOK FOR BOOK 2 IN THE BROOKLYN SHADOWS SERIES

BLOOD CONSPIRACY

AVAILABLE AT ALL MAJOR DIGITAL RETAILERS

ABOUT THE AUTHOR

Brock Deskins was born in a small town located in rural Oregon. At age twenty, he joined the army and served as an M1A1 tank crewman, dental specialist, and computer analyst. While in the military, he became an accomplished traveler, husband, and father of three wonderful children. His military career completed, attended college to brush up on his skills as a computer analyst and gain new skills as a writer. Brock received his degree in computer networking and is now devoting his full time and limited attention span to writing.

BIBLIOGRAPHY

THE SORCERER'S PATH

The Sorcerer's Ascension
The Sorcerer's Torment
The Sorcerer's Legacy
The Sorcerer's Vengeance
The Sorcerer's Scourge
The Sorcerer's Abyss
The Sorcerer's Return
The Sorcerer's Destiny
The Sorcerer's Rebirth

BROOKLYN SHADOWS

Shrouds of Darkness
Blood Conspiracy
Primacy of Darkness

THE TRANSCENDED CHRONICLES

The Miscreant
The Agent

EMPIRE OF MASKS

Highlords of Phaer
Nightbird
Mourningbird

STANDALONE NOVELS

The Portal
Amelia: Battle for Ardentia

Curious about other Crossroad Press books?
Stop by our site:
http://store.crossroadpress.com
We offer quality writing
in digital, audio, and print formats.

www.ingramcontent.com/pod-product-compliance
Lightning Source LLC
Chambersburg PA
CBHW020947180626
46814CB00003B/972